About the

Stevyn Colgan is an author, an artist, and a popular speaker at UK and international events and festivals. He has appeared on numerous podcasts and radio shows including *Freakonomics*, *Saturday Live*, *Do the Right Thing*, *No Such Thing as a Fish* and *Josie Long's Short Cuts*.

For thirty years he was a police officer in London. And for more than a decade he was one of the 'elves' that create the multi award-winning TV series *QI*. He was part of the writing team that won the Rose D'Or for BBC Radio 4's *The Museum of Curiosity* and his first novel, *A Murder to Die For,* was shortlisted for the Dead Good Readers' Awards and longlisted for the *Guardian* Not the Booker Prize 2018.

He co-hosts the (nearly) prize-winning podcast *We'd Like a Word* with author Paul Waters, and was recently elected to membership of the Eccentric Club (founded in 1781) although both he and his pet squid have no idea why.

Praise for A Murder to Die For and The Diabolical Club

'*Stevyn Colgan bestrides the territory of English rural comedy, one foot on the throat of Joanna Trollope, the other knocking the bonnet of Miss Marple off her silver head. Divine black village comedy.*'
 – Stephen Fry

'*Only the British can mix humour and homicide so charmingly.*'
 – Sandi Toksvig

'*Delightful witty fun. A joy for any fan of the great English murder-mystery. It's a literary cream tea with a glass of fizz.*'
 – Neil Dudgeon, DCI Barnaby of *Midsomer Murders*

'*My perfect book. Funny, complex, compelling, odd. The sort of book I love to read and wish I could write.*'
 – Alex Horne

'*A challenging mystery that keeps you guessing – with an added dose of humour.*'
 – Matt Lucas

Also by Stevyn Colgan

Joined-Up Thinking
Henhwedhlow: The Clotted Cream of Cornish Folktales (with Tony Hak)
Constable Colgan's Connectoscope
The Third Condiment
Colgeroons
Saving Bletchley Park (with Dr Sue Black OBE)
One Step Ahead: Notes from the Problem Solving Unit
A Murder to Die for
The Diabolical Club
The Nearly Invisible Man and Other Stories
As a contributor
I Remember: Reflections on Fishing and Childhood (ed. Joe Cowley)
Ottakar's Local History: High Wycombe (ed. Roger Cole)
The QI 'F' Annual
The QI 'G' Annual
The QI 'H' Annual
The 'EFG' Bumper Book of QI Annuals
Subject Verb Object (ed. Dane Cobain)

"The show must goon…"

Cockerings

Stevyn Colgan

unbound

This edition first published in 2021

Unbound
TC Group, Level 1, Devonshire House,
One Mayfair Place, London W1J 8AJ
www.unbound.com

ISBN (eBook): 978-1-78965-152-2
ISBN (Paperback): 978-1-78965-151-5

Cover design by Mecob

Printed and bound in Great Britain by Clays Ltd, Elcograf S.p.A.

For Chris Hale.
He started it.

Super Patrons

Lulu Allison
Claire Appleby
Sarah Atherton
Ann Aucott
James Aylett
Duncan Bailey
Bob Barr
Paul Barrier
Bruce Barrow
Julian Benton
Terry Bergin
Alexander Borg
Ruth Bourne
Mark Bowsher
Richard W H Bray
Ben Breen
Emily Brown
Lesley Bruce
Joseph Burne
Ali Burns
Marcus Butcher

Barbara Campbell
Graeme Card
David Lars Chamberlain
Sue Clark
Louis Constandinos
Gemma Cooper
Ewan Crawford
Jane Crawford
John Crawford
Ruth Curtis
E R Andrew Davis
Amanda de Grey
Miranda Dickinson
Thomas Dommett
Chris Emerson
Tony Evans
Louise Forsdyke
Alison Garner
Andrew George
Sarah Goddard
Darren Goldsmith
Johnny Goonan
Emma Grae
Ben Green
John Griffiths
Jason Grubbs
Geoffrey Gudgion
Pat Harkin
Jo Haseltine
Kel Haseltine
Maximilian Hawker
Katherine Heathcote
Cherise Hedges

David Hester
Kathryn Hill
Julian Hynd
Oli Jacobs
Clifford Jaine
Alexander Jegtnes
Marjorie Johns
Kitty Johnson
Helen Jones
Joyce Jones
Peter Kelly
Andrew Keogh
Rik Kershaw-Moore
Ian Knight
Linda Knowles
Terry Lander
Pete Langman
Ewan Lawrie
David Leach
Chris Limb
Angela Lord
Tim Lund Jorgensen
Alisdair Maclean
Wendy Mallas
Philippa Manasseh
Carol McCollough
Mo McFarland
Alan McHenry
John Mitchinson
Alison Morgan
Chris Neale
John New
Katrine Lisbygd Nielsen

Marie-Jose Nieuwkoop
Jenny Noakes
Vaun Earl Norman
Samantha Parnell
Claire Patel-Campbell
Melanie Perry
Morgan Phillips
Kim Pike
Lawrence Pretty
Paul Rawcliffe
Simon Reap
Natalie Reis
Zelda Rhiando
Michael J. Ritchie
Kate Roberts
Alan and Angella Rodgers
Sid Rodrigues
Kenn Roessler
Matt Roseblade
Bernie Sammon
Richard Selwyn
Mark Skinner
Niall Slater
Andrew Sleight
Keith Sleight
Michael Sleight
Neil Sleight
Peter Sleight
Book sloth
Toni Smerdon
Lili Soh
Mark Stahlmann
Janice Staines

Karen Staines
Roy Staines
Ruth Staines
Terry and Sue Staines
Ros Stern
Tom Stone
Tanya Stratton
Chris Taylor
James Thomas
Dougald Tidswell
Kelly Townshend
David G Tubby
Katie Urch
Mark Vent
Jose Vizcaino
Hilary Walker
Lauren Walker
Steve Walker
Gillian Wallbanks
Marion Wallbanks-Roozen
Nick Walpole
Julie Warren
Paul Waters
Pete Watt
Lucy White
Senga Whiteman
Carol Whitton
Geoff and Julia Williams
Sean Williams
Alexa Wilson
Elizabeth Wilson
Liz Wooldridge

Cockering. *Posturing, the build up before a fight. English: from Middle English cock 'to fight', 'to wrangle' (a derivative of Old English cocc). Nickname cocker used for a bellicose person. English surname traditionally pronounced as Corring.*

Chapter 1

A warning bell began to clang. The Reverend Grimson Freacke, vicar of St Lydwina's, set the handbrake of his splendidly preserved Morris Traveller and stepped out into the autumn sunshine. Warning lights flashed to accompany the bells as the ancient red and white candy-striped gates of the Snipeton level crossing lowered jerkily. The Reverend didn't mind. He was in no great hurry to get anywhere and the excitement from watching big trains thundering past had been with him since he was a boy. The modern diesels didn't have the romance and majesty of the old steam locos of course, but they still held a fascination for him and he enjoyed the brief contact with the outside world that waving to the passengers afforded.

A utilitarian Land Rover drew to a halt behind his Morris. Major Menzies Crantlemain (retired) leaned out of the driver's window looking florid and bellicose. The Reverend knew that this didn't necessarily mean that the man was angry but, it had to be said, he usually was.

'I suppose we'll be stuck here for a sodding age now,' he barked by way of a greeting.

'At least we have the weather, Major,' said the Reverend,

admiring the aerobatics of swallows dipping the nearby River Gew. 'One might call it an Indian summer.'

The Major climbed out of his car and puffed furiously on his pipe. 'Silly bloody phrase. Spent six years in the Uttar Pradesh. Couldn't tell one season from another. Except for the Monsoon. Ah, morning, Ostridge.'

'Good morning, Major.'

Professor Gerald Ostridge emerged from one of the old railway cottages nearby, tugged along as usual by Taffy, his curiously named and hyperactive West Highland Terrier. The dog choked and gurgled at the leash and growled at the clergyman, who looked up at the sky to hide his discomfort. It was fine and blue with a light dusting of wispy white horse tails.

'Good morning, Reverend,' said the Professor. 'Taffy! Stop that!'

The dog snarled, baring a startling array of teeth while straining to choking point on his leash. The Reverend Freacke smiled benignly and moved away from the dog. He had long ago realised that Taffy hated him.

'Sorry about the dog but, well, you know. He doesn't like people in skirts,' said the Professor.

The Reverend adjusted his cassock and wondered, not for the first time, whether he should perhaps adopt a more contemporary approach to his dress. Trousers did have their appeal.

'Well, any kind of drapery really,' continued the Professor. 'Curtains. Overhanging tablecloths. Bath towels. Life is a nightmare for Enid. She can't wear a skirt in the house. And trying to find slacks that fit her…'

'She should try a poncho, Ostridge,' said the Major. Since leaving the army, he'd never quite got the hang of using forenames. 'Once saw a chap in Ceylon with elephantiasis.

Balls the size of a small boy's head. He wore a poncho. Or was it a sarong?'

'The Major and I were just saying what a fine day it is for September,' said the Reverend in an attempt to bring the conversation around to something less lurid than Crantlemain's memoirs. 'The swallows haven't left for Africa yet.'

'A poncho wouldn't work anyway,' said the Professor. 'It still involves hanging cloth and… good lord. What's all this?'

He pointed at a slow-moving convoy of vehicles that was pulling up behind the Major's Land Rover. The lead vehicle was a lorry painted in a startling clash of reds and blues. A board mounted above the cab proudly proclaimed that it belonged to 'Benelli's Circus'. Its exhaust barked like a shotgun, and the engine shuddered and stalled. Behind the lorry was a beaten up old VW Beetle convertible towing a trailer bearing a large, grubby and dangerous-looking cannon. The VW was full of clowns, who tumbled out onto the road and staggered towards a nearby hedge.

'A circus! How jolly,' said the Reverend.

'They can't be putting on a show around here, surely,' said the Professor. 'Marcheline would never allow it.'

'Good thing too,' said the Major. 'Last thing we want is a bunch of in-breds gadding about and stripping the lead off the church roof.'

'Oh, that's a little unkind, surely?' said the Reverend.

'Yes, we shouldn't be so quick to judge,' added the Professor.

'Suit yourselves,' said the Major. 'But that's your pittosporum the blighters are cocking their legs against, Ostridge.'

The Major harrumphed his disapproval.

'Hello there!'

The three men turned to see a tall angular figure climb out of a Winnebago some way back in the convoy and walk towards them. He had a thick black beard flecked with grey and wore baggy blue jeans and an overly large and faded blue sweatshirt that advertised a pub in Felpersham that had closed when the Berlin Wall was pristine. It looked as if he cut his own hair without the aid of a mirror.

'Hello there,' he said again.

'Hmf,' said the Major.

'Good morning,' replied the Reverend.

'My name's Ellis. Ben Ellis. I'm the owner of this circus,' said the stranger, revealing a large, toothy smile that rivalled even the vicar's magnificent ivories. 'Are we on the right road for Morbridge?'

'You are indeed. Once you're over the crossing just keep going straight on for about a mile…'

'And keep going,' growled the Major *sotto voce.*

'… until you come to a fork in the road. Don't go straight on as that takes you into the village of Shapcott Bassett. A lot of people take a wrong turn there. It's a bit deceptive as there aren't any road markings. You actually need to take what looks like a right turn, even though it isn't, and follow that road for another couple of miles. Are you performing in Morbridge?'

'We're here at the inv–'

Any answer was lost in a sudden eruption of banging from the boxed rear of the lorry. Taffy began leaping hysterically around on his leash like a novelty balloon in a hurricane.

'He's a rather… er… excitable little chap isn't he?' said Ellis, backing sensibly away from the enraged dog.

'The damn thing is mad,' said the Major. 'No wonder Marcheline won't let you walk him in the village, Ostridge.'

'He's just a little highly strung,' said Gerald Ostridge, wrestling with his terrier and awaiting the inevitable *He should be* comment.

'I'm afraid you'll be stuck here for a few more minutes because of the level crossing,' said the Reverend.

'Ah, that's okay. We could do with a comfort break. It's been a long drive', said Ellis. He shouted up at the cab of the lorry. 'Glupi!'

Another clown appeared at the window and smiled, his teeth a ghastly yellow against the white of his pancake.

'We nearly there, Boss?' The clown's accent was foreign, maybe Eastern European. His voice grated horribly, suggesting a serious smoking habit.

'About fifteen minutes away,' said Ellis. 'Can you let them out for a leg stretch?'

'Snipeton is one of the oldest automatic level crossings in the country,' explained Reverend Freacke. 'Marcheline won't… well, the authorities won't change it. It takes a while to do its business.'

'Me too,' said the old clown, leering. All of a sudden, there was another round of banging from the rear of the lorry. The clown shouted something incomprehensible and banged on the rear wall of the cab with his fist. This was immediately met with a cacophony of angry female voices and a volley of more intense bangs and clatters from within, along with some high-pitched whinnying noises.

Glupi grunted, half-climbed and half-fell out of the cab and seemed to take a while to gain his balance. His face was lined with crevasses and his nose was large, red, bulbous and quite real. He appeared to be in his seventies at least. He smiled lopsidedly at the three astonished locals and belched loudly. The air was suddenly filled with the smell of stale liquor and garlic. The Reverend fanned the air in front of him and pretended to be shooing away an errant midge. The clown growled something in a foreign language, lit a cigarette and slouched to the side of the lorry, every step apparently requiring an effort of epic proportions. He slipped a set of bolts and opened a side door. There was a short, angry, shouted conversation between him and whoever was inside, before he made a show of walking very, very slowly back to the cab. Music began to play from speakers mounted on the top of the cab; a scratchy recording of Saint-Saens' *Volières* from the *Carnival of Animals*.

'Good Lord,' said the Major.

The Reverend Freacke clamped his hand over his mouth in surprise as an elderly white horse emerged blinking into the daylight. It was immediately followed by two others. Each horse was carrying a rider and they formed up in a line at the foot of the ramp. The riders were larger women, and similar enough in looks to suggest that they were close relatives. Their expansive bosoms were crammed into creaking basques laced taut to the point of splitting. They wore pink tutus around the places where their waists had once been and diamante headbands, each sporting a single off-white and moth-eaten ostrich feather. Not one of them looked under sixty. Spotting their small and unexpected audience, the three ladies climbed to their feet and struck wobbly ballet poses, flapping their hands in time to the music. As *Volières* segued into *Aquarium*, the rider of the first horse made a clicking noise – apparently by dropping her upper dentures onto her lower plate – and the horses walked stiffly forward, the riders balancing precariously upon their backs.

'Gentlemen... may I present the Daughters of Epona,' said Ben Ellis.

'Good Lord,' said the Major again.

A few curious onlookers had now emerged from the handful of cottages that constituted the hamlet of Snipeton. Among them was Special Constable Arthur Pews, fresh from the warm bed of recently widowed Mrs Beryl Tiggs. He fastened his tunic belt around his ample belly and walked towards the crossing, offering a loud and unconvincing, 'Well, thank you very much for helping me with my enquiries, Mrs Tiggs,' for the benefit of the neighbours. The neighbours were not especially convinced, as Mrs Tiggs had been helping Constable Pews with his enquiries, regularly and noisily, for at least two nights a week ever since her husband died, ten months earlier, and possibly before.

Pews pulled in his stomach and pushed his shoulders back in an effort to look more imposing. He quickly scanned the circus vehicles and hoped to God that no offences were being committed meaning he'd be forced to do some real police work. The cannon looked particularly alarming and he quickly passed it by and arrived at the clowns' battered and multi-coloured car. It was clearly an antique but the clowns that were now lounging in it, tooting horns and blowing whistles, were just as old; certainly old enough to have been drawing their pensions for a few years, anyway. Having emptied their bladders in Professor Ostridge's hedge, they were now doing their best to compete with the bells of the level crossing, the music, and the still insanely angry Taffy, whose self-imposed strangulation was now causing his eyes to bulge like bloodshot marbles.

With the possible exception of the driver, who was asleep at the wheel and snoring loudly, all of the clowns were riotously drunk. As Pews strolled past, one of them, a dwarf in hideous make up, smiled at him, flashing a mouth crammed full of ill-fitting urine-coloured dentures.

Pews skipped quickly along, ignoring the glaring illegality of the car's bald and under-inflated tyres. He then found himself watching three large women balancing on horseback.

'Extraordinary, isn't it?' said the Professor.

'I'll say,' said Pews, licking his lips. He glanced with ill-disguised lust at the fleshy, dimpled thighs of the ballerinas. 'I haven't seen a circus since I was...' Anything said after that was lost as the anticipated Paddington to Hoddenford express thundered through the crossing, sounding its horn and importantly announcing its presence. It delighted everyone except the crazed Taffy, who achieved startling new levels of rage. With one mighty tug, the terrier pulled the leash free of Gerald Ostridge's hand and sank his teeth into the Reverend's leg. Freacke shouted in alarm, which caused the horse nearest to him to rear up and whinny in fright. Its rider, who had been in the process of executing a *pas de deux* with one of her fellow 'daughters', was thrown into the air and landed heavily upon the roof of the Reverend's beloved Morris. The impact burst her already straining corset and her bosom exploded into view like twin airbags. The horse angrily kicked the front of the car and then bolted. The dazed ballerina slowly slid down the car's windscreen and onto the bonnet, coming to rest on her back and with one leg draped over each headlight, looking like a woman about to give birth and expecting something the size of a pig. A startled Constable Pews, his eyes fairly popping out of his head at the sight of the semi-conscious rider's frilly underwear and football-sized breasts, immediately rushed across to render what First Aid he could remember. As he crushed his lips to the horsewoman's in an attempt at artificial respiration, she regained consciousness. Finding herself half-naked and apparently being French-kissed by some pervert in a police uniform, she naturally assumed the worst and began screaming as loudly and as piercingly as her unfortunate position would allow. The other horsewomen responded and Pews suddenly found himself reeling from a hail of horsewhips. He curled into a ball on the ground and attempted to call for assistance but his radio was dashed from his hand and trodden underfoot by one of the horses.

Professor Ostridge, who had witnessed the entire incident, steeled himself for action. It was his public duty as an occasional lay magistrate, he reasoned, to go to the rescue of the beleaguered constable and he intended to do so as soon as he'd captured the now berserk Taffy. He found the dog scrabbling furiously at the driver's door of the Morris Traveller, where the Reverend and Ben Ellis had taken refuge from its fearsome jaws. After much pulling and manoeuvring, he got the animal to the rear of the car, where he tethered its leash to the bumper. He then waded into the fracas, attempting to wrestle a riding crop from one of the Daughters of Epona and getting a ballet shoe in the testicles for his efforts.

Menzies Crantlemain looked on with a growing sense of disbelief and, being a man whose military career had been spent mostly barking at subordinates from behind a desk in Whitehall or discussing past imagined glories at the Cavalry and Guards Club Annual Dinner, decided that discretion was the better part of valour and that a tactical withdrawal was in order. However, in his haste, he failed to register that he'd left the vehicle in gear. As he turned the key in the ignition, the Land Rover lurched forward and embedded itself in the rear of the Reverend's Morris, abruptly ending the short but noisy life of Taffy the dog, causing a severe case of whiplash for the already injured clergyman, and pushing the car three feet forward, where it caught Gerald Ostridge behind the knees. He fell on top of Arthur Pews, who was curled foetus-like on the dusty ground. The two men then began to scream for help as the horsewomen started putting the boot in.

The Major locked his doors, scratched his head and wondered what to do. Forty years of the finest British Army officer training hadn't prepared him for this.

Chapter 2

The good people of Shapcott Bassett awoke to another unseasonably warm September day and in the sure knowledge that today, as always, all was right with the world, because that was what they had paid for.

The sun glinted on the dewy roofs of the listing, timber-framed houses and crumbly thatched cottages that stood sentry along the length of Milk Street, which ambled its way like a crooked spine from one end of the tiny village to the other. At the halfway point stood Market Square with its charming tea rooms and shops, war memorial and garden, a newsagents' so repressed that it stacked Mills and Boon type novels on the top shelf, and the village's only public house, the King's Head. The hanging sign outside sported a picture of a rutting stag rather than the usual royal portrait because a previous landlord had used it to express his feelings about Edward VIII's behaviour with Mrs Wallis Simpson and it had never been changed. But that was indicative of every facet of life in the village. Nothing ever changed.

Retired judges pottered in cottage gardens. Ex-Army officers polished Jaguars on pristine drives. Former professors and doctors jostled each other on the bowling green and tweedy ladies with strident voices and twin-sets sang *Jerusalem* at the WI and raised money to restore the roof of St Lydwina's. Shapcott Bassett seemed to exist in a bubble of timelessness where people spoke with plummy vowels and wore baggy plus-fours to play golf; where everyone went to church on a Sunday; where the vicar was eccentric and toothsome; and where couples picnicked from wicker hampers on crisp gingham tablecloths laid out with fine bone china and silver cutlery. It was the England of *The Famous Five* and the Boulting Brothers, a place of immaculate lawns and vegetable shows, Harvest Festivals, watercolour groups and light operatic societies.

There were no fast food outlets, no cash-points and no supermarkets. The only outward signs that the twenty-first century had encroached upon the village at all were the unobtrusive CCTV camera on the side wall of Twimbley's the grocer, and an occasional, tasteful burst of classical music being used as a ringtone – if you could get a signal. Mobile phone reception was haphazard at best, which meant that even though the village was the perfect location in which to film a period drama, very few production companies would go near it. And those that did apply were invariably turned down by the village council on the grounds of 'unreasonable levels of disruption'.

In many ways, Shapcott Bassett was more like an open-plan retirement home for the upper middle classes than a living, working village. The crime rate was zero, disorder was unheard of and the most exciting headline ever to appear in the *Shapcott Bassett Argus* was 'Local Man Found Dead of Natural Causes'. Nothing ever happened to disturb the peace and quiet tranquillity, which was exactly what the residents had come to expect. And exactly what Lady Marcheline Cockering insisted upon.

She had always thought of Shapcott Bassett as *her* village and, on paper, it was. Or half of it was, at least. The Cockering family had built the village and had owned all of the properties in it for generations, and she and her younger brother had inherited the lot – along with a brewery, a slaughterhouse and several farms – upon the deaths of their parents. But Lady Marcheline's interest in the village went far beyond simple landladyship. Everything that happened in the village happened only because she allowed it to happen, and she had both the bullishness and the wherewithal to ensure that her own small piece of Creation bent to her will. Anyone wanting to live in Shapcott Bassett was required to satisfy a stringent and exhaustive set of criteria devised by her and enforced by her despotic Residents' Association. Gardens to be kept tidy and hedges trimmed. Front doors to be finished in natural hardwood or painted in one of the limited catalogue of approved colours. Washing only to be hung to dry at the rear of premises and not in view of the road... and so on. This filtering system ensured that the village only attracted prospective tenants possessed of good incomes, an air of insufferable snobbery and a spine of rubber.

Marcheline's influence also extended to the village shops. She took great pride in their appearance, frequently admonishing their keepers for dirty windows, untidy displays or flaking paintwork. Produce had to be British or, at least, from countries friendly to Great Britain – a range that seemed to get smaller with every passing year – and nothing tawdry, tacky or crass could be found on the shelves.

In short, Marcheline delighted in the picture-postcard perfection of the village and treated it like a very large and very expensive dolls' house. Whatever happened elsewhere on the globe was irrelevant. Here in Shapcott Bassett, in this little piece of rural South Herewardshire, all was well with the world because things were done the right way. Her way.

All of which was why, on this particular Monday morning, Marcheline was white with shock and Mr David George Tubby was lying dazed and bruised on the road in front of her car.

She had driven into the village in her late father's 1947 Rover P2 to buy a newspaper and some flowers from Twimbley's when something jarringly out of place caught her eye. It was a poster.

This in itself was unheard of, as Marcheline had expressly forbidden the vulgarity of public advertising. But there it was, blatantly and crookedly pasted onto the normally plain whitewashed side wall of Barsted's the Master Bakers, one corner flip-flapping in the soft September breeze. And it was not alone. As she rounded the corner into Market Square, she saw to her horror that, during the night, every available tree, every lamp-post, every wall and shop front had been bill-posted. They even adorned the backside of 'Big Bessie', the oversized marble cow that had, for over 150 years, been the focal point of the square. It was this that had distracted her to such a degree that she hadn't spotted the unfortunate Mr Tubby until he was rolling across her car bonnet. She stamped hard upon the brake, throwing the unfortunate publican onto the ground, and stepped out of the car.

'David? Are you all right?'

Tubby stood up unsteadily and staggered in small circles.

'Eh?' he said. He dusted himself down and fiddled with his hearing aid.

'Good,' said Marcheline, distractedly. Her eyes were once again locked upon Bessie's papered Carrara marble udders and rump.

'Have you seen that?' she said, pointing at the cow.

'The batteries are dead,' shouted Tubby. 'I normally hear you coming, but the batteries are dead, you see?'

The sound of Marcheline's car, travelling at a maximum twenty miles per hour and screaming like a banshee, was usually more than enough to warn people of her approach. She did have access to an almost brand new Jaguar – it was her brother's and he was currently banned from driving after celebrating a win on the horses rather too well – but she refused to use it, always claiming that it was 'for a rainy day'. The reality was that she was too scared to drive it. There were far too many buttons and electronic gadgets for her liking. Besides, the old Rover was the only car that Marcheline had ever driven and she rarely took it beyond the parish boundary or above second gear. It was Mr Tubby's good fortune to be knocked down by the one car in the village that travelled too slowly to do him any real damage.

'It's deplorable,' she said, her face red with barely controlled anger. 'Would you look at that, David' She pointed to the statue again.

Tubby shook his head.

'Criminal,' he shouted. 'Poor old Stan's having a rough time of it.'

Stan Twimbley looked shellshocked as he slopped soapy water onto his shop windows and tried to peel the posters off the glass. It was a job made all the more difficult by his lack of a left arm. He tore a poster from the window but much of it remained behind in ragged white shreds. He stood back and wiped the sweat from his forehead as Marcheline walked over to offer sympathy and support.

'It's vandalism, your ladyship, pure vandalism,' he moaned. 'I don't know what sort of glue they used, but this is going to take hours to clear. And it's not even as if the posters are attractive, is it?'

Marcheline had to agree. They were poorly printed and the details were hazy and indistinct as if they should be viewed through some kind of corrective lens. A leering clown formed the centrepiece, surrounded by animals that could have been bears. Or very large otters. It was hard to tell. Whatever they were, they had huge, toothy grins as if they were wearing human dentures. A cross-eyed elephant balanced upon an egg-shaped ball and a tiger with one leg significantly shorter than the other three roared in fuzzy defiance. The accompanying text read:

'Childrens! Boys! Ladies and Gentelmens!

Big show wit animals sensations acts!

Hours and ticketprice is make know at circuscash!

Benellis Circus! The graetest show on Earth!'

And below, in shaky handwritten letters:

'Only week, Brill Farm, Morbridge.'

'Oh no. This won't do,' said Marcheline, frowning. 'This will not do at all.'

Chapter 3

In the library of Cockering Hall the Rt Hon Lord Berkeley Cockering, Viscount Morbridge, frowned as he paged through the listings on a property website and realised just how much money he wasn't making from his portfolio. House prices had risen by thirty per cent in South Herewardshire in just twelve months. Thirty per cent! He growled and thumped his chest as a stabbing pain shot through it.

'Damned chef. I knew those oysters tasted iffy,' he growled.

Clumsily plump like an overfed puppy, Berkeley was only a few years younger than his sister but his pudding of a face made him look disturbingly childlike. The effect was enhanced by premature baldness, the pale mottled pink of his skin, and high arching brows that made him look permanently surprised and guilty like a fat boy caught with his hand in the biscuit barrel.

He sat back in his large and comfortable chair and felt the warmth of the autumn sun shining through the window. Within minutes he was snoring. It had been a late night at the golf club's annual champagne and oysters dinner.

*

Marcheline made her purchases in a peremptory fashion and then stood for a while in Market Square to gather her thoughts in the autumn sunshine. All around her, the everyday life of her village went on. Miss Dillby was putting out an A-board advertising cream teas. Fred Clacketer and his son Eric were manhandling a life-sized wooden statue of a jolly straw-boatered butcher into position outside their shop. Mrs Rabberley was feeding the doves by the ornamental horse trough and putting the world to rights with ninety-nine-year-old Mr Osyth 'Toosey' Cornock, the village's oldest inhabitant. A recovered Mr Tubby was watering the pub's hanging baskets and, somewhere in the near distance, two magpies were having a swearing match. All seemed well with the world, except for the posters. They glared at her from every hard surface and jarred with the otherwise idyllic scene. Her eye was once again drawn to the defaced backside of Big Bessie.

The statue stood on a plinth in the middle of the memorial garden and had been nicknamed in fond memory of the village's most famous daughter, Elizabeth Cockering. A fiery nineteenth-century suffragette with a fondness for bare-knuckle boxing and a deep suspicion of men, Bessie had been a formidable champion of women's rights; certainly, she'd been too formidable for Mrs Pankhurst, who, in 1908, had politely declined her kind offer by letter of twenty shotguns with which to 'bag us some Lords and landed gentry'.

What the statue actually represented was the dairy industry upon which the wealth of the Cockerings had been built. This was further commemorated in such street names as Cheese Lane, Creamery Walk and The Buttery. In actual fact, it was brewing that had made the family rich, but they had played that down as dairy farming seemed a more worthy pursuit than keeping the local drunks topped up. And, besides, a marble cow had seemed more aesthetically suitable for a permanent monument than a stack of firkins. Idly, Marcheline wondered how 'Big Bessie' Cockering would have dealt with the bill-stickers. With horse and hounds and a sporting head start, no doubt.

She was recalled to the present by the screeching sound of Stan Twimbley scratching at his store window with a paint scraper. Marcheline shook her head in anger as she watched him struggle on, quite literally single-handedly. This was her brother's doing, of that she had no doubt. Brill Farm was on Cockering land and if a circus was pitching its tent there, it could only be with Berkeley's permission. She was also under no illusions as to why he'd allowed it – to irritate and annoy her. And it had worked. That said, she doubted that he would have had the guts to arrange the bill-posting frenzy in the village. Either way, she would have words, strong words, with him when she got home. And he could pay for the clean-up out of his allowance. Meanwhile, she'd see if the law had anything to say about bill posting.

With a scowl on her face that would curdle milk, she stormed across to the tiny police station, which she found closed and with a note on the door declaring that Special Constable Pews was out 'making enquiries'. Her already bad mood now made significantly worse, Marcheline stomped back to her car and drove off towards home in a noisy cloud of dust and indignation.

Berkeley woke with a start at the sound of Marcheline's Rover pulling up on the gravel drive.

'Damn!' he barked as he dashed across the hall to the grand staircase. With any luck she'd have no interest in talking to him, in which case he'd have time to get to his rooms and change. However, luck was not on his side this morning. He barely made it halfway up the stairs.

'Berkeley!'

He froze. The entrance hall was one of the building's finest features, boasting a magnificent staircase that rose from a polished Italian marble floor to a mezzanine, where a second set of smaller staircases branched off left and right to access the two great wings of the house. Several busts of prominent ancestors stood on plinths at ground level and, on the mezzanine itself, a handful of full-length oil paintings of stern ancestral Cockerings stared down from the oak panelled walls.

Berkeley sighed and turned to face his sister. 'Oh, hello, Marsh,' he said, wiping the sweat from his waxy pork-pie face. 'You look nice.'

'I wish I could say the same for you. What on earth are you wearing?'

'It's called a onesie. Chubby Champerknowne bought it for me for a laugh. He said I didn't need a onesie so much as I needed a fivesie, which, if you ask me, is a case of the pot calling the kettle black...'

'Never mind all that,' snapped Marcheline. 'You will not believe what I've just witnessed in the village.'

Berkeley puffed out his cheeks. *Here we go again*, he thought to himself. His sister had, as usual, found something wrong with the chocolate-box perfection of her village. Or, rather, their village.

'So what's happened today, hmm?' he asked, deciding that attack was his best form of defence. 'Too many wasps in the butcher's shop window? Is the birdsong too loud? Or is the sky not quite the right shade of bl–'

'Oh do belt up!' Marcheline took a deep breath. 'While I appreciate that you don't give a damn about the amount of effort I put into keeping the village looking as it should, you could at least rustle up some consideration for its inhabitants. You may recall that they are the people who voted you into office.'

'I'm Chair of the Village Council, not President of the UN.'

'Nevertheless, the people of the village voted for you in the belief that you would address their concerns and improve the quality of their lives.'

'No they didn't. They voted for me because they're scared of you. You own half the village and you're the Chair of the Residents' Committee.'

'What rot.'

'It's the truth. They know that if they don't toe the line, their tenancy agreements are at risk. Everyone knows that you put me on the village council as your puppet.'

'Poppycock,' snapped Marcheline. 'I put you on the council to instil some sense of responsibility in you.'

'So you admit that you did fix the election then?'

'It was a free ballot. The other candidates were… were…'

'Much keener and more suitable than me and yet, strangely, I won,' said Berkeley. 'I didn't even apply to be the Chair. You applied for me. It's all about control with you, isn't it?'

'Certainly not! It's about duty and responsibility. Someone has to maintain order around here. And that means taking care of the little things as well as the bigger issues. If you ignore the little things, they begin to mount up and, before you know it, the streets are awash with… with knife crime and crack cocaine and…'

'Crack cocaine? Oh, come on…'

'The village has been attacked!'

'Attacked?'

'Yes. By a circus.'

For a moment, Berkeley's mind formed the image of a human cannonball being used to take out the village hall while hordes of ferocious predatory clowns descended upon the hapless population as if they were geriatric wildebeest. Or bewildered beasts, more like. He smiled a wry smile but stifled it upon seeing his sister's red face.

'They have plastered the village in the most appalling posters advertising their wretched show and th–'

'That's hardly an attack is it?' said Berkeley. 'When people say "attack" they mean something like a suicide bomber, or a disgruntled Emo going rogue with an AK47, or –'

'Don't be facetious. This is serious.'

'No it isn't. It's petty vandalism at the very worst.'

'I'm not just talking about one or two posters,' said Marcheline between gritted teeth. 'There are hundreds of them and they're everywhere! The village looks an absolute shambles.'

'Oh dear,' said Berkeley.

'Oh dear? Is that all you can say? This is your fault.'

'What? How is it my fault?'

'You gave them permission to set up at Brill Farm, didn't you?'

Berkeley scratched his chin.

'I thought a circus would bring a little jollity to the area and–'

'You thought no such thing, you liar!' snapped Marcheline. 'You did it deliberately to annoy me and don't you dare deny it or tell me otherwise. I demand that they leave the area immediately. And, while you're over there, you can…'

'While I'm what?'

'While you're over there telling your circus louts to pack up and leave, you can also tell them that that I will be invoicing them for the costs incurred in removing their dreadful posters; costs, incidentally, that I'll be deducting from your allowance. That might incentivise you to gee them up. And tell them that if they don't pay up I'll see that they suffer the full weight of the law. I'll have them prosecuted for criminal damage. I am a magistrate after all. Take Arthur Pews with you.'

'Aren't we jumping the gun a bit, Marsh?' said Berkeley. 'It's only a circus. And they're great fun. I saw them at the Royal Middenshire Show and they wer–'

'What they have done to the village is inexcusable,' said Marcheline. 'And you must sort it out. So go and put some clothes on. You look like a prostitute.'

'A prostitute? In a onesie?'

'I won't have you parading your sex fetishes around for all to see. You're the Viscount Morbridge for Heaven's sake.'

'My what?'

'You can't deny that you are dressed as a half-naked woman.'

The Viscount Morbridge's onesie was amusingly printed to look like he was a semi-naked woman in suspenders and stockings. A pair of nipple tassels completed the look.

'I may be many things but I am not a transvestite,' snapped Berkeley indignantly. 'Now listen Marsh, I was just looking at property prices in the area. Did you see that Duck Halt in Pardley sold for more than three mill–'

But Marcheline had stomped off, heading for the kitchen to find a vase for the flowers she'd bought and to fulminate on the morning's events with Mrs Shandcreek, the housekeeper.

Berkeley looked down at his outfit. His friend had actually bought it for him because, he'd said, it looked like 'Marcheline with her kit off'. It had seemed funny at the time. It didn't feel so funny now.

He walked slowly upstairs to the bathroom to wash and get changed. Halfway up, he felt a little dizzy and held on to the banister for support. Marcheline's tantrums were causing him palpitations. Or maybe those damned oysters were repeating on him. He'd only managed three hours sleep due to indigestion. He took a deep breath and waited for the feeling to pass. And he smiled. Allowing the circus onto Cockering land had achieved exactly the effect he'd wanted.

One of Berkeley's greatest pleasures in life was inciting little acts of rebellion that upset his sister's obsessively controlled little world. They made him feel that he hadn't entirely surrendered his manhood in order to live a comfortable life. Marcheline was bombastic and opinionated, sharing the same indomitable spirit as her forebears. In particular, she reminded him of Bessie the suffragette, whose portrait hung above the grand staircase. Physically, they were not dissimilar – broad-hipped, strong-armed and handsome. In temperament she was Bessie to the core. When she became riled, it had been known for grown men to lock themselves inside their cars or run for their lives through bull-occupied fields. Even the late Taffy had been scared of her. However, where she held real power over Berkeley was in financial matters.

Their father, the former viscount, had been a canny man. Knowing that his son would, in all likelihood, fritter away any inheritance left to him, he had made provisions in his will to prevent this. Berkeley would inherit the family title and half the estate. Marcheline would inherit the other half and complete control of the family finances. As sole manager of the Cockering-owned farms, dairy, slaughterhouse and brewery, plus the rents from the village's residents and shops, she would control Berkeley's spending by paying him a generous allowance from the proceeds. And to ensure that he couldn't simply sell off half of the Cockering property portfolio, all of the deeds had been left in their joint names. None of the family assets could be sold without the agreement of both siblings. Berkeley was, therefore, completely reliant on the 'pocket money', as he called it, that his sister paid him for, basically, doing little more than staying out of her way.

But it was nowhere near enough for him to do all of the things he really wanted to do and it was a constant irritation to feel so disempowered. He therefore delighted in creating as many small annoyances as he could to infuriate her and to prove to himself that he was not entirely under the yoke. Allowing a shabby circus to set up at Brill was his latest wheeze. But she would soon see them off and things would once again return to normal, with him doing as he was told and knowing that he would forever be 'asset-rich, cash-poor'. In recent months, his frustrations had started to manifest as dark thoughts.

He reached the bathroom, splashed his face with cold water and drew a basin of warm. He rubbed at a stubborn ink mark on his hand with a flannel. The action reminded him of a scene from a recent Shakespearian production by the Morbridge Amateur Dramatics Society.

'All the perfumes of Arabia will not sweeten this little hand,' he said in a feigned Scots accent. 'But Swarfega should do the trick.'

And as he scrubbed, his mind was filled with wishful fantasies. He was no Macbeth, to be sure, and quite incapable of anything as dramatic as murder. But surely there had to be a way to escape his situation?

He dreamed of being far, far away from the rainy grey skies of South Herewardshire, the shortening days and the constant pervasive smell of cow pats. He should be living the high life on a yacht in the Caribbean, or in the casinos of Monaco, or in the stews of Hong Kong where money was the passport to every one of his deepest and naughtiest fantasies.

But he wasn't. He was stuck here; stuck with the demands that came with being the Viscount Morbridge and joint landlord of a large and valuable estate; stuck with the complaints of his tenants, the moans of the people who ran his farms, and the arrogance and snobbishness of the sodding Village Council. And, most of all, he was stuck with Marcheline. How he yearned to be free of her incessant ordering him about.

But freedom came at a cost. If he were to walk away, he would do so with nothing. His only assets were his peerage and the properties that he knew, with absolute certainty, would never be put up for sale as long as Marcheline drew breath. He was the joint owner of at least £350 million in property and he couldn't realise a single penny of it.

The fingers in his left hand began to tingle and a cold sweat began prickling his brow. A sudden crushing pain slammed into him and he collapsed to the floor, thumping at his chest as if trying to will his faltering, arrhythmic heartbeat back to regularity. And as he lay there, feeling his life ebbing away, Berkeley Cockering suspected that maybe his wish to be free of all worldly cares and woes had suddenly and unexpectedly come true.

Chapter 4

Mrs Shandcreek was plucking a brace of pheasants as Marcheline entered the kitchen.

'Morning, Miss Marcheline. Cup o' tea?'

'Lovely,' said Marcheline, sitting herself at the kitchen table. 'What a morning! You would not believe what's happened in the village.'

'I heard from Fred Clacketer when he delivered the game birds. They'm camped over at Brill Farm, you know. Caused some ruckus at the level crossing yesterday. Vicar's wearing a neck brace. And the professor's dog got hisself killed. Not that anyone will miss that little bastard.'

'That's appalling,' said Marcheline. 'I expect you know that Berkeley invited them.'

'Prob'ly. Sort of thing he'd do.'

Meg Shandcreek had worked at the Hall for most of her adult life. The Cockering children had grown up around her and she had loved them both, reserving a particularly soft spot for Marcheline who, while never an English Rose, had nevertheless been an attractive girl with good strong features. And so old-fashioned; you could see it in her twinsets and pearls, and her pillowy hairstyle. Mrs Shandcreek liked old-fashioned people because she was an old-fashioned soul herself, and she had done all she could during Marcheline's childhood to act as a buffer between her and the visceral realities of the modern world.

She brought a heavy chopper down upon a pheasant's neck with practised ease, severing the head cleanly. The fact that she hadn't always been so skilled was evident from the missing tip of her left index finger.

'He always were a contrary boy, even when you two was growing up. If you don't mind me speaking out of turn.'

Marcheline winced as the chopper fell on the second bird.

'You're always welcome to speak your mind, Meg. You're practically family. He does these things specifically to annoy me, you know. All because I won't give in to his demands. He forgets that the village and the farms were entrusted to our care. The Cockering family have been custodians of this land for over five hundred years. We've survived a revolution and two world wars and I won't be the one who allows all of that history to be simply sold off to the highest bidder. If we don't have our traditions and our history, what do we have? Not everything in this life is about money. We have a duty to the people that live and work here.'

'Money don't buy happiness,' said Mrs Shandcreek, waving the bloodied cleaver with worrying abandon. 'And it don't buy class neither.'

'Class is a rather old-fashioned concept these days,' said Marcheline, secretly agreeing with everything the old housekeeper said. 'Many of today's most influential people are self-made men and women.'

'Then they should have used better quality materials,' said Mrs Shandcreek, now doing something nasty with entrails. Marcheline avoided looking at the ghastly happenings on Meg's chopping board by getting up and rinsing out a lead crystal vase in which to arrange the flowers she'd bought at Twimbley's. She stood back to admire her handiwork but didn't like what she saw. She moved things around a little and then stood back again. If anything, the arrangement looked worse, but she decided to leave it alone, suspecting that, whatever she did, she would never be pleased with the display. Her heart just wasn't in it today. The events of the morning had tainted even this simple pleasure.

'Will you be dining at the Hall tonight, Miss Cockering?'

'I will, yes. I can't speak for Berkeley though,' said Marcheline.

'No, don't suppose you can,' said Mrs Shandcreek.

'Will you read my leaves for me, Meg?'

Mrs Shandcreek nodded, wiped her hands on a dishcloth and took Marcheline's cup. She swilled the dregs and then turned the cup over on the saucer. She stared at the pattern of sodden tea leaves that clung to the sides and stroked her chin.

'Oh, now that's interesting…'

'Go on,' said Marcheline.

'Something lost is found. Or could be something old is made new. There are signs here of renewal. Or rebirth.'

'That sounds intriguing.'

'Or something dead is made to live again maybe?'

'Zombies in rural South Herewardshire?' said Marcheline, laughing. 'It seems unlikely.'

'I'm just the reader… I don't write the book,' said Mrs Shandcreek, putting down the cup. 'And there's something else besides…'

Marcheline smiled knowingly. 'Is it children, Meg?'

'Oh yes. I see lots of children.'

'With all due respect, Meg, you always see lots of children.'

'I misses the sound of children, Miss Cockering. Nothing warms this old house up like children do.'

Marcheline sighed.

'Well, if my brother stopped wasting his life and got on with producing an heir to the—' A sudden strangled cry from upstairs and a dull thud stopped her mid-sentence.

Chapter 5

'Have you never heard of spell-checkers?'

Glupi shrugged. 'I never played it, Boss.'

'It's not a... never mind,' said Ben, sighing. He sat back in his found-in-a-skip chair and looked around the shabby interior of his caravan home for consolation.

'You should have asked me to check the posters before you got them printed. I mean... Circuscash? That's not even a word.'

'Is where Astrid collects the monies, innit?'

'That's called the Box Office. And yes, I know there are no boxes in there.'

Glupi shut his mouth.

Ben picked up the poster from his desk and squinted at it. 'What kind of printing firm would even print posters this bad?'

'I not get better for the monies you is payin',' said Glupi who, during a recent stop-over in Bovell, had persuaded a student to run them off on his college colour photocopier in return for a gallon of home-made hooch.

'We'll be a laughing stock,' said Ben.

'Laughs is good.'

'Not when they're laughs of derision. We can't put these up. I guess we can burn them as fuel.'

Glupi's face dropped. 'But we has put them up.'

'What?'

'Last night. After we sets up the tent. I tells the Bonzini Brothers to stick 'em up in the town.'

'You did?' Ben massaged his forehead. 'Maybe we can take them down before anyone sees them. How many did you put up?'

'All of thems.'

'All of them? But you said that you'd printed a hundred posters.'

'An' I did.'

'You mean you put up all hundred posters?'

'No,' said Glupi, pointing at the poster in Ellis's hands. 'I saves that one for you.'

Ben dropped the poster and put his head on his desk. It didn't help him solve the current problem but the cool of the laminate against his forehead felt good. Worry had ploughed deep furrows into his brow and had flecked his hair and beard with grey. He lifted his head and looked once again at the appalling poster. Was that an otter? With dentures?

'Well, they say that there's no such thing as bad publicity,' he sighed. 'Maybe the posters will bring in a few punters out of morbid curiosity.'

Glupi had no idea what morbid meant but it sounded bad. His English wasn't brilliant and nor was he. And the years of alcohol abuse hadn't improved the state of his brain cells either. At seventy-six he was quite possibly the oldest and stupidest clown in the business.

'We could be free of all this worry you know. We really could,' said Ben. 'Why won't they just retire?'

'They is circus people an' circus is their lifes,' said Glupi. 'Anyways, 'ow would you afford the golden showers, eh Boss?'

'Handshakes! Golden handshakes! And you're right. I can't even afford to pay you all this month.'

'No monies again?' said Glupi, his face a painted dipsomaniac mask of tragedy. 'They's not going to like that news.'

'I don't like it either. But there's no money for wages and that's for certain. We had to use the last of the petty cash to get the horse truck out of that pound in Mallingford. I don't suppose it would have got towed if you hadn't parked it across four disabled bays.'

'I's disabled.'

'*Delirium tremens* doesn't count as a disability.'

'I's got no sense of smell.'

'That doesn't count either.'

'So what does we do now?'

'What does we do? We does what we always does,' said Ben, falling into Glupi's peculiar vernacular. 'We put on a week of shows and hope that someone other than creditors and debt collectors turn up to watch it. Our total assets currently amount to sixty-five pounds. So we sell more stuff and we pull our belts in. See if a local scrap yard will pay us something for the clowns' car. It's beyond repair now. The mechanics actually laughed at the last MOT.'

'Laughs is good.'

'Again, not in this instance. I'm considering asking Summersmith if he objects to me selling the organ,' said Ellis. 'It's probably a valuable antique Wurlitzer or something and we could trade down to something smaller and cheaper. Or we could just sell Summersmith's organs I suppose? That's if anyone wants to buy the kidneys of a nonagenarian musician.'

'You wan' me to ask about work? We's on a farm.'

Ben shook his head.

'You're all too old for farm labouring anymore and all we usually get in return are misshapen vegetables and shoddy meat.'

'Yeah, I's sick of horse.'

'What?'

'I's sick of pork.'

Glupi made a mental note to remove the horseshoes he'd recently hung over the door of his caravan. They were bit of a giveaway. He stood up unsteadily.

'Anyways, that reminds me that I come here to say foods is ready.'

'I'm not hungry,' said Ben.

Glupi left Ben's Winnebago and made his way slowly towards the centre of the campsite. A balmy day had given way to a chilly September evening and the clear black velvet sky was encrusted with bright stars. He skirted the edge of the Big Top and slipped between two of the circus vehicles that were parked in a ragged circle, like the wagon trains of old. Outside the circle, inquisitive Friesians snuffled nervously around the lorries, campers and caravans.

The acrobatic Bonzini Brothers were building a rather shaky and rheumatic human pyramid; they doubled as the gangers who put up the tent, and the day's efforts had aggravated old injuries. The smell of embrocation was carried on the soft, cool breeze. The other performers were enjoying the warmth from a modest bonfire. Most of Glupi's colleagues were as old as, or older than, him. The youngest person on the payroll – if there had been a payroll – was fifty-nine-year old Hilda Angel, the lead horsewoman. The oldest was the organist, a cadaverous ninety-one-year-old spider of a man with the rather opulent name of Summersmith Mudd.

In between there were acts like the Magnificent Coltellos, a myopic knife-throwing husband and wife team. Their careers had nearly been curtailed by Genaro losing the use of his good right arm in 1999 and Sybella sporting a prosthetic leg as the result of a clumsy rehearsal shortly thereafter. Several bottles of Chianti and an argument over how fast the Wheel of Death should be spun had been contributory factors in both accidents.

There was a juggling act that consisted of two seventy-one-year-olds who dressed up in an extra-large one-piece outfit and called themselves Hung and Lo the Siamese Twins. Their act was in demonstrably poor taste, but they had started performing long before political correctness was invented and saw no good reason to change now. Besides which, two decades of rummaging in the same pair of trousers had resulted in their relationship going some way beyond the merely professional.

The troupe of clowns – Grimpen, Cronk, Flamo the fire-eater, and his dwarf assistant Dirk – were all over 70. And family trapeze act The Flying Mannings, whose most recent review had rather cattily stated that 'the only thing death-defying about their act is that two of them have been fitted with pacemakers,' were all similarly eligible for their bus passes.

Benelli's Circus was a collection of crumbling tumblers and asthmatic strongmen, thickly bespectacled knife-throwers and arthritic acrobats. At a time in their lives when they should have been relaxing in comfortable armchairs in front of the television, they were wrapped in blankets and squatting on piles of old newspapers in a damp and muddy cow field.

Glupi squeezed himself between Hung and Lo, an action that totally undermined their act, and looked hungrily at the small stew pot that bubbled over the fire. It contained whatever vegetables and herbs the performers had managed to forage or purloin from honesty box tables, plus the last of Glupi's 'pork'. Small silver packages at the edge of the fire showed that there were some baked potatoes too.

'Smell is nice,' said Glupi by way of a conversation opener, despite not being able to smell a thing.

'Judging by the fact you're not holding a roll of tenners in your grubby hands I'm guessing that we don't get paid again this week,' said Geraint Manning. 'Am I right?'

Glupi shrugged and threw some dried grass on the flames.

'The boss has got lots on his plates.'

'I wish we did. I'm starving,' said Summersmith Mudd. The sentiment was echoed by all who sat there.

'Mr Benjamin Senior always had money to pay our wages,' snapped the big cat tamer, a crusty old gent with a huge white moustache and the unfortunate name of Colonel Sanders. 'In those days, I had a splendid coat of hunting pink and a whip of best rawhide. Now, I find myself reduced to an ex-school blazer with the badge torn off and a suede whip bought from a sex shop. Can you believe that? A ruddy sex shop!'

'You cannot be blame the boss,' said Glupi. 'Circus is not popular no more with the kiddies. They wants video games and shit.'

'You're right I suppose,' said Vera Manning. 'How can a man, swinging through the air on a rope, compete against *Grand Theft Auto*?'

'What on Earth is *Grand Theft Auto*?' asked Sybella Coltello.

'What on Earth is a video game?' asked Summersmith Mudd.

'And we're parked up in the sticks,' said Penguin Boy. 'We'll be lucky if we take enough petrol money to get us to the next dump.'

'Ben he say we can always retire,' said Glupi, and was ignored.

'Potatoes are ready,' said Wanda Balls, glamorous magician's assistant to The Great Venturini. 'Get 'em while they're hot.'

The elderly circus folk collected their meagre fare. Glupi sliced at his baked potato with a dangerously sharp pocket knife and eyed the nearby herd of cows hungrily, his thoughts filled with visions of sumptuous steak pies and roast beef with all the trimmings. The Friesians remained at the periphery of the circle, lowing quietly. Some sixth sense told them that this was not a good time to investigate the new occupants of their field.

Chapter 6

Special Constable Arthur Pews hoped that he was in for a better day. After the fracas at the crossing he'd signed himself off sick and spent the following day, and night, being fussed over by Mrs Tiggs. However, his bruised ribs meant that their lovemaking had not proceeded with its usual enthusiasm and ardour. And now, as he got into his uniform with some discomfort, he noted in the mirror that he had the makings of a splendid black eye. He touched the purpling yellow flesh gingerly and a lascivious smile appeared on his lips. Maybe, with a suitably heroic backstory, he might be able to use his misfortunes to his advantage? The possibility of what he liked to call a 'sympathy legover' with one of the other ladies he occasionally visited wasn't out of the question. He'd had a very good week after that time he'd been trampled by one of the Cockerings' prize bulls.

However, as he drove into Shapcott Bassett he began to realise that today was going to be, if anything, even worse. It was the first he'd seen of the circus's over-enthusiastic marketing campaign and he knew exactly how Lady Marcheline would react when she saw it.

'Frightful mess isn't it?' said Bertie Barsted, who was waiting outside the police station carrying a pair of spectacles he'd found. 'You weren't around at the time I take it? Conducting enquiries?'

'I was,' said Pews, unlocking the door.

'Anyone I know?' said Barsted, winking.

Pews blushed.

'Well, you look like you've gone three rounds with George Foreman so remind me not to upset her, whoever she is.'

Pews smiled weakly and stepped inside the tiny station. Barsted followed.

'But seriously, Arthur. Can't you do something about these circus types? That's what we pay our rates for, isn't it?'

Pews refrained from pointing out that no-one had paid 'rates' in the village for decades and simply shrugged. 'I'm only one man and I'm a part-timer. I can't be in the village twenty-four hours a day. And my beat covers the whole parish. I have to service Doughton Magna, Monckton Ulcery, Chepping Frogmoor and Snipeton too.'

'Then we should speak to Marcheline about getting you some help. Well, when it's appropriate and proper, of course. Poor girl.'

'Poor girl? Is she that upset about the posters?'

'What? Oh good gracious. You probably don't know do you? Berkeley's had a heart attack,' explained Barsted.

'Oh Lord. Is he…?'

'He's recovering,' said Barsted. 'Mind you, it was always on the cards I suppose. You can't eat and drink like that man does and not expect consequences. Still, let's hope he gets better soon, eh? And then Marcheline can get us a proper bobby. I mean, you know, a full-time policeman. Or maybe two. No offence intended.'

'None taken.'

'Good. We need a few more like you, Arthur. Can't have

hooligans spoiling our way of life, can we? Oh, here you go. Found these by Big Bessie this morning. Stick them in lost property will you, there's a good chap.'

He placed the spectacles on the station counter and left. Pews checked his voicemail for messages. There was just the one; Lady Marcheline ordering him to collect some invoices from her to deliver to the circus people at Brill Farm. Not asking. Ordering. Her brother's illness hadn't dented her sense of outrage it seemed, nor her unshakeable belief that the village and everything in it – including the resident police officer – were hers to employ as she saw fit. He checked the mail, locked up the station and then set off in his car for Cockering Hall. And as he drove, he watched the specialist cleaners attempting to remove the posters. Whatever glue had been used was clearly very strong. Their services would not have been cheap to hire and, from what he'd seen at the level crossing, the circus probably didn't have much money to spare. They would not welcome his visit.

Arthur Pews' day was getting worse by the minute.

Marcheline returned to Cockering Hall in a dark mood. She'd been to the cottage hospital at Morbridge to visit Berkeley, expecting to find him at Death's door. Instead, she'd found him surprisingly upbeat and as unrepentant as ever. It seemed that he hadn't taken his heart attack at all seriously, which was absolutely typical of the man. He had instead spent his time complaining to her about the quality of the hospital food.

She made a phone call and then sat in her favourite sunny spot in the drawing room, working her way through the *Times* cryptic crossword. But her mind wasn't on solving the clues. Her concern for Berkeley's wellbeing had given way to contemplation of the future and, to her mind, it was far from rosy. Her father had suffered a series of small heart attacks followed by a massive and fatal coronary just after his sixtieth birthday. Berkeley had inherited the peerage, his father's love of fine wines, rich food and expensive cigars and now, it seemed, he'd also inherited his father's constitution. And if Berkeley were to die, the peerage would die with him.

Marcheline felt robbed. Although she was the eldest child, the ancient and misogynistic rules of primogeniture meant that Berkeley had become the Viscount Morbridge simply because he'd been born equipped with a penis that he had resolutely failed to use for its proper purpose. The man railed against responsibility and any curtailing of his freedom, so the likelihood of him marrying and producing children was remote, even if he returned to full health. To make matters worse, if Berkeley did expire without siring an heir, the bloodline died with him. The Cockerings were a small family with few branches and a genetic disorder that affected male fertility. Children were few and far between and, if there was no one suitable to inherit the title, there would be no more Viscount Morbridges and five centuries of family history would come to an abrupt and unsatisfactory end. Or, even worse, some obscure male relative could emerge from the woodwork to legitimately make a claim on the title. If they were successful, it might mean that they would stand to inherit the Cockering estate, possibly invalidating the provisions of her father's will. They would be empowered to sell all of the family-owned properties.

It was this awful prospect that had led Marcheline to phone the family solicitor for advice as soon as she'd got back from the hospital. He had been able to offer her one small ray of hope; if she were to produce a child of her own, preferably a boy, he would have an automatic right of inheritance. Even a legitimate daughter would provide a direct heir in this modern age, where equality was much more valued than it had been in the past. She would have a stronger claim on the estate than any distant cousin. The title might be lost but the Cockerings would remain at Cockering Hall. However, this seemed about as likely to happen as Berkeley becoming a father. Marcheline's intolerance of children was legendary and, despite Mrs Shandcreek's constant prods and unsubtle suggestions, she had never felt the urge to have children. But now, with Berkeley's health on the wane, she began to wonder whether it was now her responsibility to the family to provide the next Viscount. If so, the question was, how? You couldn't simply have Harrods deliver. And adoption was off the table too. In order to dispute other claims to the estate, any heir would have to be a Cockering by blood. All of which meant that a certain degree of what she considered to be 'beastliness' was necessary. And that was an issue.

It wasn't that she didn't understand the mechanics of the reproductive process; she'd lost her virginity to a rebarbative Oxford Blue at the Henley Regatta at the age of twenty-one. But the man had been brutish and drunk and had displayed as little consideration for her comfort as he'd had discrimination about points of entry. Consequently, she had developed a deep distaste for the sexual act, and men in particular, which was further compounded by witnessing the husbandry that took place on her various farms. For a time she suspected that she might be a lesbian, but she found the idea of two women having sex just as repulsive as heterosexual sex, and had therefore arrived at the sensible conclusion that she was asexual. She saw such behaviour in humans as sordid and necessary only for procreation, and Berkeley's predilection for the seediest of sexual partners had merely added fuel to the fires of her celibacy. All of that grunting and straining was not for ladies who owned Minton tea-sets and who had once captained the hockey team at Roedean.

And so, she'd married herself to her work; to the village and the Hall, to the management of her farms and businesses, and her stewardship of the local woodlands. Men and babies had never been a part of her life but now, at the age of forty-three and suddenly in need of a child, she wondered whether it was too late for either.

A sense of grievance overwhelmed her and outrage grew in her bosom. At any time during the nine years since her father's death she could have listened to Berkeley's constant moans and evicted her tenants, sold the family property portfolio and lived comfortably at the Hall, a very rich woman, for the rest of her life. But she had stuck to her principles, her sense of responsibility, and her belief in what was right. The Cockering family name was more important than money. It was a name that still commanded respect, not just within the county, but throughout the upper tiers of British society. Her family tree was littered with high-ranking military officers, royal equerries, judges, bishops and knighted captains of industry. Cockering beer held a royal warrant; their small beer had been a particular favourite of Queen Victoria. Cockering forty-five-day dry-aged forerib of heritage beef was served in the top London restaurants and was said to rival the best found anywhere else in the world. You didn't just throw away all of that reputation and history for a quick buck and selfish personal gratification.

Marcheline had forgone the path of luxury, love and marriage in favour of duty and her reward, it now seemed, was the very real threat of seeing everything slip away once she herself had slipped away. The ancient family name would be no more and all that she, and the Cockerings who had come before her, had worked so hard to build and preserve, all that she had sacrificed so much for, would be lost. Within a generation, her village would become a generic, homogenous anytown made up of rentable holiday cottages and second homes that were occupied for just a few weeks a year. The iniquity of it all bubbled up inside her and hot tears rolled down her reddened cheeks.

Marcheline threw the newspaper in the bin and wandered out into the great entrance hall of her family home. And, as she stared up at the faces of her long-dead ancestors, it seemed to her that they were scowling, as if they knew that the unbroken series of family portraits might stop with her. The fact that she was a woman made their judgement all the more damning; she could palpably sense their scorn.

Her eyes fell upon the portrait of Sir Bummell Cockeringe, an eighteenth-century 'whoremasterly rogue' whose rollicking exploits had earned him a place in Aubrey's *Brief Lives* and whose adventures with the naughty upper-class Diabolical Club, and in the bawdy houses of France and Spain, were second only to Casanova's. In light of this, his eldest son Judge Parsden Cockering had, upon reaching his majority, instigated the practice of pronouncing the family name as '*Corring*' to avoid any further associations with sleaze.

Next to Parsden was the portrait of his pugnacious granddaughter, Bessie the suffragette. Then there was Lionel the deserter, Cedric the poisoner, Buxton the Blackshirt; there were as many rogues among Marcheline's ancestors as there were nobles and philanthropists, but they had all shared one thing in common; they had all had committed acts – sometimes terrible acts – with the utter conviction that they were doing the right thing, even if history had patently demonstrated that they weren't. None of them had ever experienced any doubts that they were right, and none of them had worried about the consequences of their arrogant certainty.

A new and terrible resolve gripped Marcheline and took hold. The blood that had once coursed through the veins of Bummell, Parsden, Bessie and all the others was the same blood that now pounded in her ears. Ancient blood. Powerful blood. Cockering blood. She vowed to her forebears that she would find a way to keep the Cockering name and the Morbridge title alive. Ideally she would engineer a situation that would force her brother to do his duty. But if that proved impossible, she would produce an heir herself to ensure the continuation of the bloodline. It would mean finding a man to father that son of course. But she would do it.

At the barrel end of a shotgun if need be.

Chapter 7

'That's never a happy sight,' said Audrey Manning. She pointed to a police car that was bouncing across the field towards Ben Ellis's Winnebago.

'I bet it's that filthy pervert from the level crossing yesterday,' said Hilda Angel, who still hadn't quite regained her composure.

'He's probably after sponging some free tickets for tonight's show,' said Audrey.

Arthur Pews stepped out of his car and put his helmet on. It was a little old-fashioned in the modern age of baseball caps, but the additional height gave him a little more presence and he was glad of it. Although he stood at just under six feet tall, his substantial girth and stumpy legs made him look shorter, egg-shaped and somehow comical. People didn't take Special Constable Pews very seriously. But then nothing serious ever happened in Shapcott Bassett, which was why the Chief Constable had never appointed a full-time regular officer to the parish. His colleagues at Divisional HQ in nearby Morbridge cruelly called the village 'St Peter's Waiting Room', and they had a point.

45

At thirty-three, Demelza Ostridge was the youngest inhabitant; a shy bespectacled girl who ran the mobile library and who still lived with her parents in the old Snipeton Crossing railway cottages. Apart from her, the only young people in Shapcott Bassett were the crowds of music lovers who came to the annual music concert at Cockering Hall and the occasional bird watchers who came in search of rare ducks. But any thoughts they might have had of illegal activity were soon quashed by the sight of furry-faced farmers carrying unbroken shotguns about the place. The crime rate was zero and that suited Pews very well. He was quite content to play the role of ineffective but avuncular part-time policeman, just as Grimson Freacke was happy to be the eccentric clergyman with several marbles missing. It was that sort of village.

Marcheline had chosen her tenants with all the care of a 1950s British film casting director; librarians were timid shrews, butchers were big red-faced men with forearms like hams and the village bobby was bumbling and jocular and, if not wholly respected, was treated kindly. Certainly, the uniform made him popular with the younger widows and divorcees, which was the main reason why he'd become a Special in the first place.

But now the circus had come to town and he cursed them for disturbing his enviably quiet life, and for the very real possibility of being replaced or having to risk his personal safety further. He had heard plenty of lurid stories about 'circus folk' and 'travellers', and his experience at the level crossing had done nothing to allay his fears. It was therefore something of a relief to knock upon the door of the largest motor caravan and find himself face to face with the same pleasant, bearded man he'd met the day before.

'Come in, officer, come in,' said Ben. 'So sorry about that business yesterday. Ouch. That's quite a shiner you have there.'

'Actually, I'm here about the posters in Shapcott Bassett.'

'Ah. A little misunderstanding between me and my staff. I never intended all of the... wait, did you say Shapcott Bassett?'

'I did.'

'You mean Morbridge.'

'No, they're definitely in Shapcott Bassett.'

Ben clapped his hands to his face and pulled his cheeks downwards, forming his face into a reasonable facsimile of Munch's *The Scream*.

'Let me get this straight... you're saying that my people put up a hundred posters in the wrong town?'

'Village,' said Pews. 'Or more of a hamlet really.'

'I'll bloody kill him.'

Pews looked confused and slightly worried.

'Look, officer, there's been a bit of a cock-up but I'll sort it out. I'll send some people over to remove them and –'

'No need for that,' interrupted Pews. 'Lady Cockering has already contracted a cleaning firm. She asked me to give you this.'

Ben looked at the invoice and sat down hard.

'Eight hundred pounds!'

'Apparently your people used something like superglue. Needed specialist solvents or something.'

'But I don't even have eighty pounds!'

'Oh and there's these,' said Pews, presenting a small bundle of papers to the ashen-faced circus owner. Ben feverishly glanced through them.

'Reverend Freacke's and Major Crantlemain's insurance claims,' explained Pews, helpfully. 'That... er... larger lady and those horses damaged their cars.'

'But all of that was caused by the dog!'

'Oh yes, there's the vet's bill too.'

'Vet's bill? The little sod was mashed between two cars!'

'There's still a cremation and funeral service to be paid for.'

'Funeral service!'

'I can leave this with you then, can I?' said Pews, edging towards the door. 'And if you have any questions, I wouldn't go bothering Lady Cockering. Her brother's just had a heart attack and she's a bit upset, as you can imagine. You can always contact me at the police station in Shapcott Bassett.'

He paused at the door.

'I don't suppose there's any chance of a couple of tickets for...'

Ben glared venomously.

'Right... well, I'll be off then.'

Ben slapped the pile of bills onto his desk and stifled the urge to scream.

Benjamin Ellis hated his circus. He hated the top hats and the pancake and the sawdust and swore that if he had to listen to the *yup-dup-dubba-dubba-dup-dup-dah-dup* of Fučík's *Entrance of the Gladiators* one more time he'd do someone a mischief.

Benelli's Circus had once been *Taranti's Circus* but Taranti had been a gambler and his debts had run high. In desperation, he'd approached a successful North London pawnbroker called Benjamin Ellis, for help. Ellis had looked at the various assets on offer and took a bold decision; why not pawn the lot? He'd never pawned a circus before but recognised the value of such a thing and, after consultation with his solicitors, agreed on a price. A contract was drawn up, and Taranti left the brokers with ten thousand pounds, which he successfully gambled away in under twenty-four hours. Three days later he was found floating facedown in the Thames with two bullets in his head.

This left Ellis with a circus all of his very own. Despite calls from his family to sell it, he decided that he would, if at all possible, earn a living from it. It was 1968, during the golden age of circuses, when every performance was packed with beaming faces and the bulging tills rang with the clatter of pre-decimal currency. Taranti's was a successful and profitable concern and the performers were happy to stay on under new management as they genuinely had no idea what else they'd do. And surely it was everyone's childhood dream to own a circus, wasn't it?

And so, leaving his sister and her husband to run the pawn shop, Ellis began to tour the country with the re-christened Ben Ellis's Circus. In time, he married a contortionist called Bendy Wendy and, due to frequent misspellings in local papers, the name of his circus soon mutated into the pseudo-Italian *Benelli's*.

Benjamin Jnr was born in 1979 and had a childhood that most children would envy. He travelled the country and all over Europe. He and the other circus children were educated at home and never had to go to school. And whereas other children had hamsters and kittens, he'd had lions and tigers and elephants as surrogate pets. He loved the circus and knew that, one day, he would inherit it from his parents. And so he did, prematurely and unexpectedly in 1996, when both were killed during a bizarre aerial sex act on the trapeze. Devastated, and not a little embarrassed, Benjamin Jnr had promised the performers that the show would go on.

But it didn't. Throughout the materialistic '80s and hedonistic '90s, the circus became an unfashionable anachronism, unable to compete with other, more exciting forms of modern entertainment. The general trend towards liberating animals from public performance had also led to falling gates and rising debts. To make matters worse, several high-profile cases of animal cruelty at other circuses had led many councils and local authorities to ban anything other than all-human shows, and Benelli's performers were no longer lithe and flexible enough to rival the Cirque du Soleil. The Millennium came and went, and, as the performers and animals got older and less able, Ben could only watch with sadness as his beloved circus slowly and inevitably began to die.

Takings at the box office had, by now, become so meagre that they were no longer covering even the most basic costs. And so, with a heavy heart, he'd decided that the game simply wasn't worth the candle any more. He would sell up and maybe pursue another career. He'd always fancied being a writer and had seen a number of his articles and short stories published in magazines and local papers. In general his work was very well-received, but he didn't want to be a journalist. He had started work on a novel and he longed for the peace, freedom and time to finish it. He'd also passed the age of thirty without finding a woman with whom to share his life and start a family. Somehow, there had never been the time and, anyway, the peripatetic nature of his lifestyle had hardly lent itself to long-term relationships or a stable environment in which to bring up children. But all of these things would become suddenly possible if he was able to rid himself of the circus, he realised.

However, disposing of it had proven to be next to impossible. Although he had been left ownership of the circus by his parents, they'd also given shares to each of the performers. Therefore, he could not sell it without majority shareholder agreement from his staff and they had flatly refused at every suggestion. Many had started their careers as child acts, a few even with the late Taranti, and others were the children of Taranti performers and had never known anything but circus life. Added to that was their nomadic lifestyles, and a degree of senility, which also meant that they were very rarely up to speed with current affairs and woefully ignorant of just how obsolete they were. Thinking that perhaps he'd sack the lot of them and then sell up, Ben had then discovered that it was only legally possible to lay off an employee if he paid them a substantial golden handshake amounting to a year's wage. In issuing the shares and setting these rules, Benjamin Snr had ensured a secure future for his friends after his death. But he had also unintentionally created a poisoned chalice as his only son's inheritance.

Resentment had quickly set in and, faced with seemingly little choice, Ben had begun a secret war of attrition to nudge his elderly employees towards voluntary retirement. He'd insisted on paying all bills before paying the performers, in the hope that they'd drift away to more lucrative careers. They hadn't. He'd deliberately chosen rural venues that were likely to attract pitiful numbers of customers. But still the show had gone on. For a time he'd even tried 'rediscovering' his Judaism and had insisted that the circus not perform on the Sabbath – the most lucrative days of the week. But still the circus folk stayed loyal. They'd even taken on piecework at local farms; cabbage-cutting and strawberry-picking and other similar back-breaking activities in order to raise enough money to pay the bills and buy food enough to live on. And, in doing so, the performers' strength of character and determination had touched Ben's heart and a new respect for them had grown and blossomed. He'd buried his personal grievances and shelved his ambitions in order to do all he could to earn enough money for his staff to live out their senior years with some dignity. Every day was a struggle. Their acts were outdated and poorly performed, their costumes were threadbare and their equipment was in constant need of repair. Wages were a rare luxury, and food a bare necessity. But as long as there was enough money for petrol to get them to the next pitch, they considered themselves solvent. It was a blessing that most of them had now reached the age where they could draw a state pension and no longer had to pay for medical prescriptions.

But now the circus had finally come unstuck.

At first, it had seemed like a golden opportunity; the Viscount Morbridge had been so amused by their chaotic performance at the Royal Middenshire Show that he had insisted that they come and pitch on his land. Such offers were rare and Ben had grabbed at it. Admittedly, the town of Morbridge and its surrounding villages were likely to offer slim pickings, but something was better than nothing and a rent-free pitch meant that, for once, they might even turn a profit. However, the box office probably wouldn't even cover the total of Lady Cockering's invoices, he realised, and that meant that they were now stuck here, penniless and unable to move on to more lucrative pastures. His friends, for whom he wanted nothing but good things, would have to work and work and work to pay off their debts. The show would go on. And on. And on until the last juggler, contortionist or clown was dead.

Ellis looked again at the pile of unpayable bills and felt a sudden, uncharacteristic need for a stiff drink. He reached into the bottom drawer of his desk and produced a dusty unopened bottle, and a glass. He poured himself a measure and knocked it back in one gulp. Almost immediately, he realised that he'd made a terrible mistake. Like the most powerful drain cleaner, the appalling liquid scoured its way down his throat and settled in his stomach like napalm. Blundering around the Winnebago, he took huge gulps of air in the hope of extinguishing the flames that he felt sure were engulfing his torso. Some distant memory told him that you should drink milk if you'd swallowed something aggressively caustic, which was what he feared he had surely done. He spluttered and gagged, his tongue desperately trying to escape from his mouth, as he lumbered towards his small fridge. His field of vision seemed suddenly concave as if seen through a fish-eye lens. The world became kaleidoscopic and there were strange, fuzzy, indistinct patches where colours flashed that the human eye wasn't equipped to see. Then the world closed in on him as all light and warmth was sucked out of the room.

He awoke in a pool of his own drool, and noted that it was noticeably darker than before. How much time had he spent unconscious? Or had his eyes stopped working properly? With a groan, he stood up and walked to his fridge. He grabbed the carton of milk he knew was in there, greedily gulping at the cold soothing liquid, his cauterised taste buds unable to sense that it had slightly gone off.

'Fuck,' he said as he finished the carton. His head throbbed and his fingers felt like ice. Everything seemed unnaturally loud. A fly buzzed past, sounding like a chainsaw. His elbow knocked a small pile of paperclips off his desk and they clattered and clanged like a Gamelan ensemble as they hit the floor. He tried to focus on the bottle he'd drunk from, expecting to see a hazardous chemical symbol or a skull and crossbones. Instead, the label said *Highland Fling. Geniune Scotch Wiskey.* He suddenly remembered where he'd got the bottle from and why he'd hidden it away in a drawer. It was a bottle of Glupi's homemade moonshine; an untouched, unwanted and unpalatable present from his fortieth birthday party.

He stoppered the bottle with shaking hands. The glass that had dropped from his nerveless fingers lay on the pile of bills. The spillage was sufficiently potent to have killed the fly, which had been foolish enough to chance a taste, and had dissolved the ink on the uppermost bill. The vapour rising from the spillage was still visible, distorting the air like a heat haze. Presumably the beastly stuff was dangerously inflammable.

A mad thought popped unbidden into his head. With trembling hands he placed the wet bill on the floor and struck a match. As the flame hit the paper, it flared as brightly as magnesium and, in just seconds, all that was left was ash. Ben sat down in his chair and a terrible idea formed in his mind. He knew that the circus was insured; Benjamin Snr had been a very cautious man indeed and had set the policy in place in the 1970s. And it had continued to be paid by Benjamin Jnr, who'd considered that the biannual premiums were the one guarantee he had that he and his staff were covered in the event of accidents. What he'd never done before was consider it as a way out of his predicament. He pulled out a worn manila envelope from his desk drawer and scanned through the contents. The insurance policy was incredibly comprehensive and it appeared that should the circus be destroyed – by a catastrophic fire for example – any payout would be quite substantial. More importantly, there was no clause about him having to use the money in a 'like for like' replacement. The insurance money could be divvied up between himself and the performers and they'd all be finally free.

It would be so easy to pass off a fire as an accident, he realised. It was common knowledge that Glupi operated an illegal still and he always parked his motor caravan next to the Big Top. If a fire broke out in his home it would go up like a rocket and take the tent with it. Blame would undoubtedly fall on the old clown, which was tough, but surely they'd take his age into account? And being found guilty of making illicit hooch would surely only result in a fine at worst. It was an enticing thought and, best of all, if arranged properly, it needn't endanger any lives.

Ben was so excited, and yet so terrified, by the thought of

what he was suddenly considering doing that he very nearly took another drink from the bottle to congratulate himself.

Chapter 8

Marcheline wiped the make-up from her face with an increasingly dirty flannel and looked again at the issue of *Vogue* that she'd bought at Twimbley's. Stan had been very surprised. Magazines like *Cosmopolitan* and *Marie Claire* indicated a very curious change of reading habits – her usual fare rarely went beyond *The Times* and an occasional copy of *Farmers' Weekly*. However, Marcheline undoubtedly had her reasons and he wasn't going to stir the bucket and pry. Besides, had she told him the truth, he'd probably have thought she was having a joke at his expense.

One of the cover models' faces was not dissimilar in shape to her own but somehow, no matter how hard she tried, Marcheline couldn't achieve the same uniformity of skin tone and smoothness of texture. The fact that most of her cosmetics were years old probably didn't help. The face powders were as dry as sand and the lipsticks hard and candle-like. Marcheline was wholly unaware of the degree to which photographs were manipulated in order to match some fashion-editor's idea of female perfection. She flicked through the pages and made one further attempt at turning her face into something approximating the look being sported by some Hollywood Alister she'd never heard of, and then compared it with what she saw in the mirror.

'I wouldn't look out of place in that damned circus,' she muttered and attacked her face with the flannel again.

With no interest in men and a full and busy life, Marcheline had never had time for beautifying herself. Or, rather, she had seen such behaviour as pointless vanity and wasted time that could be better spent doing something more constructive. Her regimen went no further than a sink wash in the morning and before bed, and a bath every other day using soap and water. She'd even been known to use washing-up liquid on her hair when she'd forgotten to buy shampoo. Six times a year, she booked herself a hair appointment in Morbridge where she had the same *bouffant*-style cut every time. It was so consistent that the hairdressers referred to it as the *Marcheline*.

But now she was faced with the reality of going out into the world to attract a man and the prospect was daunting. Being technology-averse almost to the point of phobia meant that negotiating the internet for help and advice was a non-starter. Besides which, she hadn't touched a computer since her school days and had no clue where to even start. Berkeley used the internet all the time but she could hardly ask his advice. Nor could she ask her friends, as they were mostly elderly ladies who found their mobile phones perplexing enough. She was also unlikely to get any tips in the arts of seduction; her choice of residents and her social status meant that all of the women she knew well were cut from the same cloth as herself. Bunty Clacketer was as red-faced and thick-forearmed as her butcher husband and was more likely to be seen spattered in pig's blood than blusher, and the only flesh that Meg Shandcreek had ever shaved and pampered was on the pigs' heads she deboned, salted and rolled as cheek joints. What Marcheline needed was some expert advice.

London was only three hours away. Where better to investigate what was currently *de rigueur* in make-up, fashion and hairstyle? She resolved to catch the train at Uttercombe in the morning.

Chapter 9

At Brill Farm Ben was weeding out the sick and infirm and ensuring that those who were fit enough to perform were ready for opening night. Tonto the Human Telephone Directory was having a panic attack and had locked himself in his caravan. Phone numbers had consisted of far fewer digits when he'd first created his act and since the advent of mobiles his anxiety had resulted in ever more frequent meltdowns. Penguin Boy had gout in one of his flippers and Le Tosseur had arthritis and was unable to juggle. Astrid the Bearded Lady's HRT treatment had cured her hot flushes but had effectively removed her livelihood, and one of the Flying Mannings had sustained a cut on her wrist after one of the Magnificent Coltello's knives had deflected off Sybilla's prosthetic thigh. To top it all, Della the elephant had stomach cramps after eating too many cooking apples from under the tree to which she was tethered and would have to sit out the performance. But, despite these setbacks, the majority of the aged troupe was fit for work and ready to put on some sort of a show.

The audience had started to arrive and consisted mostly of local residents and staff from the brewery at Doughton Magna.

A handful of villagers from Shapcott Bassett and nearby Chepping Frogmoor had also drifted in. Into this mix was added a contingent of rough-looking bikers from Hamingwell who'd discovered the circus quite by accident while on a road trip. Their appearance had quickly succeeded in frightening many other customers away and Ellis couldn't help but notice that the stalls were less than a third full. It also didn't help that a small group of animal rights protestors from Nasely had positioned themselves outside the ticket office and were handing out leaflets that described the horror and cruelty of using animals in circuses. Already, there had been a small clash between them and staff from the local abattoir.

Ben found Glupi sitting in the doorway of his camper van swigging deeply from a bottle of his homemade 'wiskey'. Ben shuddered as he remembered his own experience with the stuff. The man's insides must be made of cast iron, he thought.

'Good evenings, Boss.'

Glupi shut the caravan door and belched. A small cloud of midges dropped anaesthetised to the ground. 'I hear about cleaning bills. That's bad shit.'

'It is bad shit,' said Ben. 'Not only did you send the Bonzinis in the wrong direction, they stuck the posters up with something approximating superglue. Should I ask you what it was and where you got it from?'

Glupi looked shamefacedly at his outsize boots.

'In skip behind sofa factory when was camped in Brackhampton. Was free glue, Boss.'

Ben sighed. 'What's done is done. You ready for tonight?'

'Yeah, guess is so,' said Glupi. 'I's feeling a little bit sick though.'

Ben was not in the least surprised. The clown's diet seemed

to consist entirely of poor quality meat, very few vegetables, no fruit and all washed down with gallons of bad liquor. A sudden idea came to him.

'Then why not take the evening off? We've hardly any punters in. Grimpen and Cronk can cover for you.'

'Why?' said Glupi, suspiciously.

'Why not? You've been working really hard lately and there's been lots of driving. Get yourself into town and have a decent meal. You're no good to me ill,' said Ben. He handed the clown a twenty-pound note. 'Just don't tell the others, eh?'

'Twenty quids?' said Glupi, incredulously. 'But the bills?'

'Sod the bills,' said Ben. 'You may balls things up from time to time but I don't think I could keep this madness going without you. Go on, get out of here before I change my mind.'

Glupi shrugged and smiled.

'I'd change first though, if I were you though,' said Ben. 'If the people in the town see that you're connected with the circus...'

He waited as the old clown entered his camper van and then, in far less time than it would have taken him to have included a wash, emerged in his best suit. Glupi gave his boss a double thumbs up and then loped off towards Morbridge while wiping off the remnants of his make-up with a towel of indeterminate colour.

All was going to plan, thought Ben. Tonight, the still would be unguarded.

Chapter 10

Albert Manning, high in the upper reaches of the Big Top and hanging from a trapeze by his ankles, popped a metal bit between his teeth and steeled himself. Attached to the bit was a looped leather strap that his wife, Audrey, caught hold of. To the unenthusiastic applause of the tiny crowd, Audrey let go of her trapeze bar and hung there, gently spinning, held aloft only by the strength of Albert Manning's jaw muscles. Unfortunately, his denture adhesive was not so hardy. As he felt a gap forming between his upper plate and the roof of his mouth, he made a desperate but unsuccessful grab for his wife's arm. The crowd roared their appreciation as Audrey plummeted into the safety net, closely followed by her husband's teeth. High above, Albert drooled and shouted for someone to rescue his dentures before they were trodden on. The bikers showed their appreciation by showering the circus ring with empty beer cans and popcorn. As the no longer Flying Manning was helped from the net, Ben strode into the ring to announce the next act. His red coat bore the marks of coarsely stitched repairs and his battered top hat, crammed down hard upon his head, had been old when his father had bought it.

The show was going about as well as he'd expected, which was not very well at all. Summersmith Mudd's organ playing was erratic due to a flare-up of his sciatica, star attraction Della the elephant had now developed a nasty case of the runs and the smell was drifting inside the tent. Meanwhile, The Great Venturini had made the mistake of selecting one of the larger and dimmer bikers to be his volunteer from the audience. Having made the man's watch disappear he had consequently been hauled into the air by his shirt collar and threatened with a knuckleduster until he'd given it back. After this, his hands had shaken so badly with fear that every trick had gone wrong and his fumbled playing cards littered the floor of the circus ring. The biker had then goosed the luscious Wanda on his way back to his seat and she'd run out of the ring crying and hadn't been seen since. Their motor caravan had disappeared and the distraught Venturini, presuming that she'd fled home to her sister's house in Westcombe-on-Sea, had driven after her in the cattle truck, unwittingly taking the horses with him. Consequently, there would be no performance by the Daughters of Epona tonight either. But still, Ben struggled along.

'Ladies and Gentlemen, boys and girls... and now... Benelli's Circus proudly presents a plucky performance of peerless pyromania... the flamboyant, inflammable Flamo and his intrepid assistant Daring Dirk!'

As the fire-breathing clowns strode into the ring, Ben moved to the back of the Big Top and popped out through a tent fly. The smell of elephant ordure was much stronger outside and he held his nose as he crept around to the rear of the tent to where all of the circus people's mobile homes were parked in a circle. Glupi's camper van was actually positioned against the canvas and could not have been better placed for what he had in mind even if he'd parked it himself. His own

Winnebago was parked by the big cats' trailer on the opposite edge of the circle, next to the area of field that had been set aside for the incontinent elephant who was currently dozing under the tree. Ben was satisfied that it was just far enough away for her to be unaffected by the coming conflagration. He tiptoed his way to Glupi's van and, finding the lock usefully broken, gently pulled open the door and crept inside.

The first thing that hit him was the smell – a rich, dense fug of body odour, cheap ale, and even cheaper aftershave. Clothes lay scattered all over the floor and bed and, in a corner, stood a shop-window mannequin wearing Glupi's unkempt stage costume and orange wig. The shelves and tabletops were covered with mugs and glasses full of mould, coffee dregs, and cigarette ends. A broken cooker stood lopsidedly against a wall, the oven door missing and the space inside apparently being used to store empty bottles. On a nicotine stained window someone had written 'Bless this crapper'.

Many different smells vied for dominance but one rose above them all; a curious, sharp, almost medicinal smell that emanated from an extraordinary W Heath Robinson-style contraption of copper tanks, plastic tubes and funnels, all held together with rubber bands, gaffer tape and what looked like knotted condoms. At one end of the apparatus was a large metal bowl covered in a glass dome that sat on a hot plate. It contained a glutinous stew of something that looked like porridge, that bubbled and farted with fermenting gas. The mash was peppered, literally, with hot red chillies – presumably they provided the uniquely agonising 'kick' to Glupi's moonshine. At the other end was a copper water tank, which acted as the condenser for the illegal still. Like the rest of his elderly colleagues, Glupi hadn't been paid for months and had quickly run out of money with which to purchase those little liquid luxuries he craved. He had therefore improvised a still, and so powerful and potent was his home-made tipple that Flamo had started to use it in his act because it was cheaper than petrol.

Ben found a small tap on the copper tank and turned it on. A steady flow of the noxious liquid began to trickle onto the floor and out of the door, pooling nicely underneath the camper van. He stepped out of the noisome vehicle and pulled a box of matches out of his pocket. But then he paused; if this liquid was as incendiary as he suspected it was, wouldn't he get caught in the fireball if he was too close? What he needed was some kind of remote lighting system, a fuse of some kind. Perhaps he could leave a trail up to the camper van, like people did with gunpowder in the movies? If so he could use the vile liquid itself. Stepping once more inside the now eye-wateringly fume-filled vehicle, he found an empty wine bottle and held it under the spigot. It was barely quarter full before the flow slowed to a trickle and stopped. The still was empty. Ellis stepped outside and walked backwards away from the camper van, trailing the liquid behind him. To his annoyance, it ran out after only five feet, not nearly as far away as he'd have liked. Checking to see that he was unobserved, he quickly skipped over to his own home and collected the bottle of 'Highland Fling' from his drawer. Returning to where he'd left off, he continued the trail and wondered where to stop. The obvious place was by the ancient cannon, as that was furthest away and offered good cover. However, he wasn't entirely sure that the clowns didn't have some kind of gunpowder stash, so it possibly wasn't the safest option. Instead, he decided to end the trail in the dark shadows between the tiger's trailer and his own motor home. Placing the still half-full bottle on the ground by the front door of his own Winnebago, he crouched down and prepared himself.

This was it, his last chance to back out. For a short while he agonised over the enormity of it all, running the likely series of events over and over again in his mind. First, Glupi's camper van would go up, and then the old dry canvas of the ancient tent. Once the fire caught properly, the people would rush out – there wasn't enough of an audience to worry about anyone being crushed – and the Big Top would become a raging inferno. Then, while everyone was distracted, he'd brush over the trail he'd laid, to cover any evidence of arson. It all seemed simple enough. By the time anyone arrived to deal with the fire, the Big Top would be no more. Benelli's Circus would be out of business and the blame would fall squarely upon Glupi and his still.

He struck a match against the box and it flared. There was a mighty roar and the smell of foul breath in his face as, startled, one of Colonel Sanders' aged tigers lunged at the bars of its cage and loudly expressed its opinion of people who struck matches while it was trying to get to sleep. Ben threw himself backwards in an instinctive act of self-preservation and unwittingly knocked over the bottle of Highland Fling.

'Bloody hell,' he growled. Heart pounding, he took a deep breath. He lit another match and touched it to the trail. With a loud hiss, it caught and a beautiful violet flame raced away from him towards Glupi's camper van. Then stopped. He cursed as he realised that he hadn't joined the two trails together properly. But there was no going back now. He had to risk lighting the shorter five feet long trail. But as he stood up, he was horrified to see that the contents of the spilled bottle of Highland Fling were now flowing in a small rivulet towards his end of the still-flaming trail. As it touched, fire rushed backwards towards the bottle.

'Fuck!' shouted Ben as he threw himself to the ground just in time to avoid the small explosion that ensued. With a loud *Whooompf!* the bottle shattered and Ben's motor home burst into flame. As it was mostly clad in tired and sun-bleached wooden panelling, the fire was quick to take hold and grow, something he realised after a minute of pointless beating at it with his ringmaster's jacket, which also caught fire. He stood up and desperately looked around for a fire extinguisher. He knew there was one at the box office so he ran there, snatched up the extinguisher and rushed back.

In that short time, the fire seemed to have doubled in size and had caught the attention of the circus folk backstage who had emerged from the rear entrance of the Big Top. The Bonzinis were pulling the tigers' cage to a safe distance away from the fire, while Colonel Sanders attempted to calm the terrified old cats inside. Ben aimed the nozzle of the extinguisher at his Winnebago and squeezed the handle. The extinguisher coughed once and died. Having been used once over a decade ago and never replaced, it was long past any utility. Throwing the useless object to the ground, he looked around for something else he could use. In his panic, he barely registered that the trail had now extinguished itself and Glupi's camper van stood completely unharmed. Seeing a bucket standing outside the rear fly of the circus tent, he grabbed it up and ran back to the fire, failing to hear Cronk's cries of 'Oy!' and to note that the bucket was a good deal lighter than it should have been.

Later, he was to claim that he'd read somewhere that, in moments of great stress, the human body is capable of amazing feats of strength and that he'd assumed the same thing had happened to him with that bucket.

But, whatever the reason, he realised too late that a clown's bucket wouldn't be full of water. As the thousands of pieces of confetti-type paper hit the flames, the fire seemed to momentarily treble in size.

Ben howled as half of his beard turned to ash. He ran back towards the circus tent. A crowd of curious onlookers had started to drift away from the show to watch the hugely more entertaining events outside. News of the fire had spread and the Big Top had quickly emptied.

'Water!' shouted Ben. 'Someone get some water!'

The tyres on the Winnebago were alight now and one of them popped with a noise like a gunshot. A window exploded, showering him with glass. Suddenly Dirk appeared carrying a plastic bucket. Ben grabbed it from the dwarf, accidentally knocking him to the ground in the process, and ran across to his home and threw the contents over the fire. The resulting eruption of flame knocked him off his feet and sent Della the elephant into spasms. Trumpeting in terror and simultaneously venting urine and liquid manure at the sorts of pressures one usually associated with police water cannons, Della sprayed indiscriminately and struggled against her tether. Ben stood up and felt a punch in his left buttock.

'That was a whole week's supply of fuel for the act!' shouted Dirk. 'Glupi doesn't give it away, you idiot!'

But Ben wasn't listening. He took one more look at the blaze and fell to his knees in shock. In the distance, sirens could be heard and the bikers, not wishing to be associated with the chaos, or blamed for it, decided to make themselves scarce. But they had reckoned without Della. Snapping her rope with one final pull, the terrified animal stampeded away from the fire and, scattering motorcycles in her wake, thundered through the car parking area. The leader of the bikers howled in horror as he saw his beloved Norton turn to so much scrap beneath her huge feet.

'My bike!' he sobbed. 'My beautiful fucking bike!' He produced a knife from his jacket and stalked towards the terrified elephant.

In an instant, one of the animal rights protestors hurled himself at the biker, smashing a 'NO TO ANIMAL

CIRCUSES!' placard into the other man's face and dashing the knife from his hand. As the two men writhed on the floor, another biker slipped in the pool of liquid excrement and staggered backwards, his flailing arm knocking a brewery worker to the ground. Almost immediately, the brewers – who had finished off a few growlers between them during the show – launched themselves at the bikers. To add to the din and confusion, Special Constable Pews and the Morbridge fire brigade turned up just as the flames reached the butane tank that provided Ben's vehicle with cooking gas. In a vast bloom of flames and smoke, and a noise that made people clap their hands to their ears, the motor home launched into the air, exploded again in mid-somersault as the petrol tank caught, and then came crashing down upon Pews' patrol car. Pews took one look at the situation and screamed into his radio for reinforcements. Police from as far away as Uttercombe, some ten miles to the north, eventually arrived to help quell the riot.

As Glupi walked along the normally quiet road from Morbridge towards the circus camp, he wondered what was going on. There seemed to be blue lights everywhere as police cars, fire engines and ambulances raced past him at speed in both directions. However, fatigue, drunkenness and a belly full of gammon, egg and chips washed down with beer and a hip flask of his terrible homemade spirit overrode his curiosity and he staggered off the main road and fell into a comfortable ditch. He was asleep before he hit the soft mossy grass, and completely missed the sight and smell of a soiled and terrified elephant stampeding past him.

Chapter 11

The Reverend Grimson Freacke poured himself a cup of tea and settled himself on the sofa in excited anticipation. The reality show, *Essex: Orange County*, was his one guilty pleasure – if he could be forgiven a taste for fine port – and, for some reason he couldn't explain, he took enormous pleasure from watching the complex interplay of personal relationships among the cast. Maybe it was because the lives of this small group of uneducated twenty-somethings from Harlow New Town were so very different from his own quiet, pastoral existence. Or perhaps it was because they did things that he would never dare to do and said things that he would never dare to say and, by vicariously joining their weekly adventures, he could enjoy the sensation of being outrageous by proxy. Whatever the reason, he was hooked. And tonight looked to be something extra special, as the stars were 'having it large' in Kavos.

His television was very old and very small compared to the giant plasma screens that he regularly saw advertised on it. It didn't even have a remote control, as his late dog had destroyed it – and itself – in one unfortunate swallowing mishap. But he was happy with what he had, as he watched it infrequently and, when he did, it was usually to provide background noise while he cooked his evening meal. The TV's small tinny speaker was loud enough for his needs and he wondered why people felt the need to install multi-speaker surround sound systems. Surely the world was loud enough without adding to the cacophony? Besides, if his television was any noisier, he'd doubtless receive complaints from old Mrs Rabberley, whose ancient wisteria-covered cottage leaned against the vicarage. That said, his TV did seem to be louder than usual tonight. Or, rather, he could feel a deep, resonant bass beat through his slippered feet that seemed to be accompanying images of the sepia-skinned Essex revellers stripping to their underwear to enjoy an evening of foam party fun. And the regular *thump-thadump-thadump* was getting louder. The Reverend got up and turned the volume control down to zero but the throbbing beat was still there. *Thump-thump-thadump*. Small china items on the sideboard began to tinkle. The surface of the water in the goldfish bowl rippled as if a stone had been thrown into it. A sharp knocking on the wall told him that Mrs Rabberley had concluded that he was the source of the noise and she was making her annoyance known with the handle end of her walking stick. Meanwhile, the rumble grew in intensity. So did the angry knocking. *Thump-thadump-thadump. Tok-tok-tok.*

As the Reverend busied himself making smaller, fragile items secure, so that they didn't fall off shelves and the mantelpiece, it passed through his mind that maybe South Herewardshire was experiencing some kind of earth tremor; although that did seem unlikely. And, besides, the beat was too regular. Now that he listened again, he noted that the rhythm sounded less like a musical beat and more like a horse galloping, or a herd of horses galloping in perfect synchrony. And, he realised, it was coming from outside. He went to the front window, pulled open the curtains and was surprised to see a large elephant stampeding past his home in the direction of Market Square. Doubtless inspired more by his TV viewing than his sermons, the Reverend said 'Good Lord!' and quickly threw on his jacket and hat, running out into the street in pursuit of the animal. He didn't know if he would be needed, or indeed what help he could possibly render in a case of elephant stampede, but he couldn't simply ignore it.

Della arrived in Market Square and slowed to a halt, huffing loudly. The brisk two-mile trot from Brill Farm to Shapcott Bassett was the most exercise she'd had in years, but fear of the fire had given wings to her enormous feet. She'd initially only run about a mile before stopping and then, confused and frightened, she'd tried to find her way back, but had taken the wrong fork in the road and had found herself in the village instead. Her unfamiliar surroundings were, once again, making her feel panicky and a gnawing ache in her stomach reminded her that she had voided everything she'd eaten in the past forty-eight hours. From somewhere deep inside her animal brain came the thought that she needed food. Food was comfort. Food would make things better. She sniffed the night air, her trunk raised high, and caught the scent of vegetables. Cautiously, she walked towards Twimbley's Grocery store to explore further.

It was part of Dr Michael Sleight's daily routine to take a brisk walk into Market Square of an evening, to enjoy a couple of pints of Cockering IPA and a gossip with friends at the King's Head, and then to walk back home to his cottage in Churn Way. But tonight, he found his routine interrupted in the most surreal way by what was clearly a large Indian elephant wandering about and sniffing the air. Dr Sleight tried to remember if he'd ever read any advice regarding what to do if you found yourself unexpectedly in the company of an elephant, but nothing surfaced. Instead, he simply stood and watched as the animal waddled towards Twimbley's. A sudden, wheezing noise from behind prompted him to turn his head. The Reverend Freacke arrived at his side, silent in his slippered feet, but breathing heavily after his unscheduled jog into the village.

'Evening, Michael,' said the Reverend. 'What about this then, eh? Quite an unexpected event for a Tuesday evening.'

'Or any evening, for that matter,' said Dr Sleight. He made to walk towards the elephant.

'Wait... aren't we supposed to stand still or something? Isn't it the case that they can't see us if we stand still?'

'I think you're confusing elephants with dinosaurs,' said Dr Sleight. 'And that was only in a Hollywood film.'

'Maybe it works for all big animals. Is there someone we could call? I mean the police or a zoo or a vet or something?'

'I am a vet,' snapped Dr Sleight. 'Retired, admittedly.'

'Of course. Sorry.'

'You call who you want, Reverend. But my money is on that circus over at Brill Farm having something to do with this.'

'Of course, the circus!' said the Reverend. 'I'll just nip into the pub and make a call. I appear to have left my mobile phone at home.'

Inside the King's Head, those drinkers who didn't have their noses pressed up against the windows were listening to Major Menzies Crantlemain's blood-curdling accounts of executions involving elephants that he claimed to have witnessed during his time in India.

'Just as quick as a guillotine but much cheaper,' he explained, his speech slurred and his eyes staring wildly. 'Chap just puts his head on a flat rock, Jumbo puts his foot on top and applies his full weight and pop! Instantaneous death.' He brought his fist down sharply on a bag of crisps with a loud pop that spattered the table with shards of fried potato. Professor

Ostridge covered his mouth with his hand and ran for the toilets. He still hadn't quite recovered from the sight of his dog sandwiched between two cars.

'Ah! Just the man!' said the Reverend, elbowing his way through the crowd. 'Major, I know that you've had some experience with elephants. What do you advise?'

The Major hesitated. Like most of his stories, his elephant tales were either hugely exaggerated or purloined from braver and more interesting colleagues, and the only time he'd ever seen a live elephant was at a safari park near Liverpool. But Menzies Crantlemain was not the kind of man to lose face before an audience, especially over something as trivial as the truth.

'Don't fret, Reverend, I know what to do,' he announced with a confidence born of three decades of blustering, and bolstered by the six double gin and tonics he'd thrown back in the past hour. As he walked unsteadily towards the door of the pub, the Reverend Freacke picked up a telephone directory and began paging through to find the number for Brill Farm.

Dr Sleight had got very close to the elephant and was speaking to her in the same soothing voice he'd always used when addressing the frightened or angry pets that had come into his surgery for treatment. It seemed to be having some effect. Della was contentedly munching her way through the pile of tired and past their sell-by date vegetables that she'd found in the wheelie bins behind Twimbley's.

'That's right, good girl… easy now… good girl,' said Dr Sleight as he walked slowly forward and tentatively put his hand on her side. The elephant turned her head to acknowledge the fact that he was there, but didn't appear to feel threatened and carried on eating. Emboldened by this, the doctor picked up the trailing end of the rope that was still around Della's neck. There was just enough slack to tie her to something until the circus folk could collect her.

The rear of the shop boasted a floating extension that had doubled the size of the first-floor flat. It was supported by two sturdy concrete pillars and acted as a roof for the loading bay. Dr Sleight gently tied the rope to the nearest pillar, all the while speaking in his most comforting voice. 'Good girl... nice and easy now... someone will be here for you very soon. Easy now...'

It was more or less at this point that Major Crantlemain, red-faced and belligerent, came staggering into view brandishing what appeared to be a small, dry Hydrangea bush above his head and shouting, 'Paii! Paii!' at the top of his lungs. It was the only mahout command he knew, and he wasn't entirely sure what it meant, but his appearance and the volume of his voice were enough. With a loud, trumpeting roar, Della once again decided to get as far away from humans as quickly as she could. She strained against the tether and, to his horror, Dr Sleight watched as a large crack appeared in the concrete pillar.

Stan Twimbley didn't live in the flat above his shop – he lived in a cottage on the Hoddenford Road – but he did allow Fred and Bunty Clacketer's son Eric to lodge there in return for a nominal rent. Although this was technically sub-letting, Marcheline didn't mind as it gave the habitually nervous Agatha Twimbley a greater feeling of security by having someone live on the premises. It was she who had insisted on the shop having the village's only CCTV camera fitted. And, besides, it was good for Eric to live away from his parents, as it gave him his independence which, at the age of thirty-six, he undoubtedly needed.

Eric was a likeable man, polite and unassuming, an excellent butcher and a credit to his parents. But behind closed doors, he presented a somewhat different face to the world. In the online world of fetish chat rooms he was known to his peers as Meatman69 and, over the past decade, he'd accumulated an impressive range of hoods, gags, restraints, straps and other forms of restrictive clothing in which he liked to photograph himself, to excite his virtual friends in bondage. And, once every couple of months, when his parents thought he was in London to catch up with his old university chums, he would attend a fetish club event where a night of latex, leather and anonymous sex, all washed down with garishly coloured alcoholic shots and MDMA, would satisfy his libido for a few months. In the meantime, there was internet porn and ever-more extreme forms of masturbation; his latest variant was to tightly wrap his erect penis in butcher's string as if it was a *rosa di parma*-style beef tenderloin.

But tonight was rubber night and Eric was enjoying a peer-to-peer video chat with a latex-hooded lady from Wuppertal when the room suddenly jolted violently around him. He walked to the window as quickly as his rubber-clad and strapped-together legs would allow him to and peered down into the back yard of the shop, but could see nothing untoward. The jolt had been so strong that it had felt as if a car had run into the building. With visions of ram-raiders, he waddled back into his front room and looked out onto Market Square. There was no evidence of any illegal activity there either, just a large crowd of people standing outside the pub. Fearing that someone might spot him in his gimp mask, Eric dropped below the window sill. It was an action that undoubtedly saved his life.

Underneath the floating half of his flat and hidden from view, Della decided that if she couldn't pull free, she would push. Placing her mighty forehead against the pillar that held her fast, she dug her huge feet into the ground and, with a sickening crack, the concrete began to fracture and crumble. Encouraged by this, she pushed even harder. Dr Sleight looked up and saw the building's extension starting to sag at one corner under its own weight. It was his cue to make a run for it towards the pub. Della pushed one more time and the pillar fell free and crashed noisily to the ground. The elephant's momentum carried her forward through the alleyway between Twimbley's and Barsted's Bakery and out into Market Square, where the crowd of onlookers scattered in all directions. Behind her, a series of terrible noises heralded the collapse of the floating extension.

Crawling back to his bedroom below the eye line of his lounge window, Meatman69 suddenly felt the room tilt alarmingly. As he began sliding towards his bedroom door, he made a desperate grab for the architrave, but missed. The extension had now reached the point of no return and, with an almighty crash, it collapsed into the loading bay, the walls bursting open and spilling the contents of Eric's bedroom into public view. Eric felt himself hurtling towards the ground, but then halted. By sheer good fortune a piece of bent rebar had snagged on the hole cut into the buttock area of his thick rubber leggings and he hung, upside-down and suspended by his backside above the heads of the bemused villagers below. As the dust settled and the good people of Shapcott Bassett slowly moved in to examine the damage and, in particular, the collection of extreme German pornography that lay among the wreckage, Eric sobbed into his gimp mask.

'Fuck me,' said the Reverend Grimson Freacke, uncharacteristically.

In the near distance, an elephant trumpeted triumphantly as she was reunited with her mahout on the Morbridge Road.

Chapter 12

Wednesday morning began fine and bright, although a lack of breeze meant that a smoky, greasy pall still hung over the Brill Farm estate. It was visible from Shapcott Bassett, and several people commented upon it to Arthur Pews as he arrived at work and opened up the tiny police station. Pews cursed the circus and wished that it had never come within a hundred miles of his patch. It had caused him nothing but aggravation, pain and report-writing in recent days.

He made himself a cup of tea and sat down in his favourite old leather armchair behind the counter, idly flicking through a magazine that he'd found amongst the wreckage of Eric Clacketer's bedroom, and which he'd utterly failed to officially dispose of. He puffed out his cheeks at the ribald delights within and yawned. It had been an unnaturally busy couple of days. He considered taking a nap in the upstairs bedroom.

The police station, a tiny converted two-up two-down cottage in Creamery Walk, had been Pews' home for twenty years. It consisted of a front office and counter, a small bedroom, a bathroom, and a room out the back with a telephone and a computer that he used mostly to watch video content that his superiors would frown upon. In the tiny cottage garden he kept a coop of bantams that provided him with fresh eggs for his breakfast – when he wasn't having one cooked for him by a lady angling for a new husband – and an outdoor toilet. The door had collapsed from woodworm in 1998, so he used it as a storeroom.

The front door to the station suddenly opened and Pews dropped the magazine to the floor and stood up as if the National Anthem had just started playing.

'Your ladyship!'

'Good morning, Arthur.'

'I was sorry to hear about your brother. How is he?'

'As well as can be expected, given the fact that he seems to be utterly bent on self-destruction,' said Marcheline. 'I'll pass on your best wishes though.'

'Thank you.'

'Now, I understand you were present at that fracas with the circus folk last night.'

'I was. Nasty business.'

'Indeed. And I see that you picked up quite a shiner there.'

Pews was about to correct her but then reconsidered. The reality of being beaten up by three middle-aged horsewomen seemed rather less heroic than trying to control a small riot.

'Yes, well, things did get a little hairy.'

'I'm ashamed to say I slept through the whole thing,' said Marcheline. 'Were you also present when that animal brought down the rear of Twimbley's?'

'Not when it happened, no. I just saw the results when I returned home from Brill Farm. Nasty business.'

'Things have got quite out of hand,' said Marcheline. 'There was an emergency meeting of the Village Council first thing this morning, and they asked me to telephone the Chief Constable to demand that we have some extra police officers posted to the village, at least until the circus has moved on.'

'I see,' said Pews.

'But I needn't have bothered. You know what these Chief Constables are like, Arthur. They are obsessed with what happens in the larger towns and cities and little consideration is given to rural affairs. Plus, there have been all sorts of government cut-backs apparently. Long story short, she didn't seem very keen to help. So I'm afraid that we're on our own and it will, as usual, fall to me to sort the matter out. I am a magistrate after all.'

Arthur Pews was quite aware that she was a magistrate. She reminded everyone of the fact almost daily.

'Now, do we know what caused the fire at the farm?'

'Not really. I was muscled out of any investigation by the Morbridge CID,' said Pews. 'I did hear that there was some kind of illegal still in one of the caravans though.'

'Shocking behaviour. And the elephant?'

'Back with its owner,' said Pews. 'An elderly gentleman called Colonel Sanders.'

'A Colonel you say? Then he should know better.'

'Heh. He'll never fit one of those legs into a deep fat fryer,' said Pews, smiling.

'What?'

'You know… it's finger-lickin' goo–'

'What is wrong with people these days, Arthur? What's happened to personal responsibility and our sense of morality?'

'There is a general decline in standards across the country,' said Pews, surreptitiously nudging the copy of *Gummiliebhaber Monatlich* out of sight under the counter with his boot.

'You and I, we grew up in the same decade, didn't we Arthur?' said Marcheline. 'Where did it all go wrong?'

'Lack of respect and good manners,' said Pews. 'You can't run a country without respect and manners. And discipline too.'

Marcheline smiled. 'I hadn't realised how very similar our views are. You have surprised me, Arthur.'

'Your Ladyship?'

'Yes, indeed, Arthur,' she said, laying her hand on his. 'You have surprised me a great deal. Keep up the good work.'

She gave him a strange, coy smile and left the police station.

Pews watched her go, noting the way that her tight tweed skirt accentuated her backside, and scratched his head. Had Lady Marcheline Cockering just flirted with him? It hadn't been a blatant come-on, admittedly, but it had seemed like a flirt nonetheless. And she'd been wearing make-up of sorts. In any other circumstances, he wouldn't have noticed. Women often flirted with him. It was something to do with the uniform, he supposed, and the fact that most of the male population of Shapcott Bassett was either married or geriatric. But Marcheline didn't flirt. Nor did she wear make-up. Those were universal constants, unchanging and fixed like the waxing and waning of the Moon and the flavour of Bertie Barsted's Herewardshire buns. Arthur sat down and swallowed the dregs of his tea. He'd known Marcheline for decades and not once, in all those years, had she ever given any indication that she was interested in men. She had been wholeheartedly dedicated to her family and her village, in that order. The idea that she might have flirted with him sent a tingle down his spine, as did remembering the sight of her magnificent buttocks. And with the tingle came the sudden realisation that he had a crush on Marcheline Cockering and probably always had.

Chapter 13

Ben awoke and, for just the briefest of moments, believed that he was in Heaven. All around was light and warmth and the woman leaning over him was very pretty and smiling angelically.

'Can you hear me, Mr Ellis?'

His vision began to sharpen and what he'd taken to be the fluffy clouds of the Afterlife morphed into the swirls of an artexed ceiling. The angel, he now realised, was wearing a dental brace, which seemed unlikely.

'You're going to feel a little bit groggy as the anaesthetic wears off, but it will soon pass.'

Ben rolled his eyes left and right and saw that he was lying inside a white curtained cubicle.

'Where am I?' he attempted to croak, but his throat was sandpaper-dry and all that emerged was, 'Wheh ahhh eye?'

'Don't try to speak. You inhaled a lot of very hot air and your throat and mouth got a little burnt,' said the nurse. 'You're in the cottage hospital in Morbridge. The doctor will come and see you in a minute. And then there's a policeman who wants to talk to you afterwards.'

Ben shrank beneath the starched white sheets.

Glupi was also in a state of some confusion. He'd woken, chilled and damp in a dewy ditch by the side of the road, and had made his way back to the campsite. However, it was obvious even from a distance that something significant had happened while he'd been away, and his deep instinct for self-preservation told him that maybe it was best to remain inconspicuous for the time being. He hid among a spinney of conifers and took in the scene. There had been a fire, a big fire; that much was obvious. A thin column of smoke still rose from the shell of Ben's Winnebago – and the police car squashed beneath – and a number of the elderly performers were standing around staring at the wreckage. But more than just a fire had happened, apparently. A lorry was collecting a tangled mess of broken motorcycles, and a vet was sedating Della the Elephant. Most worrying, however, was the sight of his own caravan undergoing stringent forensic examination by the police.

His still was being slowly dismantled and each piece was being bagged, labelled and stored in a stack of crates marked 'evidence'. Police officers were everywhere, interviewing performers and punters alike. Glupi skirted around the outside of the camp, unnoticed by all, but, even if he had been spotted, he doubted that the other performers would recognise him as he so rarely got out of costume and greasepaint. However, he wasn't about to chance it.

He wondered what he should do. He could hardly return to the camp. He had a cast-iron alibi in respect of where he had been during the previous evening, but the police were obviously interested in the contents of his caravan and would therefore be interested in him. At the very least he'd be prosecuted for the still. And then there was Ben. He hoped that he hadn't been in his vehicle when whatever had happened to it had happened. But, even assuming he was still alive, Glupi doubted that he'd be very pleased to see him either. No, the circus could take care of itself, he decided, and he would lay low for a while.

He strolled away from the campsite and towards the low hills above Shapcott Bassett. The woods were thick and deep there and, he was sure, would provide everything he needed for an indeterminate stay. His stint in the Red Army in the 1960s would stand him in good stead now.

Chapter 14

After leaving the police station, Marcheline went to offer Stan Twimbley her sympathy and to promise that repairs to the shop would be organised as soon as possible. She then visited Fred and Bunty Clacketer, to reassure them that no one was likely to blame them for what their son got up to behind closed doors. Eric himself had gone to stay with some friends in London for a while. Then she took morning tea at Miss Dillby's, as was her custom when the daily round afforded her the time, all the while doing her level best to control her blushes whenever she recalled what had happened in the police station. She had been just as surprised by her own behaviour as Arthur Pews had been. Quite why she'd suddenly decided to test whether she still had any kind of female allure was a mystery. And why on the village bobby of all people? As pleasant a fellow as he was, Pews certainly wasn't known for his discriminating good taste and, frankly, would probably respond to a come on from any female still capable of surviving a bout of lovemaking. But something had made her try her hand at flirting and there had been a reaction, a definite reaction. Marcheline admitted herself some small pleasure in the fact. But what could she do with this knowledge? What was the next step? She felt hopelessly and uncomfortably out of her depth.

She finished her Lady Grey and stared at the tea leaves in the bottom of her cup and, remembering Meg Shandcreek's predictions, once again found herself pondering her uncertain future. She remembered her epiphany beneath the stern portraits of her ancestors, and self-pity quickly turned to determination. As practical as a sperm bank was, it seemed to her coldly clinical and, besides, the donor would be anonymous. She much preferred the idea of having some say in the paternity of her prospective child. This meant that she needed a man and, in order to get one, she needed to bone up on her courting skills. It had been a long time since she'd flirted and trying it on with Arthur Pews had made her feel uncomfortable, but she had to admit that the experiment had been rather a success. Pews had quite definitely developed what she called 'doe eyes' towards her, so perhaps the task wouldn't be so difficult after all. If she could successfully run an entire village, several businesses and organise the lives of the people around her, surely she could attract the attentions of a single man? She simply needed to approach the business of motherhood as she did any other project – with good research and forward planning.

The more pressing question was who she should attempt to woo. Shapcott Bassett was hardly a hotbed of suitable young Lotharios and what single men there were offered a poor choice. Beyond the village there were younger men working in the brewery and the slaughterhouse but they were mostly married and, besides, they were her employees and were therefore not really suitable for her purposes. Pews would no doubt be willing, but he wasn't the sharpest knife in the box and, besides, his willingness extended to far too many women she knew. And, as she had no intention of ever having anything to do with the father of her child beyond conception, a local man would be awkward. She didn't want to have to face them on a regular basis or put up with their demands for time with the child. All of which meant that she needed to look further afield, further even perhaps than Bowcester, Pockheal or Pawley at the other end of the county. Ideally, he should live sufficiently far away to ensure that he would never see her or the child ever again, maybe even as far away as London. If so, her trip today would be a good way to test the waters.

She finished her tea and then drove her Rover slowly and noisily to Uttercombe station where she caught the 10.32am express train to Paddington. Three hours later she was stepping out of a taxi in Oxford Street. Her first stop was Selfridges. She then, quite by chance, happened upon a sex shop. Marcheline knew that the whole sordid business had been commodified in recent years and that shops of this kind could be found on the High Streets of most large towns but she'd never seen one for real. However, as perverse as the idea of a shop for sex sounded to her, she had to concede that it was the sort of place that would surely hold the secret to bewitching a man. Taking a deep breath, and some comfort from the fact that no one was likely to recognise her, she stepped inside.

The interior of the shop wasn't at all what she had expected. The exterior looked no less respectable than some of the fashion outlets nearby – although the mannequin in the window did seem to be wearing some kind of undergarment made entirely of red string – but she'd expected things to be less salubrious inside. Instead, to her surprise, it was light and airy and clean. There were no strange men in overcoats or other seedy types, as she'd imagined there might be. Instead there were quite a few young men and women and even couples walking about, carrying shopping baskets just like they would in Twimbley's. For a brief moment, she suspected that she had somehow accidently wandered into the wrong shop, but closer inspection revealed that the long ivory-coloured object in the basket of the young woman nearest her was not a prize-winning leek. The sheer size of the dildo was extraordinary, of a girth and length that she'd only previously seen exhibited by horses. It was surely inconceivable that the slim, attractive woman who'd picked it up intended to… Marcheline cleared such thoughts from her mind and walked slowly around the store looking at the displays. And, as she did so, she subtly perused other women's baskets in an effort to see if there was any kind of consistency to their purchases, any hint as to what was popular with the gentlemen. But other people's shopping choices simply added to her perplexity by presenting her with a range of objects that she couldn't even identify, let alone figure out what they might be used for.

A quarter of an hour later, Marcheline was none the wiser. What would someone want with an enema flush bulb or a cruelly spiked Wartenberg Wheel, for example? And the huge range of vibrators, clamps, gags, restraints, pumps, lubricants, magazines and sex furniture had left her feeling completely out of her depth. The sheer breadth of choice was bewildering.

'Can I help you at all?'

A young sales assistant appeared at her side and smiled brightly. She was dressed in a tiny pink leopard-print skirt and a see-through black fishnet vest over a pretty pink bra. 'Love the outfit,' she said. 'I work with Harris Tweed a lot at uni. Beautiful stuff.'

'Uni?'

'This is just a part-time job. I'm studying fashion design. You don't think I work here by choice do you? Mind you the staff discount is good. Keeps my boyfriend happy anyway!'

'Well, quite,' said Marcheline, smiling clumsily.

'Tell you what, come with me back here and we'll have a chat.'

The saleswoman led Marcheline to a small room off the main shopping area. They sat in a matching pair of large pink leather beanbags shaped like breasts complete with nipple cushions.

'My name's Clare,' said the saleswoman. 'And something tells me that you're new to this kind of shop. I guess it can be a bit overwhelming, seeing all this stuff.'

'Oh dear, this is all so... well, you know,' said Marcheline.

'Makes you realise just how many different ways people like to please each other, doesn't it? Do you have an idea of what sort of thing are you looking for?'

'To be frank, none at all. You see, I need a man.'

'I'm afraid we don't sell them yet,' said Clare, beaming. 'So, this man... what's he into?'

'Into?'

'What turns him on?'

'I have absolutely no idea. I haven't met him yet.'

'Ah, I see. You're on the pull.'

'I am?'

'You're looking for a man.'

'Yes. And I need something that will make me more... alluring. Something that a man might find irresistible.'

'Blokes are all different and they all like different things,' said Clare. 'But I've never met a man who didn't like a good pair of bangers. You could try a push-up.'

'I see. And how would that help?' asked Marcheline, wondering what men's liking for sausages had to do with it and why physical exercise, even such a very small amount, would be any kind of aphrodisiac.

'You've got a good rack. My advice is to get those puppies doing the work for you. A push-up and a matching set of undies; something sexy and girly. You'll be fighting them off, trust me.'

By the time Marcheline had finished her consultation, she had considerably increased her vocabulary, and purchased two bra-and-knicker sets complete with suspender belts and stockings, a full-length semi-transparent black nightie, a 'saucy nurse' outfit and a pot of yellow herbal tablets that, apparently, would 'produce a boner in a corpse'. She had also bought a device called the Suckmaster 3000 Penis Pump in the mistaken belief that the machine would handle some of the 'beastliness' for her, thus reducing the amount of hands-on work she would have to endure. It looked rather like one of the milking machines she regularly saw in use on her farms and she assumed that it performed a similar function. And, as a thank you for making her first purchase, the store had also presented her with a choice of free gifts. Marcheline had plumped for something called a butt plug. It looked too small for a butt of wine but she imagined it was just the thing for stoppering an open bottle to keep the contents fresh.

Chapter 15

Ben had spent most of the day dozing, or pretending to doze, which had been enough to keep the big bad policeman from his door. But, by six o'clock in the evening, he was feeling ravenously hungry and the fact that the two other patients in his ward were already eating didn't help matters as the delicious smell of their meals were drifting under the curtains drawn around his bed. All of which meant that there was no putting it off any longer; if he wanted to eat, he would have to reveal that he was well enough to eat. And that meant that he was also well enough to be interviewed by the police. He ordered his food and, while he waited for his dinner to arrive, he got out of bed and went to the bathroom to use a proper toilet for the first time since he'd been admitted and to explore the extent of his injuries. It wasn't a pretty sight. His head had been shaved of what little hair hadn't been turned to ash in the explosion and there was a deep gash on the top of his head that had been stitched. His eyebrows and lashes were burnt down to stubble, as was most of the right hand side of his beard. It hurt to breathe. He did his business and then wandered back to his bed.

'You look better,' said the nurse. 'I assume you won't need a wee bottle or bedpan any more?'

'Fie... fine now,' Ben croaked.

'It could have been a lot worse you know,' said the nurse, changing his bedding. 'I heard you were in some kind of explosion. I can't imagine that very many people walk away from an explosion.'

'Don' really know wha' happened,' said Ben. It was the same lie that he told the detective who turned up a short while later to interview him. But the police officer was having none of it. Nor of Ben's apparent inability to speak. He needed a conviction and he was determined to make sure that he got one.

Detective Sergeant Brian Blount was a bitter man. Three years previously, his disastrous handling of a high-profile murder investigation had led to his demotion and a transfer to Morbridge Division where, as the Chief Constable put it, there was 'scant opportunity for him to do any further harm to the force's reputation'. He'd been lucky to survive the inquiry into his actions with his job and his pension intact. But the embers of ambition still burned, as did a very real sense of grievance.

Blount knew that he wasn't the brightest or most imaginative of coppers but he had earned his inspector's pips by dogged determination and by never being afraid to claim the credit for a good result, even if the majority of the work had been done by his subordinates. The murder of bestselling author Shirley Pomerance had been a difficult and complicated case, and he believed that he'd acted properly throughout. The fact that he'd been pointed in the wrong direction and had subsequently made a number of significant blunders was, he claimed, something that could have happened to anyone.

He'd just been unlucky. He was a good policeman, a reliable and steadfast policeman, and he spent his days hoping for a sufficiently serious case with which to redeem himself and regain his former rank. However, the fact that he now worked at Morbridge – the quietest police division in the most law-abiding county in England – meant that his dream was unlikely to be realised. The little market town provided no challenges for him whatsoever, beyond an occasional domestic burglary or car theft. And besides, Chief Constable Jo Raynott would not be an easy person to convince. She was one of a new breed of progressive, university-educated senior officers, bursting with innovative business practices, psychological insights and left-field ideas about policing. In her brave new world inspectors were expected to be 'enablers' rather than supervisors. She encouraged mind-mapping, plenary discussions and something called 'thought showers', and Blount, if he was honest, had absolutely no idea what she was talking about most of the time. He didn't engage in 'outcome-focused services', and he wasn't sure if he could ever be the 'client-centred agent of change' that she wanted him to be. He caught villains, not 'high harm causers', and he was determined to catch and prosecute as many of the bastards as he could, thereby building an impressive catalogue of successful investigations that even she could not ignore.

And now he had a potential arson case to play with – possibly even an attempted murder if he pushed hard enough. Ben Ellis was the conviction he needed to expunge his past failures, the key that would unlock the doors to a brighter, happier and more financially secure future when he was reinstated as a detective inspector. He would not let such an opportunity slip through his fingers.

'Right, let's go over this again,' he said, looming over the bed. Blount was extremely tall and cadaverously thin and resembled nothing so much as an angle-poise lamp in a cheap supermarket suit.

'I ca... can't teh you any... more,' said Ben, making every syllable sound like an agonising Herculean effort. His throat was very sore, he was tired and his painkillers were beginning to wear off. The last thing he'd needed was a police interrogation, so he'd decided to gild the lily regarding his injuries in an effort to shorten the interview. 'I've tol' you wha' appen' fie times now.'

'Four actually,' said Blount, 'But let's make it five. I'd like to hear it again.'

'Bu my throa...'

'Yes your throat is burned, I understand,' said Blount. 'Perhaps then you can answer me with nods or head shakes? Now... you say you were passing by the clown's caravan. That's Glupi the clown, yes?'

Nod.

'And you say you saw liquid trickling out of the door.'

Nod.

'And you thought it might be a burst water tank or something.'

Nod.

'But before you had a chance to check, the camper van behind you burst into flame.'

Nod.

'Your camper van.'

Nod.

'Just like that.'

Nod. Nod.

'And you have no idea why your camper van should just spontaneously combust? Was there something inside that made it particularly flammable?'

Nod.

'So there was something inflammable inside?'

Head shake.

'But you just nodded when I asked if there was anything flammable.'

Head shake.

'I think he was nodding to say that he had no idea why it should have spontaneously combusted,' said a voice from across the room. Blount frowned at a stout man in pyjamas sitting up in the bed opposite.

'If you wouldn't mind, your Lordship, this is a police investigation.'

'Sorry, couldn't help overhearing. Just trying to help, old boy,' said Berkeley. 'Blount isn't it? Detective Inspector?'

'Sergeant,' growled Blount.

'I'm so sorry, do carry on. Don't mind me.'

Berkeley returned to reading his magazine and Blount turned back to his suspect. Now that it was obvious that the Viscount Morbridge was listening in, he dropped his voice to a near whisper. 'So, you say that the liquid escaping from the clown's still – which you swear you knew nothing about – had run in a little river across the grass and formed a pool under your vehicle. Then a spark from something "must have set it off". Is that what you're saying?'

Nod.

'Well, here's the thing,' said Blount. 'There wasn't an unbroken trail of liquid from the clown's caravan to yours. There were two trails of the liquid, one ending at your camper van, the other at the clown's. But there was a gap – which I suspect may have been the starting-point for both trails – somewhere between the two vehicles. There's no way that happened by accident. Someone laid those trails deliberately and intended to burn down both vehicles, and I believe that you are that person.'

Furious head shake.

'You were seen to throw a bucket of something like petrol over your camper van,' said Blount.

'By assident. I thawt it wa water.'

'You thought it was water? So what about the bucket of highly inflammable confetti?' said Blount. 'Did you think that was water too?'

Nod.

'It all sounds very unlikely.'

'Is true,' said Ben, 'Why wou I burn dow my ow home?'

'Who knows?' said Blount. 'The insurance perhaps?'

'My van... wasn't... worth a bean,' said Ben. 'And issurass polcy was insi thu van.'

'The insurance policy was inside the van? But insurance companies keep copies, Mr Ellis,' said Blount.

'Buh I ha no idea who issurass compny is,' wailed Ben with genuine anguish. And it was true. He didn't know who his insurers were. The policy had been set up by his father and, during the three decades that he'd paid the premiums by post, the original brokers had been absorbed, bought out, merged and re-badged so many times that he'd no longer bothered to memorise their name and address. He had a feeling that there was a name like 'Milford' or 'Milchester' in the most recent incarnation, but he couldn't be sure, and every piece of correspondence relating to the policy had been in the Winnebago. Given his nomadic lifestyle and penchant for obscure locations, the insurers had contacted him annually by posting a renewal to the pawnbroker's shop in London, still run by his aunt and uncle. The next renewal letter wouldn't arrive for at least another five months. His sloppiness now made any kind of claim very difficult.

'How can you not know the contact details for your insurance company?' asked the detective.

'Do you?' said Ben.

Blount seemed momentarily stumped.

'Look, they sen me a renewal evey year an I pay it by pudding a chegue in post,' said Ellis. 'An before you ass, my chehbook and all my bank corresponens were also in van. All gone. Eveything. Gone. My whole life wa insie tha van.'

'And you expect me to believe that?' said Blount.

'To be honess, nod a word,' said Ben. 'Buh is true. Ha you considered tha it mi ha been that animal rights group who wuh demonstratin owside? They ma their feelings qui clear abou circuses.'

'We're quite familiar with the activities of that group. We've been watching them ever since that pond business at Harpax Grange last year. We're verifying their alibis as we speak,' said Blount. 'We're exploring every avenue of investigation, Mr Ellis.'

'I think that unfortunate fellow has had enough now, don't you?' said Berkeley, chipping in once again. 'Poor bugger can hardly speak as it is.'

'Your Lordship, I...'

'Your Lordship nothing,' said Berkeley. 'It's pretty obvious that he's not going to tell you anything different if you ask him a sixth time or a seventh or eighth time. I'm meant to be recuperating and I can hardly rest and relax with your inquisition going on. And I do play golf with the Chief Constable's wife, you know. I'd much prefer to be able to put in a good word for you.'

Blount looked at Ellis's tired, pleading eyes and then sat back in his chair and frowned. As strange as events had been, everything the man had said made sense. The only thing that didn't were the two distinct trails of flammable liquid the forensics people had discovered. The Fire Brigade investigator was convinced that someone had intended to burn down both camper vans, but, for some reason, only one trail had been lit and Glupi's caravan had survived. The question was... who had done it and why? Both vehicles were worth next to nothing. Blount could feel the case, and his chances of promotion, slipping away from him and decided to try a different tack.

'Alright, just one more question, Mr Ellis. Maybe two. Then I'll call it a night. For today anyway. This Glupi character... what can you tell me about him?'

'Noh much,' said Ben.

'Well, let's start with a name.'

'Adalbert suthing.'

'Adalbert something?'

'He di tell me his surname once, long time ago. Ha lots of Zs in it.'

'Polish?'

'Silesian.'

'Where's Silesia?'

'Poland.'

'Are you being deliberately obstructive Mr Ellis? Because I could have you done for wasting police time you know.'

'I'm noh been ostructive,' said Ben. 'Silesia was once a country buh is now mostly in Poland with other bits of it in Germany an Czech Republic. Glupi calls hisself Silesian.'

'But you said he'd worked for you for years. Surely you must know his full name? What does it say on the payroll?'

'Ne'er earn' enough money to ha any kin' of payroll,' said Ben. 'He's very private. Jus' always been... Glupi.'

'So where is he now?'

'No idea,' said Ellis. 'I sent him into town for a nigh off lass night and I han't seen him since. Han't you found him?'

Blount rubbed his forehead. Ellis had just provided Glupi – a possible alternative suspect – with an alibi for the evening.

Either the circus owner was a complete idiot or a very clever and manipulative criminal. Or, depressingly, he was telling the truth.

Ben didn't feel clever and manipulative. He felt like an idiot and a complete rotter. He'd intended to make the clown his scapegoat even though Glupi was probably the closest thing that he had to a best friend. However, he balanced that against the aggravation he was now getting from Lady Cockering over those damned posters, and the fact that he actually knew very little about the man. He'd inherited Glupi, along with the rest of the circus, following his parents' deaths and, even after nearly four decades, all he knew was his first name and where he was born. Glupi kept himself to himself. Besides which, his volatile nature, his ability to start a fight no matter how genteel his surroundings and his penchant for strong liquor had made him a friend that you sometimes preferred to disown. He had the unique accolade of being the first and only person to be thrown out of the *Opportunity Knocks* studio by Hughie Green, who'd decided that foul-mouthed drunks dressed as clowns were not his idea of good television. And he'd once ruined a 1976 episode of *Seaside Special* by waving his manhood at the cameras while standing behind 'Diddy' David Hamilton when he was on air. But whatever his faults, Glupi was funny. The children who came to the circus adored his abusive edgy style and he loved performing for them. And that, more than anything else, made Ben feel guilty about his attempt to make Glupi take one for the team, albeit unknowingly. But what other choice could he have made? The alternative was taking the blame himself and possibly facing charges of arson and attempted insurance fraud. And then where would the circus be?

But now he felt like an idiot because he'd stupidly provided Glupi with an alibi. He was back to square one and, to make matters worse, Glupi would probably be charged with operating an illegal still. He'd made a complete mess of things and now his situation was worse than ever.

'Ca I geh some sleep now, officer?' he asked.

'Yes, that'll do for now,' said Blount. 'But I will be asking more questions, Mr Ellis. A lot more questions. None of this adds up at the moment and I smell something rotten. Don't leave town.'

'Where woul' I go?' said Ben, forlornly.

The police officer stood up and towered over the bed like a dangerously livid giraffe.

'I'm watching you,' he said and left the ward. Ben breathed a sigh of relief.

'Bet you thought he'd never go, eh?'

There were only two other beds in the ward. One contained a frail-looking skeleton of a man who was noisily sound asleep. In the other was a large, red-faced forty-something who was wired up to a bank of monitors and a saline drip. Ben hadn't really taken a good look at him before as he'd either been asleep or hidden behind curtains, but had recognised him when he'd interrupted Blount's questioning.

'Lord Cockering,' he said. 'I met you at the Royal Middenshire Show. You invited us to come here.'

'I am, you did and I did,' said Berkeley. 'I say, your throat seems to have suddenly got better.'

Ben coughed shamefacedly.

'You don't have to fake it with me,' said Berkeley. 'But I advise caution with that Blount chap. He's a bit of a weasel and as unimaginative as they come, but he's tenacious. He doesn't give up easily.'

'You know him?'

'Know of him,' said Berkeley. 'He used to work over at Bowcester and made a thorough arse of himself over the murder investigation of some famous writer. He is therefore keen as mustard to prove that he isn't ready to be put out to pasture yet. Let's hope he doesn't winkle the truth out of you, eh?'

Ben shrank a little lower in his bed.

'The truth? What do you mean?'

'Well, you know… arson, insurance fiddle, all that sort of thing. Damned awkward.'

'What?'

'These things are awfully thin,' said Berkeley, shaking the curtains around his bed. 'And you, old chap, have been pretty vocal during your sleep. Despite your sore throat.'

'I have?'

'Indeed. You've been mumbling on about insurance policies and splashing whisky about. And something about tigers and elephants. None of it made much sense until I heard you being interviewed.'

'I…'

'Don't worry, mum's the word,' said Berkeley, tapping his nose. 'That's why I butted in. I'm no stool pigeon and your secret is safe with me. Besides, I have a similar problem myself and can sympathise. In fact, it may be that I know a way in which we can be of some help to each other. Benjamin isn't it?'

'Ben.'

'Excellent. Pleased to meet you, Ben. My name's Berkeley. I have a feeling that you and I are going to become firm friends.'

Chapter 16

At Brill Farm the confusion of the past twenty-four hours saw no sign of abating. The farm manager, a Mr Flockton, had insisted that the circus pack up and go. While he appreciated that it was Lord Cockering who had booked them to appear, and had secretly rather enjoyed helping the man to cock a snook at Lady Marcheline, the fire had been just a little too close to the farmhouse for his liking and fragments of shrapnel from the exploding gas bottle had peppered the cowsheds. Thankfully, no real damage or harm had been done, but Benelli's Circus had outstayed its welcome. However, moving the circus on was no easy task. Ben was in hospital; Venturini the magician had completely failed to return with the horse truck. The keys to the other truck large enough to tow the tent trailer had been in Ben's Winnebago, and were now just so much molten slag. As a compromise, Mr Flockton had insisted that the Big Top be moved several fields further away from the house until the circus could get its act together, and had loaned them a tractor for that purpose. It had taken the elderly performers an entire day to take the tent down, move it, and erect it again and they now found themselves camped in the wettest, muddiest, and least accessible field on the estate, a fact that guaranteed to make any future box office takings even more meagre.

That evening, and despite their obvious exhaustion, the circus folk managed to throw together something approximating a full programme, with Albert Manning stepping up into the role of ringmaster. But it had been a very lacklustre affair. Flamo had been forced to siphon what little petrol remained in the clown's car and Dirk had swallowed some by accident, resulting in projectile vomiting. Without Glupi to keep them in line, an inebriated Grimpen and Cronk had been unusually crude and their abusive ad-libs had resulted in a score of complaints from people who'd insisted that a clown act should not consist of two drunks sitting in the ring laughing uncontrollably and using words like 'bell-end' and 'twat'. Della the elephant was still sedated and unable to do anything other than snore and break wind. There was no magic show and no horse act. Even Hung and Lo had failed to inflame the more politically correct members of an audience that had barely been large enough to fill the front benches. Everyone had complained about the mud and filth outside and the show had ended with the performers having to help push the audience's cars free of the quagmire in which they'd become bogged down. The job had been made even more unpleasant by the unwanted attentions of a few nosy and occasionally randy bullocks.

The only people who'd escaped the madness were the Daughters of Epona, who, as the result of their impromptu brace of days off, had taken the opportunity to get plastered. Quite where they'd got their booze from was anybody's guess, but the constant sound of **ABBA** tunes punctuated by raucous male voices from their trailer was an indication that they had struck up a relationship with some locals and that they, at least, were having a good time.

After the show, Geraint Manning called everyone together around a camp fire to discuss their situation. 'I've been to the hospital to check on Ben and the good news is that he's well enough to be discharged tomorrow morning,' he explained. 'The bad news is that he is apparently still helping police with their enquiries and is not allowed to leave the area. There is also still no sign of Glupi – not so surprising considering that he is now apparently a wanted man because of that still of his – which is leading people to make assumptions that he may have been involved in the fire too.'

'It's all terrible, terrible,' said Hilda Angel, deep in the throes of a gin-fuelled mood slump.

'If you ask me, Ben did it,' said an equally soused Cronk.

'No one is asking you,' said Geraint. 'But I don't mind saying that this terrible business has made me seriously consider my future.'

'You mean if Ben is convicted we'll all be jobless?' asked Cronk.

'That wasn't what I was saying.'

'I tell you what I'm going to do,' said Hilda, rising unsteadily to her feet. 'I'm quitting.'

'Quitting?' said Vera Manning. 'Are you serious?'

'I've had enough,' said Hilda, 'In fact, me and my sisters have all had enough. We're fed up with being poor, being lonely and being chained to a circus that is trudging slowly towards its own grave. I know that Ben has done his best for us but none of us are getting any younger and, while I can't speak for all of you, I can't go on camping in wet fields any more. The chill goes straight to my back. I'm going to find myself a proper job and maybe even a man to grow old with. I'm sorry. I'll miss you all but I just can't do this anymore. Last night was the final straw. And I'm sure I speak for a few others here.'

With that, she burst into tears. She was comforted by her

sisters, Joan and Maureen, who led her away to their caravan for more gin and Swedish pop.

'I never thought the Eponas would be the first to quit,' said Flamo. 'They're the youngest of us.'

'Let's face it, we've all thought about it,' said Geraint. 'At least they've had the guts to admit it.'

'My sister has been asking me to go and live with her in her bungalow in Kendon-On-Lea ever since her Tommy died,' said Summersmith Mudd. 'Retirement by the seaside. I'm tempted. Wouldn't you be?'

There was a general murmur of agreement.

'Well, if that's how we all feel we could put it to the vote, but it does have to be a majority of us in favour,' said Geraint. 'Raised hands if you think it's time for us to quit?'

The forest of raised hands, or gouty flipper in the case of Penguin Boy, provided the final nails in the coffin of Benelli's Circus.

'Well, that's that then,' said Geraint. 'So what do we do now? Finish our week here and then what? I don't have the money to go anywhere else.'

'Ben needs to make those kinds of decisions,' said Flamo.

'Whatever happens I say we go out with a bang,' said Grimpen. 'We should do one last show, the best show we can put on.'

'Oh yes, we should bow out in style!' said Genaro Coltello.

'Who agrees?' asked Grimpen.

Again, a forest of hands and other sundry limbs were raised unanimously.

'So how about we cancel the next few performances – we have a pitiful box office as it is – and we can use the time to put together the best possible show that we can for, say, Wednesday?' said Geraint. 'We can advertise it as the circus's final ever performance. That should bring a few extra punters in. We can contact the local press, maybe even some local radio or regional TV. It'll be a nice surprise for Benjamin and a wonderful swansong for us.'

His suggestion was greeted with cheers of approval.

Chapter 17

Ben lay awake in his uncomfortable hospital bed, his injured throat throbbing. Had he been aware of his performers' decision, it might have lifted his gloom. If they were leaving of their own volition, then he was free from the Golden Handshake clause of his father's will and the long, hard journey was finally at a satisfactory end. However, his thoughts were currently focused on not falling asleep in case he let slip any further indiscretions. His nocturnal confessions were a complication that he hadn't foreseen and he had resolved to stay awake until Berkeley had gone to sleep first.

His interview with Blount had been an ordeal. However, now that he'd had a chance to ruminate upon it, he'd come to realise that the police had nothing on him. Plus, Berkeley had spent the evening convincing him that he probably hadn't committed a crime anyway.

'Look, even if you had set fire to your own home,' he'd said. 'That's not a crime, Ben. It's a fundamental right of every Englishman to be allowed to burn down his own castle if he damned well feels like it. As long as there's no danger to anyone of course. As I understand it, you were the only one hurt?'

'Yes but…'

'And it was on private land. Which I own, incidentally. Did the fire damage any property belonging to anyone else?'

'Only the grass. Although I'm told that the gas cylinder and petrol tank took a few chunks out of some cow sheds,' said Ben.

'Cow sheds are ten a penny,' said Berkeley. 'I'm not looking to prosecute you for a few dents and scorches. After all, I let you camp there. I'd be hoist on my own petard. And I'd be inflaming local people's prejudices about travellers like you. No slight intended.'

'None taken,' said Ben.

'And you weren't in any way involved with making illicit hooch?'

'No. That was all down to Glupi.'

'That's good. The police chap in charge of licensing and alcohol-related stuff is a ghastly little man called McNabb, and he's nearly as awful as Blount. Of course, there's still the attempted insurance fraud and arson.'

'Look I can explai–'

'Ah, but you haven't actually made a fraudulent claim, have you? So you've committed no crime there either. Mind you, even if you had, I do know some damnably good barristers who would take your case as a personal favour to me, if it got that far of course. After all, the onus is on them to prove intent.'

Or you decide to tell them, thought Ben to himself. But, despite everything, he'd found himself warming to Berkeley. He'd been very forthcoming about his own problems; his difficult relationship with his sister and her intransigence when it came to selling off any of their jointly owned properties and releasing the capital. The Viscount Morbridge's problems really were not dissimilar to his own. And the man was charming, funny and really rather blasé about his recent dice with death.

'The thing about something like that is that it makes a chap take stock,' he'd explained. 'And I've realised that here I am, in my forties, and I've achieved nothing. Not a sausage. Now, some chaps might have an epiphany and find religion or do great charitable works or something like that. But I'm rather more self-centred than that I'm afraid. All I can think about is that my father died almost a year to the day after his first heart attack, which might well mean that the bell is tolling for me now. God knows I'm the spitting image of the old duffer plus several stones more. Seems the old sod left me his dicky ticker as well as the title. And what that says to me is that I should treat this coming year as potentially my last and do everything that I've always wanted to do, within reason of course, before I join the Choir Invisible. But if I want to tick off all the things on my bucket list, I'm going to need money. And, one way or another, I'm going to make sure that I get it.'

'You could live another fifty years,' said Ben. 'Medical science is advancing every day. Maybe your father would still be alive now if he'd died today… If you get what I mean.'

'I do,' said Berkeley. 'But good healthcare depends on money too. The Queen Mother, God rest her, wouldn't have notched up her century if she'd grown up on some wretched sink estate in South London. I'm a bloody Viscount and look at me. I'm lying here in a public ward in a tiny cottage hospital and, frankly, I'm amazed I'm still above the sod. Don't get me wrong, lovely staff and they do their best with what they have, bless 'em, but a man of my means should be able to afford to be flown by chopper to Harefield and attended to by some boffin from Harley Street. But no. Instead I have to wake up every morning in the knowledge that I own half of a bloody parish valued in the tens of millions that I cannot realise a single penny from. If I had my way, I'd have the finest medical care a man can buy and spend the rest of my life indulging in pure, selfish hedonism to test that care to its limits.'

'It all sounds wonderful,' said Ben. 'If that were me I'd settle down in a nice little house somewhere and finish my novel. But I'm in the same boat that you are. The only assets I have are tied up in the circus, and there's no way to free them up.'

'Oh I don't know,' said Berkeley. 'I have some very clever friends who work in the city. I'm pretty sure that they could locate your insurance policy. That is, of course, if you fancy trying to burn it all down again. I imagine the police might view that as a trifle suspicious, however.'

'Trust me, I'm done with all that,' said Ben. 'I've learned my lesson.'

'Exactly,' said Berkeley. 'So what I propose is this. It seems to me that I'm doing you a favour by keeping mum about your little... accident. So if you do me a favour by helping me to get my hands on my rightful inheritance, we'd be quits.'

'Isn't that blackmail?' said Ben.

'I see it more as a business partnership with mutual benefits,' said Berkeley. 'You do something for me and, in return, I'll not only keep quiet but I'll set you up with enough money to buy that nice little retirement place you want. How does that sound?'

'Too good to be true,' said Ben.

'Marcheline and her holier-than thou sense of duty have robbed me of my rightful inheritance. I'm never going to be able to realise any money from the properties I own unless I can persuade her that there's more to life than just being a glorified landlady,' said Berkeley. 'I need to make her sell up. And I think I know how to arrange that. You help me do so and I'll see you alright.'

'That all rather depends on what you want me to do.'

'Nothing illegal, I assure you,' said Berkeley, smiling. 'In fact, I think you might even enjoy it.'

Chapter 18

Marcheline woke on Thursday morning with a renewed sense of purpose. She'd decided not to return to Shapcott Bassett the evening before as planned; Berkeley was in hospital and she had no appointments or meetings to attend. She'd therefore booked into one of the better London hotels and had enjoyed a very comfortable night's sleep.

After breakfast, she popped out to a nearby newsagent and returned to her room with a large stack of fashion magazines, a pair of scissors and some glue. Three hours later, the stack of magazines was on the floor and on the bed lay a kind of human collage; a composite woman made from cuttings. Like Dr Frankenstein assembling the 'Adam of his labours,' Marcheline used the knowledge she'd gained from a day of visiting stores and salons to choose the hairstyle, the clothes, the make-up, the shoes, the nails, the jewellery and the accessories that would transform her into the kind of woman that she believed a man might be attracted to. The collage would be the template for her rebirth.

She took a photograph on her phone and then carefully glued all of the pieces into a notebook that she could show to the people she would soon be visiting. If her transformation looked even half as good as the jigsaw woman she'd created, she'd be very pleased indeed.

The next job was to book the various appointments she needed. And if they didn't have the appointments, she'd make them open a window in their schedule, just for her. Money was a great motivator and she intended to spend quite a lot before returning home. And why not? Berkeley had been spending a sizeable monthly allowance for years, while she'd shown a great deal more restraint. Today it was her turn. She reached for the phone and asked Reception if they'd be so good as to send a copy of the local *Yellow Pages* to her room.

At the cottage hospital, Ben and Berkeley were saying their goodbyes.

'You mean *au revoir*,' corrected Berkeley. 'We'll be seeing a lot more of each other, I'm sure. I'd have loved to come see the circus, especially as I booked it to come here. But I have to stay here until Sunday evening, apparently. Another few nights of this damnable food while you'll be living the high life, eh?'

Ben refrained from pointing out that his 'high life' was most likely going to be sleeping on someone's sofa after an evening meal of baked beans straight from the can. And, if what Geraint Manning had told him during his visit was true, some of the performers thought that he was an arsonist. So there might be some awkwardness too. He rather envied the fact that Berkeley was going to have several more hassle-free days with a comfortable bed and warm meals. Even hospital food was better than no food.

'I have your mobile number,' said Berkeley. 'I'll call when I've set things up.'

'Sounds ominous,' said Ben.

'Anything but,' said Berkeley, reassuringly. 'It'll be easy money, trust me.'

Ben smiled an unsure smile and walked towards Reception to sign his release forms. A cloud of worry and trepidation hung over him as he tried to imagine just what sort of work the Viscount Morbridge might have lined up for him in return for his silence. His words had sounded sincere enough, but Ben was acutely aware that his liberty now lay squarely in the man's pudgy hands. Berkeley Cockering had him over a barrel.

Blount sat in an unmarked police car in a lay-by very near to Brill Farm and cursed the bad luck that had robbed him of what had seemed, at first, to be just the sort of arrest he needed to impress his superiors. Instead, he had nothing. The animal rights protestors all had good alibis; they had never left their position in plain view of the audience and couldn't have set the fire. And the same story had been repeated with every other person that Blount had interviewed. The only person who didn't have a corroborated alibi at the time of the fire was Benjamin Ellis, and Blount was as sure as any man could be that the man had been up to something illegal. But, after nearly twenty-four hours, he had no physical or witness evidence to support his hunch. Yes, there had been traces of Glupi's 'wiskey' on Ellis's clothing, but that was the case for almost every one of the circus folk who regularly spent some of their meagre pensions on the vile stuff. But that was all he had. He had no confession nor even any kind of a motive other than, possibly, a botched arson with a view to insurance fraud. But even that seemed unlikely. Ellis's caravan and contents had been worth almost nothing. His investigation was scuppered, and, with it, his chances of a reinvigorated career.

He'd spent his Thursday morning at the campsite in one last-ditch attempt to hang something on Ellis but had, once again, drawn a blank. While a few of the more cynical circus folk suspected that he might have deliberately started the fire, most couldn't see the logic in this if the only property damaged was his own. Most affected by a difference of opinion were Mr Hung and Mr Lo, who hadn't shared a pair of trousers all day, and Dirk, who was still smarting from his treatment.

'I don't know what everyone else was doing at the time but I quite clearly saw him throw a bucket of fuel at his own camper van,' he'd said. 'That was after he'd pushed me to the floor and torn it from my grasp, mind you. Who does that to a little person like me?'

'He assaulted you?' said Blount, hopefully.

'Not really assaulted,' admitted Dirk, 'But you can't tell me he didn't know what was in that bucket. I mean, what else would I be carrying? I'm a bloody fire-eater's assistant.'

'He was in a panic. His home was on fire,' interrupted Colonel Sanders. 'And it was dark. Damned if I could tell the difference between water and Glupi's home-made hooch under those circumstances.'

'You would if you'd ever drunk the beastly stuff,' said Summersmith Mudd. 'I once took a sip and… well, talk about eye of the needle…'

And so it had gone on; a division of opinion coupled with a complete lack of any usable evidence. On top of everything, Blount had developed a nagging suspicion that Ellis had done a bunk, as he'd been discharged from hospital that morning but no one had seen him at the camp all day.

As he left the site, Blount resigned himself to the fact that he'd never be promoted now. With a heavy heart he returned to Morbridge police station to start work on the remainder of his small and altogether more mundane case load. The Ellis case was, apparently, dead.

After leaving the cottage hospital Ben hadn't gone directly home, because he had no home to go directly to. With his Winnebago destroyed and his future uncertain, he'd taken a minicab to Shapcott Bassett to cleanse the antiseptic hospital air from his lungs and to see for himself the damage his posters had wrought on the village. However, the specialist cleaners had earned their massive fee; all vestiges of the flyposting were gone and Ben found himself delighted that they were. It was the first time that he'd seen the village and the prettiness of the place quite took his breath away. Other than some obvious building work behind the grocery store, where a gang of scaffolders were setting up, Shapcott Bassett was his idea of Heaven; a glorious dollop of rural England wonderfully presented and maintained. From the camel-coloured stone walls and brightly painted red Victorian post box, to the polished brass doorknobs and the late summer hanging baskets, it was his ideal picture-postcard village made real. In his idle hours, he'd often fantasised about the life he could be living and of the rewards that a less peripatetic lifestyle could bring him. He liked the idea of being part of a community with roots, a community of people that didn't include trapeze artists and clowns and knife-throwers. And maybe even settling down and meeting someone special, and spending his days writing the great novel that was in his head. It was all completely beyond his means, of course, and always would be. He had the circus and he would have the circus until he died. But the dream was beautiful.

Feeling thoroughly sorry for himself, he'd made for Miss Dillby's charming little tea rooms and then spent the afternoon watching the daily life of the village, accompanied by a succession of pots of tea and toasted teacakes. Enjoying his anonymity, he'd chatted to a birdwatcher from Wintlebury who'd come to see the rare Nagle's Red-Headed Merganser, a type of duck found in only a few spots across the UK. Then he'd met a nice couple from Nasely called Mr and Mrs Shunter who were exploring the northern boroughs of the county. The husband, an ex-policeman called Frank, had remarked how much he was enjoying visiting a place where there were no crimes for him to get caught up in. Then he'd chatted to a couple of Agnes Crabbe fans – the great crime author had lived her entire life in the county, and visitors flocked to the area to see if they could find the real places that had inspired her fictional murder scenes.

Time had flown by and he'd been genuinely surprised when Miss Dillby had politely informed him that it was nearly 5.30pm and she wanted to shut up for the day. He'd therefore settled his bill and phoned a Morbridge cab firm – Berkeley, who had an account due to his disqualification from driving, had kindly offered him the use of it – and was driven to Brill Farm. It was time to face reality.

After a degree of confusion, due to the fact that the Big Top appeared to have hiked across several fields to a new location, he was dropped off at the end of a muddy lane. A short, breathless walk brought him to the tent where he was, to his relief, enthusiastically greeted by his staff, who quickly apprised him of their decision to retire.

'And you're sure about this?' said Ben.

'Quite sure. It's time for us to go our separate ways,' said Geraint Manning. He held out Ben's top hat and scarlet jacket. 'Here, you'll need these for next Wednesday. It's your place to be ringmaster one last time. You look good, by the way.'

Before leaving the hospital, Ben had taken the time to shave off what was left of his beard and he looked ten years younger, despite his injuries. He took the proffered costume.

'Thanks,' he said, smiling, 'And yes, let's do it. One last show.'

Geraint nodded and walked away. Ben ducked under the 'POLICE CRIME SCENE' tape that surrounded the burnt and upturned remains of his camper van and sat down on a partly melted and uncomfortable plastic chair, one of the few remaining recognisable items among the piles of ash and charcoal. He looked around. The chair was a kind of metaphor, he realised. It represented all that had gone before; a barely functional and uncomfortable thing that he now needed to walk away from. He had no home, no personal effects, no memorabilia. Nothing was salvageable. His past, like the chair, was behind him. Yes, there were some unpaid bills but, even though he'd now learned about the damage done by Della the elephant, he felt strangely unconcerned. This was what he had wanted for so long. The circus was no more. He would sell anything that was saleable and then do the right thing by dividing the profits among the performers. Then he'd use his share to settle the debts. Or declare bankruptcy. Either way meant that he'd be left with nothing but his health, his imagination and his creativity. But that was all he needed. He could start a new life.

He put on his jacket and sat the top hat carefully upon his wounded head. Of course it was only right that he joined his friends for one last triumphant performance. It was just a shame that Glupi had disappeared. Not for the first time, he wondered where the elderly clown was.

Chapter 19

Glupi checked his snares and was rewarded by the sight of a fat buck rabbit struggling to get free. He broke its neck cleanly and looked forward to sampling its tender meat later that evening. He dropped it into a carrier bag, where it twitched among the bodies of a fresh roadkill squirrel and a pheasant, some horse mushrooms, hazelnuts, sweet cicely, mallow and a selection of wild herbs and berries. A man could eat like a prince and all for free, if you knew what to look for. And Glupi did know, having grown up in a poor family that had supplemented its meagre daily income with foraged food. That, combined with his army training, meant that he felt anything but homeless or in need.

He had been surprised by how much he had enjoyed the experience of sleeping in the woods. He'd built a shelter that was warm and waterproof, his bed of ferns was softer and more fragrant than both the bed in his caravan and the ditch in which he'd slept the previous night, and he was eating very well indeed. All that was missing was a decent drink, but he'd considered that and was already stockpiling wild berries, nettles and oak leaves for when he could conjure up a demijohn and lay his hands on some yeast and sugar. He reasoned that if he was going to be living this way for a while, a bottle or two of homemade wine would help make the experience more pleasurable.

The Sun was beginning to set, and an early autumnal coolness pervaded the woods as he arrived at his bivouac. He shivered slightly as if someone had walked over his grave. Glupi had found a lovely spot in which to set up camp and it suited his purposes admirably. He'd built it deep in the woods that grew up the sides of the low chalk hill known as the Big Knapper. He had food and shelter and fresh water via a small offshoot of the River Gew that also, handily, contained delicious freshwater crayfish. All in all it was a very contented clown who set his fire and began preparing his evening meal.

Chapter 20

At the Cottage Hospital, Berkeley made his plans. Despite his show of bravado to Ellis and the hospital staff – especially the pretty little nurse with the dental brace, who'd quite taken his fancy – his recent heart attack had scared him a great deal. And with that fear had come a fierce determination to get his hands on what he believed to be rightfully his. His sister's intransigence, always a source of deep irritation, was the obstruction that he had to clear in order to live whatever life remained to him in the style to which he aspired. In his mind's eye he'd seen his sister die a hundred different ways, some more ghastly than others, but he always felt a little guilty after such thoughts as, truth be known, he didn't hate her. She was just thoroughly infuriating. Besides, at heart, Berkeley was nothing if not a milksop, and he had little of the passion and fire that saturated the Cockering bloodline. What he did have, however, was guile.

Berkeley had long ago abandoned the idea of dragging Marcheline through the courts to get equal rights of access to the family business accounts. Such a prolonged and messy process would undoubtedly result in the lawyers being the only people to come out of it better off. And because he was already in receipt of a very generous monthly allowance, his apparent greed might make him seem like an unsympathetic victim and weaken his case. He'd also given up on the idea of stealing the money and running off to some foreign paradise with no extradition treaty with the UK. It was quite doable; all he needed were the account numbers, and a few clever computer people who owed him a favour to do the rest. He would hardly be leaving Marcheline destitute, as she'd have the Hall and her extensive portfolio of properties which, if she sold even one tenth of them, would make her a very rich woman indeed. She would never be a pauper, that was for sure, and that was why he felt no guilt about the plan. However, he had no idea how much money there was to steal. He'd always been too busy having fun to get involved in the dull business of talking to accountants and paying bills. He had left all of that to Marcheline. He therefore had no idea how much profit the farms, slaughterhouse and brewery generated. Theft was a risky business in itself, but with the prospect of a potentially disappointing haul on top, it just didn't seem worth it. Besides which, he'd be a wanted man and unable to return to the UK for life. He didn't much like that idea at all.

One thing was for sure – there was real, tangible money tied up in bricks and mortar, if he could only get access to it. He needed to somehow manufacture a situation where Marcheline would suddenly have to raise a large amount of money. If the amount was large enough, she would have no other choice than to sell off some properties. And once that ball was rolling, he would be entitled to fifty per cent of all proceeds. What he needed was something like a huge lawsuit or... an expensive divorce settlement.

In recent years she had berated him numerous times for not setting down and producing an heir. But, just recently, she seemed to have developed something approximating

121

broodiness. It was a subtle yearning, to be sure. She certainly wasn't lingering near baby stores or cooing over pictures of toddlers. But mention of children had become much more frequent since she had passed her fortieth birthday, and her discussions with Mrs Shandcreek were nearly always peppered with talk of tiny feet pattering. Was she considering the idea of having a child herself, he wondered? If so, he realised, he might have the perfect opportunity to kill two birds with one stone. She was such a stickler for tradition that it was unlikely that she'd entertain a baby outside of wedlock, so she might be susceptible to propositions of marriage. If he could get her paired off with someone of his choosing, and then quickly divorced before the complication of children set in, it would be a cinch. The husband would be bound to get a large settlement and Marcheline would have to sell some of their properties to meet the tab. All that had been missing from his machinations until now was a suitable bachelor of the right age who was sufficiently on his uppers and in no position to refuse. Ben Ellis fitted so neatly into the jigsaw of his plans it was as if he'd been laser-cut to do so.

Berkeley reached for his mobile phone.

'Ah Ben? Hello. Berkeley here. Would you mind popping back to the cottage hospital tomorrow morning? You know that little favour I said I'd ask of you...'

Chapter 21

Ben woke on the Friday morning with a mounting sense of trepidation. Berkeley's phone call of the evening before had been annoyingly vague: 'Pop over to the hospital. And make an effort will you? I'll need to take a photo of you,' was all he'd said, but it had felt somehow ominous.

He arrived wearing the least shabby shirt that he'd been able to borrow from a Bonzini Brother of similar height and stature. He'd also unwisely removed the stitches from his head. He had made an effort, as requested, although he had absolutely no idea why it was necessary. He found Berkeley in an ebullient mood.

'Come in dear chap, come in and sit down,' said the Viscount. 'You look very well, if I may say so.'

'Amazing what a good night's sleep can do,' said Ben. 'Plus, a great weight has been lifted off my shoulders.'

'Really?' said Berkeley.

'We've decided to retire,' said Ben. 'We're putting on a final goodbye show next Wednesday. Then, we're selling up and going our separate ways.'

'Then I will endeavour to ensure that I'm there to see you off,' said Berkeley. 'And I'm so pleased they didn't form a lynch mob. Of course, they might still do so if they found out what you'd tried to do, but that's our little secret isn't it?'

'Yes it is,' said Ben, resignedly. 'So what is it you want me to do?'

'Nothing too grievous. I want you to seduce my sister.'

'You want me to do what?'

'Seduce my sister. Have you met my sister?' asked Berkeley.

'No I bloody haven't,' said Ben. 'And good thing, too.'

'What do you mean?'

Ben explained about the posters and the Snipeton level crossing debacle and the resultant pile of invoices he'd received as the result. And since returning to the campsite he'd also learned about the damage to Twimbley's that had resulted in the scaffolding he'd seen being erected. There were surely more big bills to come.

'But these bills... were they addressed to you? Does she know your name?' asked Berkeley.

'No. Everything was addressed to "the irresponsible oaf supposedly in charge of a circus". Why do you ask?'

'It makes things so much easier, because you won't have to create a false identity,' said Berkeley. 'You can just be yourself.'

'Myself?'

'I believe that being yourself is the key to a successful seduction,' said Berkeley. 'Or so I've read in magazines.'

'You're not seriously suggesting that I seduce your sister? A woman who, if she knew who I was, would skin me alive?'

'I am,' said Berkeley. 'You know the form... eyes meeting across a crowded room... engaging her in conversation... the old chat-up and schmooze. You're not a bad-looking chap. And she's not terribly *au fait* with the whole dating game. I think she'd fall for you hook, line and sinker.'

'But she hates me!' said Ben.

'No, she hates "the irresponsible oaf supposedly in charge of a circus". You said yourself that she doesn't know you from Adam. You'll be fine.'

'She'll find out who I am eventually.'

'I don't see how,' said Berkeley. 'Marsh isn't the kind of woman who sullies herself with the *hoi polloi*, no slight intended. That's how she would view you and your people. She's a frightful snob and selects the people she chooses to do business with as carefully as she chooses her tenants. She won't turn up at the circus, I assure you; she'll send an intermediary – probably the local constable or one of her confounded village councillors.'

'But why do you want me to seduce her?'

'As a favour to me,' said Berkeley. 'As things stand, Marsh has a great degree of control over my life, and the life of every tenant in the borough. But she is only able to maintain that control because she has no other distractions. I want you to provide that distraction. It's such a little ask.'

'Look, I don–'

'And I am doing you a big favour by keeping my trap shut in return.'

He smiled a cold, reptilian smile. The words sounded more like a threat than an explanation.

'But I don't even know what she looks like,' protested Ben.

'Ah, easily sorted. I've a few photos on my phone,' said Berkeley, handing the device over. 'She's not hideous, by any means.'

Ben scrolled through a series of blurred photos, each portraying a woman with a frightening Margaret Thatcher-like hairstyle, apparently getting angrier and angrier and lunging towards whoever was operating the camera. 'Hates having her photograph taken,' explained Berkeley. 'But she's a handsome woman. And could look a damned sight more attractive if she made the effort, in my opinion. The meat is in all the right places. You could do worse, old chap.'

'But I can't just seduce a total stranger,' said Ben. 'I'm out of practice... and I might not be her type.'

'My dear chap, she doesn't have a type,' said Berkeley. 'And I firmly believe that she's currently on the hunt for a man. She may even be desperate.'

'Oh, thanks.'

'You know what I mean. She isn't used to male attention. She'll be swept off her feet by your silver tongue.'

'But what if there's no chemistry? I'm not sure I can do this.'

'Of course you can,' said Berkeley, his smile evaporating. 'And you really don't have much of a choice, do you? Now, come around here and let me get a good photo of you. Best we find a way to disguise that head wound, though. First impressions and all that.'

Marcheline was also thinking about first impressions as she looked at her reflection in the full-length mirror mounted on the wall of her hotel room. What she saw made her feel quite giddy.

She'd had a very busy Thursday and a second very comfortable night at the hotel. She would always have very warm memories of this hotel room, she realised. It had been her chrysalis during her transformation. The caterpillar had become a butterfly. Gone was the Marcheline bouffant, to be replaced by a medium-length bob, cut high at the back. She'd also taken advantage of a nail bar, a facial and some expert advice on applying make-up that had cleverly accentuated all of her best features. When it came to her clothes, she hadn't entirely abandoned her love of wool. She'd paid the kind young lady from the sex shop to accompany and advise her on a shopping spree. As the result, the dour greys and greens had been replaced by a violet plaid tweed skirt and jacket ensemble over a chenille blouse that showed off what Clare had referred to as her 'rack' to best effect. She'd paid a very handsome sum to have the outfit beautifully tailored to fit and accentuate her figure. Walking in heels had taken some getting used to after so many years in flats, but she'd remembered her teenage deportment classes and had the blisters to prove that she had remastered the art. Her two-night stay in London had not been wasted.

'My goodness,' she said, turning around to look at herself from all angles. Her appearance was a revelation. Anyone she knew could be excused for not recognising her if they met her on the street, so extreme was her metamorphosis.

A short repetitive burst of Berlioz's *Symphonie Fantastique Opus 14* broke her reverie. She picked up her phone.

'Berkeley. What's the matter?'

'Hello, Sis. Nothing's the matter, all good here. How are you?'

'What do you want?' said Marcheline.

'Succinct and to the point as ever,' said Berkeley. 'I was just ringing to let you know that I'm being discharged Sunday evening and will be coming home to convalesce.'

'Well, that's a blessing,' said Marcheline. 'But I'll be locking the drinks cabinet. Do you want me to pick you up?'

'Lord no, it would take us hours to get home the speed you drive. I'll get a cab. Appreciate the offer, though.'

'Then do you need anything brought to you at the hospital?'

'Not a thing,' said Berkeley, 'But I was wondering if you could do me a favour this evening? I've only just remembered, what with having a heart attack and everything, that I arranged a meeting that I obviously now can't make.'

'And you can't cancel it?' said Marcheline.

'Damned if I can remember the chap's number and he's not in my phone,' said Berkeley. 'I'm sure I have it at home somewhere among all of my correspondence, but you'd never find it. I'm not the best when it comes to filing. Anyway, I wondered if you'd meet him for me? Shouldn't take long.'

'I'm really not sure I can…'

Marcheline bit her tongue. If she refused his request, it could lead to unwanted questions and might raise his suspicions. She didn't have the busiest of social lives and rarely went out of an evening. Besides, she thought, perhaps this was an unexpected opportunity to try out her newfound flirting skills.

'Oh, I suppose so,' she said. 'Who is this man and why am I meeting him?'

'His name is Benjamin Ellis,' said Berkeley. 'He's a business associate of mine. He's looking to retire and write a book and I suggested that he might like the area. After all, we do have a vacant cottage in Creamery Walk now that old Jack Clancaster has passed on. I rather like the idea of having an author in the village. A nice addition to the cultural demographic.'

'You know I don't approve of favouritism,' said Marcheline. 'He'll have to be vetted by the Residents' Committee just like anyone else.'

'Of course,' said Berkeley. 'But this will give you a first look at the chap. And I thought you could at least sing the praises of the village? You are so very good at keeping it looking nice.'

'Very well. When and where?'

Marcheline jotted the address down in her notebook and then, just to be sure that this wasn't one of Berkeley's ruses to cover him while he went out to some damned drinks party or gentlemen's club, she called the cottage hospital to make sure that he really was not going to be released until Sunday. All seemed to be in order, so she relaxed a little and returned, once again, to admiring her new image in the mirror.

Her phone buzzed and she picked it up again and saw a text from Berkeley that said simply, 'This is him.' The accompanying photograph showed a slightly worried-looking man wearing a Panama hat. He looked a little beaten up but, all in all, he was quite presentable. Quite good-looking in fact. Marcheline raised an immaculate eyebrow and smiled.

'There you go, all arranged,' said Berkeley. 'Eight o'clock at the Hogman's Arms near Uttercombe. Far enough from here that no one will recognise you both, not that they would recognise you now that you've smartened up, mind.'

'I still don't like this,' said Ben.

'What's not to like?' said Berkeley. 'You don't have to lie. All I've told her is that you're a business associate. You can say that you're in the entertainment business and are looking to retire to the country. That's true, after all. And that you want to write a book. That's true too. Just talk about that and you'll win her over. Women love romantic and creative types. You might even get lucky.'

'This is your sister we're talking about.'

'Desperate times require desperate measures,' said Berkeley. 'Here, this will help things along.' He handed over a brown envelope. 'I'll even let you keep the hat.'

Ben left the hospital with a sense of foreboding. So dark and brooding were his thoughts as he got into the waiting taxi that he utterly failed to notice the dishevelled and surprised-looking detective sergeant in the unmarked police car that was parked opposite the entrance.

Blount had spent his Thursday working through a backlog of unexciting petty theft and burglary allegations, all the while putting off closing the Ellis arson case on the crime computer. But eventually, with booking-off time approaching, he'd resignedly logged on and was then reminded of the fact that he'd only created a skeleton record to date. He was missing most of the details, such as Benjamin Ellis's full name, date of birth, place of birth, etc. As Ellis had been interviewed as a suspect, those kinds of details were needed by law. Blount had sworn and sworn loudly at the prospect of having to once again visit Brill Farm. But then he'd realised that the cottage hospital would have the information he was after and he could pop in on his way to work in the morning and get them. Which was, coincidentally, why he happened to be sitting in the car park just as Ellis was leaving.

At first he hadn't recognised the circus owner, his appearance being so different. Gone were the beard and the scruffy clothing, replaced by a clean-shaven chin, a suit, and what looked like a Panama hat. But what had actually drawn Blount's attention to the man was that he was counting a fat wad of cash that he'd taken out of a brown envelope. The realisation that it was Ellis took him completely by surprise. As did the revelation – kindly supplied by a nurse whose husband was a Morbridge police officer – that Ellis had apparently been given the money by Berkeley Cockering. Blount returned to his car and considered this new development. What possible connection could there be between a titled aristocrat and a penniless circus owner, other than the fact that they'd shared a hospital ward? Why would Cockering pay a substantial amount of money to a man who had just caused a dangerous fire on a farm owned by him and his sister? And why had he allowed the circus onto his land in the first place? Had the arson actually been something that the viscount knew about, possibly even organised? And why had Ellis so drastically changed his appearance? Blount knew that he now had no choice but to keep the suspicion of arson case open a little longer. Something was definitely going on. He didn't know what it was, but he resolved to continue his observation of the man. Sooner or later, Ellis was bound to slip up and reveal the true nature of his criminal activity. And when he did, Blount would pounce.

That evening, having finished her appointments in London, Marcheline caught the train back to Uttercombe and was both pleasantly surprised and slightly unnerved by the lecherous looks she got from other commuters. If this was the effect her new look had on men, she could hardly fail to find a father for her child. She looked again at the photo of Ben on her phone.

He really was quite presentable.

Chapter 22

Ben ordered his third gin and tonic, cursing his luck. On the surface he was having the kind of evening that many men dreamt of; Berkeley had given him a generous amount of cash to spend as he saw fit and he was shortly to meet a lady who was apparently in want of a man. It was no different to meeting someone via a dating website, he reasoned. However, this meeting was not of his own choosing and it wasn't a traditional date. This was a premeditated act of artificial seduction and there was a degree of pressure upon him to be successful. That did put something of a dampener on things.

He took a swig of the gin to bolster his resolve. With a wry smile he recalled that the term 'Dutch courage' had originated with British soldiers discovering the warming properties of *jenever*, the Netherland's national gin-based beverage, which they availed themselves of before marching into battle. He felt like a man about to go over the top.

He looked around the bar. The Hogman's Arms was a nice enough mid-range motel; the kind of place where travelling salespeople, or delegates attending conferences, spent their nights. It was also, judging by the advertised day room rates, a place where meetings of an entirely more intimate and probably clandestine nature were held. Ben tried to see if he could identify the classic boss-and-secretary cliché among the drinkers but there were no obvious candidates. This crowd was composed of young, smart, dynamic-looking business types. He realised, with some small degree of humour, that the various tableaux before him looked just like the stock images you saw on business websites. It was as if they were performing a parody of their own trendy lives, with their craft beers, designer suits and heads thrown back in laughter to show off their bleached teeth and perfect hairstyles.

He turned back to the bar and caught a glimpse of his own reflection in the mirrored wall behind the bowls of lemon slices and jars of olives. And in doing so, he was suddenly acutely aware of the gulf between these young go-getters and himself. They had all probably been to university at an age when he'd been learning to juggle and ride a unicycle. They would have steady incomes – good incomes – while he lurched from near-bankruptcy to nearer-bankruptcy. They undoubtedly lived in overpriced minimalist apartments with expensive sound-systems and wine fridges and Govinder Nasran prints on the walls, while all he had to show for a lifetime of toil was the burnt, skeletal remains of a thirty-year-old motor home and a battered old top hat. He knew that there were people out there who fantasised about running away to join a circus rather than live their humdrum lives of nine-to-five banality, with their predictable weekends off, monthly wage packets and crippling mortgages. His own father had been one of them. But, as he sat, staring at his reflection in the motel bar, Ben knew that he would happily trade his life for theirs in a heartbeat.

He let his eyes rove around the room again, looking for the fearsome-looking matron he'd seen on Berkeley's phone. There was no sign of her yet. And he realised that he'd drunk his third double gin and tonic in just three gulps. He ordered a fourth.

Marcheline parked in the car park and wondered what she should do with her shopping. There was quite a lot of it. As the motel was just outside Uttercombe, there had been no point in going home to Shapcott Bassett just to come all the way back to meet this Ellis fellow. But she didn't fancy taking her shopping into the bar where the blatantly designer-branded bags and boxes would be open to public scrutiny. And, of course, there were her sex shop purchases. But leaving her shopping in the car was problematic too; the aged locks on the Rover wouldn't take much forcing and the thought of someone breaking in and finding the penis pump was a particularly disturbing prospect. Therefore, the obvious answer was to book a room at the motel and stash everything in there. A sudden thrill rippled through her as she realised that she could possibly make better use of the room later if this writer fellow, Ellis, demonstrated some hint of romantic interest in her. Feed him plenty of drinks, flutter her eyelashes and who knew where the night would lead? She immediately dismissed such silly thoughts. She didn't even know if he was single. And, even if he was, there was no guarantee that he'd find her attractive. He could even be gay for all she knew.

Ben had slowed down. His sixth and seventh gins had gone down far too easily and, upon ordering his eighth, he noted that he was no longer entirely sure where his feet were. They seemed to have fallen asleep, but not the tingly annoying sensation you got when your circulation returned. It felt more like his feet were anaesthetised. His eyesight had started to fail too; he had developed an inability to focus and his eyeballs seemed to be acting independently of each other. He imagined himself looking something like a chameleon. Or, indeed, Chameleon Girl, who had toured with the circus in the early 1980s before eloping with his cousin, a contortionist called Elastic Lasseter.

His eyes alighted with some difficulty upon a woman who had just entered the bar. She was tall and curvaceous and looked to be in her early forties. She was the only person in the bar who wasn't wearing a business suit, favouring a classy violet jacket and skirt combo instead. Ben glanced at his phone and tried to focus his erratic eyes on one of the photographs of Marcheline that Berkeley had provided. There were some similarities in the face but it was clearly not the same woman. She favoured him with a small, coquettish smile as she found a seat at a table and indicated to a waiter that she would like to be served.

Marcheline studied her phone, and glanced again at the man at the bar. He looked just like the photo that Berkeley had sent her. She wondered why he didn't come over and introduce himself. Then it occurred to her that he had arranged to meet Berkeley and probably didn't realise that she was substituting for him. Berkeley did say that he didn't have the man's number so he wouldn't know who she was. A very naughty idea popped into her head and it quite took her breath away.

Marcheline had never been a bad girl. She'd never played pranks at school, she'd never lied to a teacher and she'd never have dreamed of truanting. Things were much the same now that she was an adult. Berkeley called her unadventurous and dull, but it was more that she couldn't understand why anyone would get any kind of a thrill from bad behaviour, either watching it or taking part. But now, as she considered doing something quite out of character, she started to understand the appeal. Her heart rate had suddenly doubled in her excitement. Here was the perfect flirting opportunity. It wasn't as if some business deal was riding on their meeting tonight, as he was just an associate of her brother's who was looking to relocate to the area. If she tried and failed and left the bar, no one would be any the wiser and she could always tell Berkeley that the man hadn't shown up. But if she succeeded... all sorts of possibilities could open up for her.

She took a deep breath, stood up, then sat down again and mentally scolded herself for even thinking such a thing. It was a ridiculous notion. Her face flushed with embarrassment.

'Er... excuse me?'

She looked up into the smiling and slightly inebriated face of Benjamin Ellis.

'Would you mind if I joined you?' he said. 'The crowd in here is a little... er...'

'Young?' said Marcheline.

'What? Oh god no, I wasn't suggesting...' spluttered Ben. 'I was going to say boisterous. Hi, I'm Benjamin.'

Marcheline extended a hand and, all of sudden, found herself using her middle name instead of her first.

'Leticia,' she said. 'Nice to meet you Benjamin.'

Chapter 23

At the campsite, Glupi moved silently from tree to tree, skirting the edge of the field and looking for the best place from which to make a dash across open ground to his caravan. With no immediate prospect of a return to a normal life, or what passed for a normal life for him, he'd decided to collect some extra clothes and a few necessities to make life in the woods more comfortable. Never the most sanitary of individuals, he nevertheless didn't relish spending the next few weeks or months with only one pair of underpants to his name. With an impressive turn of speed for someone of his age and level of *delirium tremens* he arrived at his caravan, pulled open the door and stepped inside.

Everything was as he'd left it, except for the notable absence of his illegal still. He rooted among the piles of unwashed clothes and found a battered old suitcase, which he proceeded to fill with the self-same unwashed clothes. Into the case too went what few remaining cans of food were in his cupboards, some pots and pans and cutlery and any other small items he could carry. Forcing the bulging case closed, he clicked the locks shut and turned to leave. Standing silhouetted in the open doorway were his clowning comrades, Grimpen and Cronk.

'I knew it was you,' said Cronk. 'I saw you run across the field and I said to Grimpen, "That's Glupi, that is."'

'Hey guys. How is it hangin'?'

'We weren't expecting to see you back here,' said Grimpen. 'Have the police let you go?'

'Ain't caught me yet. I's just getting some of my stuff.'

'There's a detective keeps visiting and asking questions about the fire,' said Cronk. 'He seems to think that Ben tried to burn us down.'

'Ben? Never.'

'And I reckon he'd nab you for the illegal still if he saw you here. So I guess you'd better carry on laying low.'

'We won't say nothing,' added Grimpen. 'We ain't seen you.'

'Hey, thanks, guys.'

'But look, the reason we came over here is to tell you that we've decided to retire. Took a vote in your absence,' said Cronk. 'Next Wednesday. Final performance.'

'After all them years?' said Glupi. 'Do Ben know?'

'Yeah. He seems really happy about it,' said Grimpen. 'Never seen him look so relaxed. I think it's a big weight off his mind. And the fire hit him hard.'

'Which he probably started,' said Cronk.

'Oh don't go on,' said Grimpen.

'We will just have to agree to disagree.'

'Anyway, that's it. We do one last show, sell up, split the money and go our separate ways,' said Grimpen. 'The show won't be the same without you, though. We would have told you but we didn't know where you were.'

'You could be there you know,' said Cronk. 'If you turned up looking like you do now, no one would recognise you. Or you could change your clown make-up and call yourself something different and who would know? You could be in the show then.'

'That's a good idea,' said Grimpen. 'Best disguise in the world.'

'No,' said Glupi. 'I not become different clown. Was Glupi all my lifetimes. If circus is dead, Glupi is dead. But I come watch the show.'

'That's a shame,' said Cronk. 'So, if Glupi is dead, what do we call you now?'

Glupi scratched his unshaven chin.

'Bert,' he said.

Ben had quite warmed to the charming and educated woman who called herself Leticia, who had suggested that they spring for a bottle of champagne and was now regaling him with a history of the county. She'd revealed very little about herself other than that she was a lady of independent means who owned a number of properties in the area and who took a strong interest in local affairs.

'It's always been cows in this part of the county,' she said. 'Down south it's all pigs – the Herewardshire Hog is quite famous – but up here it's dairy and beef. Always has been, right back to Robert Bakewell and the first British breeding stocks. As a matter of fact, that burger you're eating probably came from a local farm. Oh, I'm so sorry, I'm such a bore when it comes to local history.'

Ben smiled. 'It's fascinating.'

'Oh, you're just teasing me now.'

'No really. It is. And I was just thinking how glad I am that I ran into you tonight. To be honest, I was meant to be meeting someone else, but she hasn't shown up. Is it me or is it warm in here?'

Ben took off his hat and laid it on the table.

'Oh dear, what happened to your head?' asked Marcheline.

Ben cursed himself for forgetting about the injury, now quite free of pain thanks to the gin.

'Er... an embarrassing and silly accident,' he said. 'I fell down some stairs.'

'You poor lamb,' said Marcheline. The sight of his injuries had brought out her softer side; the tender, caring side of her personality that had been bottled up for so many years. She was a kind woman, to be sure, but having to run several farms meant that she had never become overly sentimental. She had never hesitated to put a suffering animal out of its misery. But these new feelings were very different. 'And this person you were meeting... is it anyone I might know?' she asked.

'Lady Marcheline Cockering. A bit of a bigwig around here I'm told.'

'Gentry eh? You do move in posh circles,' said Marcheline. 'I hope you're not too disappointed that she didn't show.'

'Definitely not. If anything I'm delighted. I wouldn't have met you otherwise.'

'Oh, you charmer!' said Marcheline. 'So you haven't yet told me what you do.'

'I'm in the entertainment business,' said Ben, smiling. 'Or I was. I'm just about to retire, hence my looking for somewhere to retire to. I want to write a novel. I've been plotting it in my head for twenty years. I just need the time to get it down in writing.'

'How exciting. What's it about?'

'Listen, I'll tell you in a minute but I must visit the little boys' room first. Back in a moment.'

Ben scuttled off to the Gents, and Marcheline sat back in her chair, very impressed with her own performance. She put her new-found confidence down to the champagne. It was also having an effect on her long-suppressed libido, and she was quite definitely feeling the first stirrings of something that might be called physical attraction. His injuries didn't detract from his looks at all and parts of her were experiencing little tingles that she wasn't used to. She felt light-headed and slightly goosepimply. The fact that this Ellis chap was articulate and clever, as well as quite good-looking, made her wonder whether he was a possible candidate to father a child. That he was also artistic, and his rough hands showed that he wasn't a stranger to hard work, were bonuses in his favour. Marcheline's thoughts turned to the hotel room. Did she dare? It was certainly the right time of the month for her and, besides, when would another opportunity like this present itself? All that stood in the way were her own self-doubt and inexperience. What if he didn't find her attractive enough?

She reached into her handbag and took out the small medicine bottle she'd bought in the sex shop. Perhaps, if the 'herbal supplement' tablets did what the label claimed they would, it would load the dice in her favour. 'Take two tablets with food for sustained erection,' she read. She popped the lid and tipped one of the tablets onto her hand. It was very small, about the size of a coffee sweetener, so she tipped out three more.

'Ah well, in for a penny,' she said and was about to drop them into Ellis's champagne when it occurred to her that they might not be soluble. So, instead, she ground them to a powder using the back of a spoon and then sprinkled the powder underneath the beef patty of his half-eaten burger. Surely he wouldn't notice the addition?

Half an hour later, Ben was quite definitely starting to notice. He squirmed uncomfortably in his chair. Something was going on inside his trousers that he had no conscious control over. A warm sensation had settled over his groin like a hot towel and his rapidly inflating penis was nudging its way uncomfortably up and out of the waistline of his underpants. Disguising his action as a scratch, he quickly pushed the stiffening organ to one side where it then popped out of the leg hole. The tip, he noticed, felt almost painfully sensitive.

'Are you alright?' asked Marcheline. 'You seem a little… distracted.'

'Fine,' said Ben, a little too loudly. 'Horsefly bite. Itches like Hell.'

'Oh dear,' said Marcheline, sipping another glass of champagne.

Ben smiled weakly. The damned thing was still growing and every slight move he made caused it to rub against the cotton of his pants. A dull throbbing began. He'd always known that what he called 'Little Ben' had a mind of its own, often deciding to engorge in the most unsuitable of situations. He was reminded of a train journey he'd once made in which an unwanted and unexpected erection had been so obvious in the shorts he was wearing that he'd had to stay on the train for an extra two stops until it had subsided sufficiently to be called decent. He now found himself faced with a similar dilemma.

Another fake scratch revealed what was, he was sure, the most impressive stiffy he'd ever had and, to make matters worse, the throbbing had become quite urgent and the ultra-sensitivity of his circumcised glans made it entirely likely that he'd ejaculate into his clothes if he wasn't careful. And it wasn't as if Leticia was helping. She was quite tipsy now, and her blouse had popped its top button and gaped alarmingly every time she leaned forward to speak. She was a good-looking woman and, in other circumstances, he'd be thoroughly enjoying the view. But, at this moment, it was stimulus that he could do without. He carefully adjusted himself again.

'Is it weeping?' said Marcheline.

'What?' said Ben in alarm.

'The bite. Perhaps it's infected,' said Marcheline. 'You might need antibiotics. Want me to take a look?'

'It's fine,' said Ben, knowing full well that it was anything but. He shut his eyes and began visualising the sort of images that might cause his tumescence to disappear: garbage bags torn open and stinking; a roadkill badger, its guts on display and peppered with fat little maggots squirming with excitement; a blocked drain exuding effluent; the inside of Glupi's caravan.

'Or maybe I should kiss it better?' said Marcheline, leaning forward and touching his hand. He opened his eyes to see that, in leaning so far forward, she had accidentally exposed half a nipple.

'Be right back,' said Ben and he made a wild dash for the gents. Crashing through the door and into a cubicle he hurriedly turned the lock and undid his belt, waist button and fly. Lowering his trousers and underpants gently, his erect member sprang into view, the head huge and swollen, great veins standing proudly all along its length. The damned thing looked like a sex toy – a monstrously large sex toy made of angry purple rubber. Something was terribly wrong, that much was obvious. Deciding that maybe cold water might help to soothe the inflamed organ, Ben lifted the lid off the cistern and wondered how to get his penis to the water or vice versa. There was no way he was going to use the water in the toilet pan. He cupped his hands and dipped them into the cistern and then let the cool water dribble over his organ. It felt good. But what he needed was prolonged exposure. He needed to dunk his penis somehow.

There seemed to be two options open to him: either he found some sort of receptacle, like a cup, in which to put the water; or he had to contrive a way to get his organ into the cistern. Unlocking the door to the cubicle, he peered outside and looked around for some item that could be used as a cup or bowl. There was nothing. He could, at a stretch, manoeuvre himself under the cold tap of a basin, but the chances of someone walking in were high and he didn't fancy having to explain his actions. In fact, it sounded as if someone was just coming in to use the facilities right now, so Ben ducked back inside his cubicle and slipped the latch. Likewise, there was nothing in the cubicle except for the toilet brush and its holder, but using that was just too horrific an option to consider. But then he noticed that the lid of the cistern itself was slightly concave. Maybe a shallow cold bath would do the trick? Carefully, he removed it and placed it upside down on the toilet seat and used his cupped hands to transfer some clean water from the cistern. It wasn't much, barely quarter of an inch in depth, but he straddled the toilet, bent at the knees, and slowly lowered himself into the water.

The cool bath felt wonderful but, all too quickly, his raging penis brought the temperature up to a level where he could no longer feel the benefit. Besides which, it made no difference to the swelling. His next thought was maybe to use the cardboard tube inside the toilet roll as a makeshift cup. He quickly tore all of the remaining paper off the roll and dropped it into the toilet. Then he crimped and folded one end of the tube and tried to collect some water in it. It failed dismally, the seal being anything but waterproof. But popping the damp cardboard tube over his penis had felt good. A sudden inspiration made him grab up a spare unused toilet roll and dunk it in the cistern. When it had taken up all of the water, he fished it out and manoeuvred his penis inside.

'Oh god that feels good,' he murmured quietly under his breath.

At their table, Marcheline looked at her watch and frowned. Benjamin had excused himself over ten minutes ago and hadn't returned. Horror stories of people climbing out of toilet windows rather than face returning to their dates surfaced in her mind. Was that what he'd done? Surely he couldn't be doing anything legitimate or innocent that took ten minutes?

'Excuse me,' she said to a passing waiter. 'My friend has been in the lavatory an awfully long time. Would you mind checking that he's alright?'

'Certainly madam, what's his name?'

'Benjamin.'

The waiter nodded and smiled in a reassuring way before heading for the gents.

The wet toilet roll felt like bliss. Although there seemed to be no immediate effect on the size and firmness of 'Little Ben', Big Ben was feeling less panicked. He sighed with relief and sat down on the toilet seat with the cistern lid resting on his knees. And, now that he had a quiet moment or two, he began to wonder how he'd got into this predicament in the first place. While Leticia was an attractive woman, and she seemed to be quite keen on him, there was no way that her physical proximity could have caused such an extreme reaction. He'd heard that some kinds of spider bite could cause erections, but that seemed an unlikely scenario. For a start, he wasn't aware of any bite marks on his body. And didn't the spiders responsible live in South America and look like tarantulas? He'd also read that hormone imbalances could cause random erections – it was why men got them at night. But this seemed to be a much more serious issue than so-called 'morning wood'. All he could think of was that he'd been slipped a dose of Viagra or Cialis or some other drug that he was frequently offered in spam emails. But by whom? Leticia? Or had Berkeley spiked his tea at the hospital earlier in the day to make him more likely to perform? Ben wouldn't have put it past the man.

Thoughts of Berkeley set him to wondering how the man would react when he learned that he hadn't seduced his sister as he'd been asked to do. It wasn't his fault that Marcheline hadn't shown up. Would he spill the beans about the arson to the police out of spite anyway? And why wasn't all of this worry causing him to deflate?

'Benjamin? Is there a Benjamin in here?'

Ellis jumped and, in doing so, dropped the cistern lid. It fell to the floor with a loud clunk and broke cleanly in half. Water ran out under the door.

'Hello?' said the voice. 'Are you okay in here? There seems to be a lot of water on the floor.'

'I'm fine!' squeaked Ben. 'I'll pay for any breakages.'

'You don't sound fine,' said the voice. 'Your lady friend asked me to check on you. You have been in here a long time.'

'I'm fine,' said Ellis again.

'You're not doing drugs in there, are you, sir?' said the waiter. 'We have a very strict house policy on drugs.'

'It's just a bad tummy. A very bad tummy.'

'Any suggestion of drugs and we are obliged to contact the police, sir.'

'I'm not doing drugs!' snapped Ben. 'Look, I'll be out in a minute, okay?'

Inside the cubicle, Ben cursed Marcheline's impatience and went to pull the toilet roll off his penis, but found that it was stuck fast. Either the swelling had become even more severe, or the waterlogged toilet roll had squeezed the cardboard tube smaller but, whatever the reason, it was not coming off. He began tearing frantically at the wet paper, pulling it away in thick clumps and dropping them into the toilet. The subsequent and prolonged series of loud splashing noises might, at least, satisfy whoever it was outside the cubicle that he was putting the facilities to the use for which they were intended. However, the toilet pan was filling up rapidly, so he flushed it before adding any more. All too late he realised that the pan was already blocked. As water began flooding over the rim, he tore desperately at the last of the toilet roll. The water was now cascading onto the floor and flooding out under the door of the cubicle, carrying lumps of wadded paper with it like tiny icebergs.

'I'm getting the manager!' said the waiter.

'No, please don't…'

But, with a slam of the door, the waiter was gone and Ben rushed to try to make himself look decent, forcing his errant erection back inside his trousers.

Marcheline watched the waiter go into the toilet and then come out a few minutes later. To her alarm, however, he didn't come back to her to reassure her that all was well. Instead, he walked briskly into the kitchens and then re-emerged with another man and they had both headed back to the toilets. She cursed herself for her stupidity in doubling the dosage. Perhaps he'd had an allergic reaction? What if he'd gone into anaphylactic shock? What if he'd had a heart attack?

'Oh God, what have I done?' she said, and staggered to the gents' toilets. She crashed through the door and found the waiter banging on the cubicle door. The room was awash with water and hunks of tissue. Spotting several dark masses moving across the floor, she felt her bile rise. Closer examination would have shown them to be parts of the cardboard inner tubes of two toilet rolls, darkened by saturation, but she wasn't going to look that closely.

The waiter banged on the cubicle door again.

'You need to come out of there now, sir. I've brought the manager, Mr Buston, with me. If you don't come out we'll be forced to open the door.'

Mr Buston turned on Marcheline.

'Madam, you shouldn't be in here. This is the gents.'

'Indeed. But as I am the person who asked your staff to check on my friend I have every right to be in here.'

Marcheline was not an easy woman to sway at the best of times and the two bottles of champagne she'd helped to empty had made her even more bombastic than usual.

'But what if...' began the manager, but Marcheline had taken charge.

'Benjamin! Are you alright?'

Inside the cubicle, Ben attempted to wrench his fly closed, but material from his underpants had become stuck between the teeth. With one last mighty tug, he yanked the zipper upwards. To his horror it broke off in his hand and his penis sprang out of his fly like an obscene Jack-in the-box.

'Fuck!' he yelled.

'Right, we're coming in,' said Marcheline. She turned to Mr Buston. 'You! Open the door. Something is obviously very wrong in there.'

Inside the cubicle, Ben forced his organ back inside his trousers as best he could and steeled himself for action. He would have to make a break for it and get as far away from the hotel as possible.

The Manager fumbled among his bunch of keys to find the one that could open the cubicle lock from the outside. But he was too slow. The door suddenly swung inwards and Ben burst from the cubicle and, glissading on a wad of wet tissue, skidded across the floor and collided with the opposite wall. His head clunked against a basin and, as he lay there, wet and red-faced, with blood oozing from the re-opened wound on his head and his impressive erection poking out of his trouser fly, he passed out.

'I'd best take him to our room,' said Marcheline, removing her pashmina and draping it over his embarrassment.

Chapter 24

Outside the Hogman's Arms, Brian Blount yawned and, once again, tried to make any kind of sense of circumstances. After spotting Ellis at the hospital, he had followed the man's taxi to a motel outside Uttercombe, where, to make matters even more confusing, he had seen Marcheline Cockering arrive. Only, it wasn't the woman he knew. Like Ellis, her appearance had changed dramatically, which, in his eyes, was very suspicious. If there was one constant in life, it was that Lady Cockering was constant.

He frowned. First, Ellis had met Berkeley Cockering at the cottage hospital and had been given a wad of banknotes. And now he was at the same hotel as the Viscount's sister. That couldn't be coincidence. But he couldn't begin to fathom a scenario in which the three of them were not at odds with each other. And yet, he'd seen for himself that Berkeley had protected the man while he was trying to interview him. And he'd been told by his spy at the hospital that the Viscount had been chatting to Ellis like they were old friends. To further confuse matters, Blount had just peered in through the window of the hotel bar to see Ellis and Marcheline laughing and drinking champagne.

Blount returned to his car and tumbled the known facts over in his mind, looking for any kind of connection or coherent narrative. But the various snippets of information bounced off each other and refused to stick. Nothing made sense. Eventually, his weariness overtook him and he dozed.

He was rudely awoken less than an hour later by the scream of a man in fear of his life. And who was standing naked in front of Blount's car.

Benjamin was having the strangest dream. He was inside a farmyard barn with high wooden rafters and a thatched roof. He was on all fours and, when he looked down, he could see that he had cloven hooves instead of hands. His arms were white with mottled black patches and, now that he looked again, he realised that they looked more like legs. What's more, something very strange was going on at the other end of his body. He twisted his head around to look and saw, with some surprise, that he was apparently a Frieisan cow.

'Ah yes,' he thought. 'This is cow country.'

'Yes it is,' said a milkmaid in gingham and pigtails who, apart from being the spit of Leticia, was furiously milking him with her hand. He started to say something but all that emerged was a lowing moo.

'There there,' said the milkmaid. 'Soon be finished.'

Her arm movements seemed to suddenly kick up a gear and Ben let go another loud moo.

'I hope that means that you're enjoying this,' said the woman who had now, unaccountably, turned into a nurse in a curiously shiny uniform. The barn then dissolved and Ben awoke to find himself lying naked and prostrate on a hotel bed where terrible things were being done to his manhood. The Suckmaster 3000, which hadn't been designed at all for this kind of work, consisted of an over-sized plastic test tube, to which, at the closed end, was attached a rubber hose that terminated in something that looked like a remote control. Holding the control was Leticia, dressed as a nurse, her PVC outfit failing to conceal her sexy underwear, just as it was designed not to. The test-tube part, meanwhile, was over his still erect penis and appeared to be trying to remove the organ by suction.

'Mooo...' groaned Ben.

'More? You like that? Shall I turn up the power?' asked Marcheline. She tapped a button and the tinny whine of the electric suction pump contained within the control box rose by an octave. Ben took a sharp intake of breath.

In the device's accompanying leaflet, the manufacturers made the wholly unverified claim that the pump could increase the length of a man's member by anything up to fifteen per cent. They had nothing to say, however, about its use as a mechanical milking machine on an already hugely engorged and chemically stimulated organ. Ben, however, had plenty to say and would have done so had not the Suckmaster 3000 quite literally taken his breath away. The low pressure inside the tube was making him fear that his penis was about to explode. He reached down to try to remove the device but found that it was going nowhere thanks to the vacuum and the patent rubberised collar that ensured a good seal around the base of the shaft.

'Are you nearly there? If you need some inspiration...' said Marcheline. She stood up and slowly undid the long zip down the front of her nurse's outfit. The outfit flew open, revealing a curvaceous body wearing a very nice bra-and-knickers combination, suspender belt and stockings. With a smile on her lips, she put the remote control down on the bed and used both hands to undo the front-fastening clasp of her bra. 'How's this?' she said and, in one quick movement, whipped it open, straddled his body and pushed her naked breasts into his face. Now in danger of suffocating as well, Ben waved his arms and legs frantically in an effort to get her off him. A fat nipple pushed urgently into his mouth.

Marcheline groped blindly for the hose with which she could reel in the handset and turn off the pump. The man was surely good and ready now and it was time for her to do her duty for the Cockering family. But she had reckoned without Ben's desperate and understandable need for oxygen. With one mad, frantic last attempt to extricate himself, he thrashed like a madman and one of his wildly kicking feet caught the remote control and, more importantly, the button that produced the highest degree of suck. As the ghastly machine began to wrench even harder on his penis, he found himself in such desperate straits that only one course of action was left open to him. He bit down hard on Marcheline's nipple while simultaneously launching himself off the bed. She shouted in alarm as she crashed onto the carpeted floor.

Ben sprang to his feet and rushed to the door. In an instant, he was running nakedly down the hotel corridor, the hose dragging along behind him like an umbilical cord and threatening to tangle itself around his legs, and the control box smacking off the walls and floor. He stopped for a moment to pick up the box and, hopefully, to do something about the excruciating suction that was threatening to un-man him. But in the flight from the room, the front of the control box had been smashed in and several of the buttons, most crucially the stop button, were missing. Frantically, he jabbed his fingers in the holes where the buttons had been but nothing seemed to make any difference. He then turned his attention to the hose and wondered if he could pull it off the test tube without removing his genitals into the bargain.

'Benjamin!'

The sound of the obviously insane woman's voice set him running again. He had to get away, as far away from her as he could and find some way to stop the demented machine's ghastly attentions. A fire door beckoned and he crashed through it and out into the car park. In desperation, he put the hose between his teeth and clamped his jaws together. As the rubber split and air rushed in, he felt the pressure inside the tube drop and the pain in his groin began to ease.

'Benjamin!' Marcheline appeared at the open fire door.

Ben screamed. And inside the car directly in front of him he saw Detective Sergeant Brian Blount smile.

Chapter 25

'So tell me again… what exactly have they been arrested for?' asked the Custody Officer. He glanced across at the two dishevelled and shamefaced prisoners who were sitting on a bench in his custody suite at Uttercombe. He'd let them get dressed into their own clothes and Ben, for one, was delighted that his arrest and detention had finally subdued his privates. He shuddered as he spotted the remains of the Suckmaster 3000 in a sealed property bag on the Custody Officer's desk.

'Him, suspicion of arson and outraging public decency,' said Blount. 'Her, indecent exposure.'

'You do know that that's Lady Cockering, don't you?' whispered the custody officer.

'Yes,' said Blount. 'That doesn't change anything.'

'It bloody well does. It means that you had better have a watertight case or your life won't be worth living. She's a magistrate, for starters. And her brother is besties with the Chief's wife. You can't charge her with indecent exposure.'

'Just because she's a toff?'

'No, because you don't have the evidence.'

'But she was topless in public,' said Blount.

'So are half the sun-lovers on Brighton beach in July,' said the Custody Officer. 'That doesn't make it a chargeable offence. For indecent exposure there has to be genitals. Were there genitals?'

'Dear God, no.'

'Then I can't charge her,' said the Custody Officer. 'My advice is to go for breach of the peace. Nicely nebulous.'

'Breach of the peace?' said Blount. 'That's not nearly enou–'

'Now, about this other person... Ellis. Outraging public decency you say? Who was outraged?'

'Well, I was.'

'Cops don't count. There's case law says so,' said Custody. 'And it has to be a public place...'

'It was.'

'And has to be capable of being seen by two or more people, who have to have been present, whether they saw it or not. Was there anyone in the car park besides you?'

'No. But people could have seen if they'd come to the hotel windows.'

'And did they?'

'I don't know.'

'Breach of the peace, then,' said Custody. 'So what's the arson charge in connection to?'

'He is the prime suspect for a fire that happened two nights ago at Brill Farm.'

'Ah, now we have something. What did he set fire to?'

'Er... his caravan,' said Blount, feeling increasingly uncomfortable.

'His own caravan? That's not a crime,' said Custody.

'Not *per se* I agree,' said Blount. 'But I strongly suspect insurance fraud.'

'So it's a fraud investigation?' said Custody.

'Yes, yes it is,' said Blount victoriously.

156

'Best I phone the DI then,' said Custody, reaching for the phone.

'There's no need for that,' said Blount.

'Yes there is,' said Custody. 'Standing orders. I don't know what you do over at Morbridge, but here all fraud cases must be investigated by an officer not below the rank of Detective Inspector.'

'But…'

'I'm sure Ma'am Banton will be delighted to hear that we have one in the bin.'

Blount sat down and his heart sank.

Ben and Marcheline were feeling very sorry for themselves. During the booking-in procedure, Ben had learned that his assailant was none other than Berkeley's sister, the person he'd been supposed to meet and seduce. And Marcheline had been equally shocked to learn that the object of her less-than-tender ministrations was the owner of the circus and the very person to blame for the fly-posting of her village and the damage to Twimbley's. But even more painful had been the revelation that Berkeley, her own brother, had employed someone – the very person she blamed for all of the trouble in her perfect village – to seduce her, apparently just for kicks. It made her very sad and, at the same time, extremely angry. She would make him pay for what he'd done, and pay dearly. As for Benjamin, she had to confess that she felt a little sorry for him, despite everything. He genuinely hadn't known who she was when he'd met her in the bar that evening and he'd been delightful company. And then she'd abused him, firstly with the tablets and then, after he had failed to wake up in the hotel room, with the pump. Her actions had been inexcusable and, she realised, in many ways her behaviour had been no better than Berkeley's. She'd taken extreme action to get what she wanted and, in doing so, had caused Benjamin Ellis a great deal of physical pain. The modern day Cockerings had acted as unscrupulously as their many abhorrent ancestors had done in the past, and she felt thoroughly ashamed of herself and her bloodline. To add to her sense of shame, Ellis had refused to charge her with any kind of assault.

Ellis was staring at the floor, considering his fate. Once again, the arson had come back to haunt him and he knew that Blount wouldn't let it lie until he had some kind of conviction. But more hurtful was the thought that he'd genuinely liked 'Leticia'; they'd got on so well and had so much in common. And even though their meeting had been off the back of a nasty little plot, he'd genuinely taken a shine to her. But it had all been a lie. She was just another Cockering, using him to get what she wanted. He was therefore somewhat surprised to feel a cool hand touch his. He looked up into the tearful eyes of Marcheline.

'I'm so very sorry,' she said.

Detective Inspector Nicola Banton was doing her best to try to make sense of Blount's suspicions. And, having once been Blount's deputy before his fall from grace, she couldn't help notice that he was having difficulty adjusting to their reversal of roles.

'He's an arsonist, Bant... er... ma'am. I swear he is.'

'But he burned down his own Winnebago, Brian.'

'Yes, but he wanted to burn down the clown's caravan too, I'm sure he did,' said Blount. 'There were two distinct trails of flammable liquid, both with a common starting-point between the two vehicles.'

'Sounds like he would have done us all a favour,' said Banton.

'The forensics team had to be shaved and deloused. But you still haven't found the clown?'

'He's done a runner because he knows we'd nick him for that still.'

'But he hasn't made an allegation against the Ellis person?'

'No.'

'And you have no witnesses that saw Ellis start the fire or lay the trail of fuel?'

'Not yet.'

'Forensics?'

'Not as such.'

'Then what do you have?' asked Banton.

Blount glared at his former Detective Sergeant. Her promotion to DI had been inevitable; she was effortlessly clever and exceptionally good at her job. But it was nevertheless frustrating that she now outranked him. Secondly, he knew that she was fully acquainted with his terrible handling of the investigation into the murder of author Shirley Pomerance three years previously. She had been there and had seen how he had let his obsession with catching a particular suspect blind him to the truth. It occurred to him that he was now exhibiting what appeared to be worryingly similar behaviour.

'I swear to you, Ba... ma'am, there's something going on,' he insisted. 'Why else would he be meeting with the Cockerings?'

'I don't know. But find me some evidence of what they're up to and I'll be happy to charge them,' said Banton. 'We can keep these two in overnight to answer the breach of the peace charges at court tomorrow. But, as things stand, once they finish at court they walk.'

And, with that, she walked.

The tirade of swearing that had followed had made Ben smile a little. Unless Blount was one of those cops he'd seen in TV dramas who was willing to fabricate evidence or 'plant' stuff on him – and, from what he'd seen, he doubted that Blount had the balls for that – then they would be free by lunchtime tomorrow. All he had to do was stick to his story.

He looked again at Marcheline and was surprised to find that he felt genuinely sorry for her. She didn't deserve his sympathy after what she'd put him through, but he couldn't help noticing how lost and alone she suddenly looked. All of the bluster had been knocked out of her with her arrest. Far from being the imposing figure he'd heard about, she looked like a frightened little girl and his anger had quickly melted away. Having heard her side of the story, he could understand – if not approve of – the action she'd taken to try to preserve her family line. Her motivations for acting the way she had were certainly more virtuous than her brother's. And it was flattering that she'd attempted to seduce him in the more traditional way, even going so far as to dress up in the nurse's outfit, before turning to mechanical means to obtain what she wanted when he'd remained unconscious. It was surely an offhand compliment that she'd seen him as suitable to father the next generation of such an old and respected family. And no permanent damage had been done, even though his genitals felt like they'd been through a mangle. Therefore, as far as he was concerned, they were quits. He doubted she'd be asking him to pay for the poster removal or the repairs to Twimbley's now.

He lifted his hand out from under hers and placed it on top.

'Don't worry. Everything's going to be all right,' he said.

'Right you two lovebirds,' said the Custody Officer. 'Let's sort you out some rooms for the night. It won't be as comfy as the Hogman's Arms but the breakfast is good.'

And with that, Ben and Marcheline were led to separate cells for their overnight stay behind bars.

Chapter 26

At Uttercombe Magistrates Court the next morning, Marcheline experienced the most humiliating day of her life. To begin with there was the ignominy of standing before the bench in a neighbouring town to plead guilty to an offence of Breach of the Peace. She knew both of the magistrates on duty and the looks on their faces were almost pitying as they heard the evidence against her. She felt utterly ashamed and resolved to submit her resignation as soon as she was able. She was no longer fit to occupy the chair.

Saturday morning was traditionally the time of the week when people that she had always referred to as 'the yobbery' were processed by law. She had sat in on many such sessions and had always expressed the deepest contempt for the hungover and shamefaced persons brought before her. But now, as she watched each defendant step up into the dock, she realised that they were just normal people who'd had a bit too much to drink and, consequently, had seen a good night out go bad. With few exceptions, they were all working people: an assistant shop manager, a gardener, a bank clerk, a dustman. They weren't habitual drunks or violent louts. They were just like the people in her village, the people she thought of as friends. The realisation that she had been such a snob made her feel sick to her stomach. The court could fine her whatever they liked, but nothing could hurt her more than the sudden understanding of the sort of person she was. She'd let everyone down. She'd done terrible things to Benjamin Ellis, who, to his credit, had been an absolute gentleman throughout the entire legal process. She'd always assumed – and the bill-posting hadn't helped – that circus folk were irresponsible travelling thieves and tricksters. But if the rest of Benelli's Circus were anything like Ellis, it was her prejudices that were criminal, not them.

Ben too was considering recent events. Despite the deception and the herbal erection tablets and the less than tender ministrations of the Suckmaster 3000, he had genuinely fallen for 'Leticia'. The fact that she had been acting out of desperation to save her family lineage had somehow made her actions more understandable and, in a curious way, almost noble. To care that much about something was a worthy and strong character trait, even if her methods had been ill-considered and fuelled by an overindulgence in champagne. He reserved the greater part of his ire for Berkeley, whose greed and willingness to blackmail him to get what he wanted had created the entire situation in the first place.

'Lady Marcheline,' said the head magistrate. 'Few cases have come before me in the past twelve years that have distressed me as much as this. I can only assume that you, a fellow magistrate, were found in such... er... circumstances because of some temporary loss of reason caused by excessive drinking. Given your clean record and exemplary service to the bench, I am inclined to be as lenient as I can be. However, that does not detract from the fact that both you and Mr Ellis exhibited disruptive and unacceptable behaviour at the Hogman's Arms and caused damage to said premises as the result. Do you have anything to say?'

Marcheline pulled herself up to her full height and lifted her head high. 'Only that I am deeply ashamed about what has happened. I have let you all down. I have besmirched my family name. I have disgraced myself and I will, of course, tender my resignation as a magistrate forthwith. I accept any punishment that the court deems suitable.'

Ben and Marcheline stood together in the dock and accepted their punishment; a fine, a binding-over to keep the peace for twelve months, costs of repair and clean-up payable to the Hogman's Arms, and a lifelong ban from said premises and all hotels belonging to the chain.

Blount watched the proceedings from a seat by the witness box and frowned. Despite his best efforts, despite his policing experience, despite the many books he'd read and tried to understand about the psychology of criminals, he simply could not work out what the connection was between the two defendants, the Viscount Morbridge, and the fire. Was there some sinister collusion going on among the landed gentry of South Herewardshire? It wouldn't be the first time that a bunch of posh sorts had got together to run some kind of a clandestine insurance fiddle or tax-avoidance scam. And it wasn't uncommon for rich people to hire criminal types to do their dirty work for them. Various conspiracy theories popped into his mind but none of them quite fitted the circumstances, and none of them could explain the involvement of a penniless circus owner with no criminal record. Once again, he could feel his chances of promotion slipping away from him. His mortifying stepdown in front of Nicola Banton had been an embarrassment. And the fact that he had just learned that

Clifford Jaine – his other former detective sergeant – now owned his own private security firm and lived in a big expensive house in posh Binster simply fuelled his frustrations still further.

The case finished and the defendants were shown where to settle their fines. Blount stood and stretched his aching back. The only way he was going to find out what was going on was by dedicating all of his waking hours to following Ellis about. He could see a good many more uncomfortable nights in his car in his immediate future – at six feet six inches tall he was not designed for compact spaces – but he would learn the truth and see that justice was done, even if it crippled him.

Ben and Marcheline walked out of the court together and into a dull, grey autumnal lunchtime. The events of the past twenty-four hours had taken its toll of them both but the outside world neither knew nor cared and went about its business as usual.

'Do you fancy a coffee?' said Ben.

'I'm surprised you're even speaking to me,' said Marcheline.

'I wasn't exactly a boy scout either, so let's call it quits, eh? Fresh start,' said Ben. 'So, coffee?'

'That would be lovely,' said Marcheline. 'Oh, but can you afford it? I don't mind paying.'

'Berkeley's paying,' said Ben, waving the last few twenty-pound notes that the peer had furnished him with. 'Just as he paid our fines. I say we have lunch on him too.'

'Yes, he deserves to pay,' said Marcheline with a terrible glint in her eye.

At the cottage hospital, Berkeley Cockering lay in his bed wondering if his plan was working. He'd sent three or four texts to Ellis with no response, but there wasn't a great deal he could read into the silence. It was possible that he was entangled with Marcheline, which would be excellent news, or it could be simply that he'd run out of phone credit. The man did claim to be broke, after all. He dialled the number again and it rang for thirty seconds before going to voicemail.

'So you aren't out of credit, you're just not answering,' he said to no one in particular. 'All I'll say is, Mr Ringmaster... beware the fury of a patient man.'

'Good grief, I couldn't eat another thing!' said Marcheline. 'I don't know where you put it all, especially after those big breakfasts we had at the police station.'

Ben patted his stomach and smiled. The remains of two mixed grills littered the table. Half of Marcheline's had found its way onto his plate. 'It's a skill you pick up when you never know where the next meal is coming from,' he said. 'Eat large and live off the reserves. Like a bear hibernating. But without the hibernating. And the bear. Sorry, bad analogy.'

Marcheline laughed. 'I just have to look at food and I put on pounds,' she said, nibbling at a chip. 'This won't help my figure at all.'

'Nothing wrong with your figure,' said Ben. 'Who wants to cuddle up to a bicycle frame, eh? Men prefer curves to bones.'

'There's curvy and there's fat,' said Marcheline.

'You forget, I did see rather more of your curves last night than I'd expected to when I met you in the bar,' said Ben. 'And, trust me, you are not fat.'

Marcheline flushed fire engine red. Ben's phone began to buzz on the table top.

'Berkeley again?' said Marcheline.

'Yes,' said Ben. 'But I'm done with him, and that's for sure.

If he wants to drop me in it, fair enough. I did wrong, I accept that, and if he wants to tell the police, I can't stop him.'

'It is only his word against yours,' said Marcheline. 'I think there's a good chance that the police would take no action anyway.'

'But if they did, who would the magistrates believe, eh? A viscount or some guy from a circus?'

With some regret, Marcheline had to admit to herself that his words were true. Her colleagues on the bench were as snobbish as she had been.

'I'd almost welcome it right now,' said Ben. 'I'm sick of all the lying. Maybe I should phone him back and say, "Do your worst." Call his bluff.'

'Or…' said Marcheline, her lips pursing in thought. 'Maybe we could use this opportunity to teach him a lesson.'

'I just wish I knew what he was thinking,' said Ben. 'I genuinely have no idea why he wanted me to seduce you.'

'Because he's a vindictive and petty little man!' snapped Marcheline, a little louder than she intended. Several of the other diners turned to look at her and she smiled back apologetically. 'He did this to deliberately upset me. He's always doing things to upset me. Inviting your circus here, for example. The man is obsessed with money and is constantly badgering me to sell off the family estate. But I will not do it. My ancestors fought hard to build what we have today, and we were one of the very few old families who managed to retain our estates after the wars. I will not see all of that history, all of that sacrifice and sense of duty thrown away just so that Berkeley can lose it all in the casinos at Monaco.'

'It seems a lot of effort just to annoy you,' said Ben.

'There will be a deeper motive behind it,' said Marcheline. 'I suspect that he blackmailed you into seducing me so that he could then break my heart by revealing that you owned the circus and that he'd put you up to it.'

'Sounds about right. What a nasty, petty-minded little man he is.'

'And greedy.'

'So, did it work?' said Ben.

'Did what work?'

'Did I manage to seduce you?'

Marcheline blushed again. 'You did a very good job.'

Now it was Ben's turn to blush. He reached across the table and held her hand. 'Once I met you, I didn't need blackmailing,' he said.

Marcheline smiled back at him and squeezed his hand. 'That's all very well but Berkeley mustn't be allowed to get away with what he's done to us. I presume that he has no idea of what transpired last night or this morning. But word will undoubtedly get back to him in a day or so. I'm well known enough in the area and he knows plenty of people in Uttercombe. That said, it is the weekend, and he's in hospital, so I reckon we have maybe twenty-four hours before he finds out. We should use this opportunity to our advantage.'

'You mean... get our own back on him?' said Ben. 'Well, whatever you're planning, count me in.'

'I will go home and have a think,' said Marcheline. 'I have a desperate need for a long, hot bath. Those police cells stank of disinfectant and Lord knows what kinds of people had been in... God, listen to me. I'm no better than any of them.'

'You just had one bad day,' said Ben. 'So, can I call you tomorrow?'

'I'd like that,' said Marcheline. 'Oh Lord, I just remembered. I have to go back to that motel to collect my possessions and my car. How embarrassing.'

'Want me to come with you?' said Ben. 'I have time. And use of Berkeley's taxi cab account.'

'You're very sweet,' said Marcheline, pecking him on the cheek.

As they left, Blount saw the kiss and filed it away in his confusing mental dossier of facts. It added no clarity to the situation whatsoever. If anything, the waters had become even murkier than before.

Chapter 27

Bert – the clown formerly known as Glupi – had not been idle since his return from the campsite. He had intended to live rough in the woods until the troupe moved on, when he would then re-join them. But, having learned that the circus was soon to be no more, he now found himself facing an uncertain future.

He'd joined the army as a young man and it had taken care of him. It had fed him, clothed him, billeted him and told him what to do until his demob. Then, in his early thirties, he'd worked as a labourer on a succession of farms, gradually working his way westwards across Poland and into Germany, where he'd become a landscape gardener for Bremen City Council. Again, in every place he'd worked, he'd been fed, watered and given somewhere to live. In Bremen, he'd quickly developed a reputation as both a funny man and a hard drinker among the large Polish immigrant population. He'd also left no one in any doubt that he was someone it was best not to cross. His frequent brawls and street-fights were responsible for the craggy, beaten-up look he sported in later life.

It was during a spectacular bender at the 1972 Freimarkt that he'd first put on the pancake and big shoes after being asked to fill in for a friend who was part of a busking troupe. Glupi the Inebriated Clown was an immediate hit among the audience of what was one of Europe's biggest fairground festivals, and he had been invited to tour with Benelli's by Benjamin Snr. He'd been with the circus ever since, once more happy to let others dictate what he did and where he lived.

But now, at the age of seventy-six, and with nothing to his name but the clothes he stood in, Adalbert Szewczyk felt understandably lost and, he realised, alone. Once the circus was gone, he had no one. He had lost contact with his own family in the 1980s and, while there had been the occasional romances and flings along the way, he hadn't had what you could call a 'significant other' since his late fifties. He hadn't minded; he was happy in his own company and quite often too drunk to get lonely. The past few days in the woods had been serene. But they had also been sober and had given him time to reflect upon his lot. With the Big Top permanently closing its flies in a week's time, he had to consider his future. It wasn't terribly rosy.

To begin with, a nagging thought had been growing in the back of his mind. From what he'd heard, there was a strong suspicion that Benjamin had burned down his own home. But, apparently, the fire had also been intended to destroy his caravan too. Why would Ben want to do that? The man had been cross about the poster campaign, admittedly, but not cross enough for arson, surely? He had also, uncharacteristically, given the clown the night off work and given him money that the circus could not afford. A genuine act of friendship? Or had it been to get him out of the way?

These were disturbing thoughts, but he didn't have time to dwell upon such things too deeply. His first and most obvious priority was to find somewhere to live. His caravan was still out of bounds and he was keen to avoid entanglements with the law and, in particular, the Excise men, who took a very dim view of home distilleries. So he had explored the woods in the hope of finding an abandoned cottage or an old shed in which to squat. Disappointingly, all he'd found was a folly on the border of Brill Farm and the Cockering estate that probably attracted too many visitors. But searching further afield he had struck gold. At the far edge of what looked to be a field turned over to meadow, he'd found a small brick-built cowshed. From all appearances, it looked as if it hadn't been used or visited for decades, but the corrugated iron roof was sound, the interior was dry and it would be a simple matter to lash together some kind of a door. The shed and meadow appeared to belong to the rather grand manor house that he could see nestled among some trees around three-quarters of a mile away. He doubted that the owners ever came down to this quiet corner of their estate and so he'd probably be quite safe from discovery.

His reverie was broken by the sound of a screaming car engine. Even from this distance, he could see the vehicle and the trail of dust it left as it drove up the long drive to the distant manor house.

Marcheline arrived back at Cockering Hall in a fug of unfamiliar emotions. An uncomfortable visit with Ben to the Hogman's Arms to apologise and pay for her room and the damage done to the toilets and corridor walls had been followed by a slow drive home in second gear, which had given her time to reflect on the past two days. It was fair to say that she had learned humility the hard way. It had never occurred to her before that the face she had presented to the world all these years was an unpleasant one. She'd tried to make the world a better place or, at least, that part of the world within her sphere of influence. But such had been her conceit that it had never crossed her mind to wonder if her idea of 'better' was shared by others. It had always been her way or the wrong way. But now that the scales had been torn from her eyes, she could see herself as others did – a snobbish, self-centred virago who had been prepared to sexually assault a man she hardly knew because he had sperm and she didn't. With thoughts of Ben, her mind quickly cantered through the spectrum of emotions from shame to self-pity to feelings of guilt and then affection.

The circus owner had awoken something within her that she'd thought lost. Whether it was love, it was too early to say. Maybe it was the thing that Meg Shandcreek had seen in her tea leaves. Something lost is found, she'd said. All she knew for sure was that she had developed feelings for the circus owner and that she had never, to her knowledge, felt this way about anyone before. It made her wonder why. Why now? And why Ben? All she could put it down to was the curious conjunction of circumstances that had led to their meeting. And, perhaps, the fact that in her zeal to make her small world as perfect as she could, she'd populated it with men who were cast from the same mould as herself. She and they were like the hooked sides on a piece of Velcro; no matter how much you tried to make them connect, they never would. Or the poles of a magnet – it took opposites to attract.

She parked the Rover in the garage next to Berkeley's dusty, unused Jaguar, and made her way into the Hall, carrying her London purchases. While in the motel room collecting her shopping, she'd taken the opportunity to fix her hair and make-up and get changed into a very attractive and flattering panelled Jersey dress. It had taken Meg Shandcreek a few seconds to recognise who she was.

'Oh Miss Cockering! You'm a feast for the eyes,' she'd said, with uncharacteristic enthusiasm. Her compliments were as rare as hens' teeth. 'You look like a film star!'

'Thank you Meg, but I'd hardly go that far,' said Marcheline. 'I certainly don't feel very special. In fact... would you put the kettle on please? I need to share a few things with you regarding my trip away.'

Mrs Shandcreek listened carefully, occasionally nodding or shaking her head when she felt it necessary, as Marcheline told her all about the momentous events that had re-shaped her life in the past forty-eight hours. Meg had stayed quiet until the very end, sensing perhaps that Her Ladyship needed to share her experiences with someone, rather than bottle it all up inside. Most surprising of all had been the tears. Mrs Shandcreek couldn't remember seeing those since Marcheline's childhood.

'So there you go,' said Marcheline, dabbing at her eyes with a handkerchief. 'I'll call for extraordinary meetings of the Village Council and the Residents' Committee on Monday and announce that I am stepping down as Chair of both. And, naturally, I've offered my resignation as a magistrate.'

'None of that matters, councils and committees and courts,' said Mrs Shandcreek. 'You'm well rid of it all I reckon. What matters is you. This man, Benjamin, you like him?'

'Yes, I do. I mean, I barely know him, but...'

'Don't need to share a bed to know you like a man,' said Meg.

'He is very kind and very gentle,' said Marcheline. She'd been about to add 'forgiving' but remembered that she'd spared Meg the more lurid details of her Friday night. All that Meg knew was that Marcheline had met a man, they'd had too much to drink and had been arrested as the result. She'd also been spared the knowledge that Berkeley had been involved. Although she didn't dote on him in the way she did his sister,

Meg was very loyal to them both. Marcheline didn't want to put her in a situation where she'd feel pressured to pick sides.

'That counts for a lot,' said Meg. 'Finished your tea?'

Marcheline handed over her teacup and saucer. With one swift movement, Mrs Shandcreek inverted the cup and then looked closely at the pattern of wet leaves remaining stuck to the inside of the cup.

'Don't tell me. Children,' said Marcheline with a wry smile.

'There's always children,' said Meg.

'Oh, and didn't you say something the other day about something lost will be found?'

'See the shell there?' said Meg, pointing to a vaguely ovoid cluster of leaves. 'That means treasure, something found. That wheel there means change. And the beetle means renewal.'

'Change, eh? There have definitely been some changes these past few days. And I think I might have found something that I'd lost too. So where are the children in those leaves, Meg?'

'There,' said Meg, pointing to an amorphous glob of wet leaves. 'That's a pear. Means a birth.'

'It looks nothing like a pear!' said Marcheline, smiling. 'Could just as easily be an egg.'

'Egg means a birth.'

'I think you see what you want to see, Meg. It's like those Rorschach ink blot tests. They say more about you than about the future I suspect. I mean to say... that little pile of leaves there looks like a bat to me.'

Mrs Shandcreek peered closely at where Marcheline was pointing and frowned.

'So it does.'

'What does a bat mean?' asked Marcheline.

'Death,' said Meg, sombrely.

Chapter 28

Ben spent a restful night on a comfortable couch in Hung and Lo's caravan and was woken gently by the distant sound of the church bells of St Lydwina's calling the faithful to prayer. He yawned and stretched and smiled. Today he was meeting up with Marcheline and the thought filled him with happiness. What an extraordinary series of events had led to their meeting. How did such things happen? Was it fate or was it no more than capricious chance? All he knew was that she filled his every thought.

In her bed at the Hall, Marcheline heard the bells and smiled sleepily. The topic of conversation among the congregation today would undoubtedly be the fact that she wasn't there. Lady Cockering never missed a Sunday service – that was a matter of fact. Well, not any more it wasn't. St Lydwina's could do without her this morning. And maybe next Sunday too if she felt like it. It wasn't that she was being irreligious; it was more about doing what she wanted to do rather than what she had always believed she had to do. Her attendance at church every week was simply about duty and keeping up appearances.

Her mobile phone buzzed on the bedside table and she picked it up. It was a text from Ben that said, simply: 'Cublington's Folly. 12 midday. Bring a bottle.' Marcheline spread her limbs starfish-like in the big bed and revelled in the sensation of the cool Egyptian cotton against her bare skin. She'd never slept naked before. It felt wonderful. It felt naughty. It felt like liberation.

A less comfortable night had been had by Blount, whose car was once more parked in the lay-by near to Brill Farm. He cursed the church bells and the pain in his back, and completely failed to wriggle himself into a less crippling position on the back seat.

Bert stood back and admired his handiwork. Having constructed a makeshift broom from birch twigs and wire cannibalised from a long redundant and broken fence, he'd swept out the cowshed and used water from the Gew to wash the walls clean of cobwebs and birdlime. He'd then stuffed an old duvet cover with soft fragrant ferns to make a comfortable mattress and was using his old army greatcoat as a temporary blanket. A bundle of his dirty clothes stuffed inside a pullover made a pillow. The door was still an issue but he had found a rusting sheet of corrugated iron behind the cowshed and it would keep out most of the draught. His best find, however, had been an old fly-tipped barbecue. As rusty and dirty as it was, he could cook food on it and then burn wood to warm the shed during the night. What was missing now was something in which to sit; an old armchair or something that he could fashion into one. He also needed to stock his larder, and so he set off into the woods for a morning of foraging.

Marcheline arrived at Cublington's Folly at precisely midday, but Ben was nowhere to be seen. The folly, a curious miniature copy of the Basilica di Santa Maria del Fiore in Florence, was covered completely in seashells and had been built on the edge of the Cockering estate over a decade of summers by an eighteenth-century groundsman after whom it was named. It sported a limpet-encrusted dome at one end and a 'bell tower' at the other; a mere thirty feet high and decorated with dog-whelks and scallops rather than the near-300 feet of Giotto's beautiful white marble *campanile*. But it was a pretty thing and the bleached white seashells gleamed in the autumn sunshine.

'Hello!'

Marcheline looked up and saw that Ben was waving from the very top of the tower.

'Come down here! It's probably not very safe!' she shouted.

Ben disappeared from sight and re-emerged a few seconds later from a door at ground level.

'There's a great view from up there,' he said. 'I could just about see your house over the woods.'

'That thing has no foundations and is only held together with lime mortar and seashells,' said Marcheline. 'It isn't safe. I should put up a sign or something. It's on Cockering land and I'm sure I'd be liable if someone had an acci–'

'Felt pretty solid to me,' said Ben, emerging from the doorway. 'And I know a thing or two about firm erections.'

'You're never going to let me forget that are you?'

Benjamin smiled. 'Come with me.'

Taking Marcheline by the hand, he led her around to the side of the folly, where two melted plastic chairs stood next to the trunk of a felled tree. The chairs had been made usable by the addition of some plump cushions. The makeshift table, meanwhile, sported a clean tablecloth, two wine glasses and two place settings.

'If Madam would care to take a seat,' said Ben, indicating one of the chairs.

'This is interesting,' said Marcheline, settling into the distorted chair. 'Who's your furniture supplier? Hurricane Katrina?'

'Actually this is a metaphor,' said Ben. 'These chairs came from my camper van. They're all that remains of my former life. This is me having my last meal as Benjamin Ellis, circus proprietor. After this, everything is new.'

'A renewal,' said Marcheline. 'That's interesting.'

'Hmm?'

'Oh nothing. I brought some wine.' She lifted a bottle out of a cool bag.

Ben spotted the black butt plug wedged in the top of the bottle. 'Hang on, is that a… ?'

'What?' said Marcheline, innocently.

'Nothing. Never mind,' said Ben. 'You pour and I'll sort the food.'

Ben had prepared a tasty picnic using the last of Berkeley's money. Over brie and cranberry jelly baguettes, crisps and pickles, and a Danish pastry dessert, they learned more about each other – their very different childhoods, their interests and passions, and the things that they both wanted from life. Neither of them had realised until now just how much of their lives had been dictated by a sense of duty to those around them. And when the food was all gone, they moved the tablecloth down onto the grass and lay on it, watching buzzards soaring lazily high above them.

'I've been thinking about how to get back at Berkeley,' said Marcheline. 'And I've had a bit of a brainwave. We should use his greed against him. Hoist him on his own petard.'

'Irony. I like it,' said Ben. 'But how?'

'What if we tricked him into thinking that I have a secret hoard of cash hidden somewhere? We could send him on a wild goose chase trying to find it. Make him look really foolish.'

'Like a treasure hunt?'

'Yes. We could invent some cryptic clues,' said Marcheline. 'He likes that sort of thing.'

'Won't he suspect something, though? They'd have to be convincing.'

'I've been doing cryptic crosswords since I was a little girl,' said Marcheline. 'And so has Berkeley. He'd relish the challenge and I'm sure we could pull it off. That's if you still want to take part?'

'I don't know. The words "pull it off" still hold some terrors for me...'

'I'm serious,' said Marcheline, punching his arm.

'Ow! Yes, count me in,' said Ben. 'Anything that teaches that wretched brother of yours a lesson is a good thing.'

'I thought, perhaps, that I'd lead him to believe that I have some gold stashed away,' said Marcheline. 'Lots of people invested in gold during the banking crisis a few years ago. It's just the kind of story that he'd swallow.'

'Clever,' said Ben.

'And the best thing about it is that, once his greed has been exposed, I can then play the hard-done-by sister for ever more. He'll have been caught trying to steal from me so he won't dare put a foot wrong in case I call in the police. He'll have to behave or else.'

'Genius. Evil genius.'

'But can I trust you enough to involve you?' said Marcheline, with a cheeky smile.

'Hmm, good point,' said Ben. 'You know what us circus types are like. Gypsies, tramps and thieves. Just like the song.'

'You're not making a very strong case for yourself.'

'Do you really think I'd dare to cross you? I've seen what you can do with a Suckmaster 3000…'

'I warned you!' shouted Marcheline and launched herself at him. They rolled in the soft grass, with him holding her wrists as she attempted to playfully slap his face. And then, suddenly, they were kissing; deep, sensual kisses full of urgency and fire. They began tearing at each other's clothes.

From a hidden spot on top of the Big Knapper, Blount dropped his binoculars and wondered whether it was strictly professional to continue his observation. In the end he thought, 'Who will ever know?' and returned to the show. The fact that Ellis and Lady Cockering were now, apparently, an item despite what had happened at the Hogman's Arms was important, if confusing, new intelligence.

And from behind a birch tree much nearer to the action, Bert watched as his employer and some posh-looking lady made loud, passionate love. He decided to hang around until they'd finished. Maybe they'd leave the chairs behind. They'd be perfect for his new home.

Chapter 29

Berkeley arrived back at Cockering Hall on Sunday evening and was surprised to find that Marcheline wasn't there. She always came home straight after church to change and to help Meg with the Sunday roast before spending the rest of the day in the greenhouse and garden. It was what she did every Sunday and she was nothing if not a creature of habit. But she was definitely absent and, more surprisingly, there was no sign of Mrs Shandcreek either. The house was completely empty.

'This is damned queer,' he said. He dialled his sister's mobile.

Less than a mile away and spooning Marcheline in post-coital bliss, Ben heard her phone ringing.

'I bet it's Berkeley,' he said. 'Ignore it.'

'I intend to,' said Marcheline.

The phone stopped. And then Ben's phone rang.

'He's calling you now,' said Marcheline.

'He can sod off.'

'No, wait. You should answer it,' said Marcheline, sitting up excitedly.

'Really?'

'Yes! We can plant the seed. Quickly! Before it goes to voicemail!'

Ben took a deep breath and accepted the call. 'Hello?' He switched on the phone's loudspeaker so that Marcheline could listen in.

'Where the hell have you been this last day and half?'

'You don't want to know,' said Ellis, winking at Marcheline. 'It's all very gynaecological.' There was an audible gasp at the other end of the phone. 'She's a bit of a wild one, your sister, isn't she? You didn't tell me that.'

Marcheline slapped his head gently and mouthed the words 'Stop it!'

'She is? She's obviously a darker horse than I suspected. So all is going to plan?' said Berkeley.

'Depends what the plan is,' said Ben. 'You said seduce her, and I've been seducing her several times a day since Friday evening. What happens now? More seducing?'

'Do you think she's falling for you?' said Berkeley.

'I don't know. Is that important?' said Ben.

'Very much so,' said Berkeley. 'I want her to fall head over heels. So much so that she'd consider a marriage proposal.'

'Marriage!'

'How else did you think we were going to get the money out of her?' said Berkeley. 'Wait… you're not falling for her too are you?'

'Of course not. I barely know her. Except in the Biblical sense.'

'Good. Keep it that way.'

'But marriage… I'm not sure I can…'

'You'll do as you're told,' snapped Berkeley. 'You will woo her. You will marry her. You will divorce her. Then you hit her for a massive settlement and she'll be forced to sell some properties to pay the fees. I get fifty per cent of whatever she

182

gets, you get a nice fat reward and you don't go to prison. How does that sound?'

'Cold,' said Ben, with genuine feeling.

'Needs must as the Devil drives,' said Berkeley.

'There must be an easier way to get your money, surely? What about the gold?'

'Gold?'

'Yeah. Can't we just steal that from her instead?'

A long, silent pause.

'Gold,' said Berkeley, again.

'Yes, her hoard of gold. I assumed you knew.'

'Ah, yes, of course I did,' blustered Berkeley. 'I just don't know where it is.'

'That's my point. I might be able to help with that,' said Ben. 'But listen, I don't feel comfortable chatting about this in the open. Anyone could overhear.' He winked at Marcheline but was surprised to see that her face was looking sombre, sad even. 'Can you meet me tomorrow?'

'Very well. But somewhere where we can be anonymous. Everyone knows my damned business around here. There's a pub in Pardley called the Green Man. About ten miles away. Use my taxi account. I'll meet you there at 12.30pm.'

'I'll be there,' said Ben and hung up, smiling. 'The hook is baited.'

But Marcheline wasn't smiling. She was crying.

'I suspected that he wanted to deliberately break my heart out of spite, but I had no idea that he had planned to go so much further, to destroy my life and everything I've worked for, just for money,' she sobbed.

Ben drew her to him and hugged her, kissing her on the face and tasting her salty tears.

'I didn't know either,' he said, 'but we'll get him back. We'll destroy him.'

'But now I have to go home and face him and pretend that none of this has happened, when all I want to do is throttle the life out of him.'

Ben hugged her even harder. He looked over her shoulder at the folly beyond.

'Hey, where did our chairs go?' he said.

At nearby Brill Farm, the atmosphere was one of great excitement; every performer was doing what they could to ensure that Wednesday's show would be the very best performance of their lives. There had been no word from Venturini or the luscious Wanda, and the horses were still AWOL, but the Daughters of Epona were determined to put on some kind of spectacle and were deep in conversation with Colonel Sanders about incorporating Della the elephant into their act. The Flying Mannings had resurrected an old routine that they hoped they could still pull off. And Strongitharm the Strong Man had teamed up with the Bonzini Brothers to work on a very special human pyramid.

In the clowns' trailer there was also talk about the act they would perform on the night. Impressively, the three of them – Grimpen, Cronk and Dirk – were already several sheets to the wind and it wasn't that long after lunchtime. Glupi wasn't the only clown who brewed his own tipple – Grimpen and Cronk had stockpiled a fine collection of home-brewed wines, and Dirk could produce a brain-damaging alcoholic ginger beer in just forty-eight hours.

'Thing is, we need something special for Wednesday night,' said Grimpen. 'A real fucking showstopper.'

'Like what?' said Cronk. 'The old food fight routine?'

'Nah. Been done to death,' said Grimpen. 'Plus we can't spare the food.'

'What about the invisible clown?' said Dirk.

'That doesn't impress kids any more,' said Grimpen. 'They've seen too many special-effects films.'

'Then what?' said Cronk.

'If I knew that we wouldn't be sitting here discussing it would we?' said Grimpen. 'Here, I'll tell you what I wish we could do…'

'What?' said Cronk.

'That,' said Grimpen, pulling back a grubby net curtain and pointing out of the caravan window at the aged cannon.

'You're joking, right?' said Dirk.

'It would be amazing to do the act one last time,' said Grimpen.

'Are you nuts?' said Cronk.

'Bazoom the Human Cannonball! Man alive, I used to love doing that act,' said Grimpen.

'I know,' said Cronk. 'But that was twenty years ago. I doubt you'd fit down the barrel now.'

'Cheeky bastard,' said Grimpen.

'And anyway, that thing is ancient. I don't know why you kept it.'

'That is a classic bit of circus kit and probably worth a bob or two to a collector. It's an investment that is. And, remember, a few years ago we talked about bringing the act back using Dirk here. Until he bottled out and went to work with Flamo instead.'

'I didn't bottle out,' said Dirk, indignantly. 'I developed claustrophobia after I got locked in Venturini's escapology chest.'

Grimpen sighed. 'What I'd give to feel myself flying through the air again, one last time…'

Chapter 30

Marcheline's Monday was a flurry of activity. She woke early, before first light, and long before Berkeley, and spent several hours scouting out the suitability of possible hiding sites for her treasure trail of clues. The early hour meant that there was no one around, other than busy farmers who were unlikely to ask awkward questions.

She'd got home the night before to find Berkeley apparently drunk and asleep in a chair. It had taken all of her self-control not to shake him awake to berate him for his disgraceful and callous behaviour and for drinking so soon after a heart attack. However, on balance, the fact that he was asleep had served her purposes better. It meant that she'd been able to avoid the inevitable questions about where she'd been and why she'd so drastically changed her appearance. And so she'd plumped for an early night and, getting up at 5am and finding Berkeley still slumped in the chair and snoring loudly, she'd tiptoed out of the house and driven off. If Berkeley had heard her car leave – and it was testament to how drunk he was if he hadn't – he hadn't indicated so by phoning her to ask where the hell she was going so early.

By 10am she had selected several excellent hiding places for her treasure trail, visited a jeweller's in Morbridge and then hidden the first two clues for Berkeley to find. She then drove into Shapcott Bassett, as was her normal morning routine, to collect the papers and some fresh flowers from Twimbley's. She noted that, without exception, the villagers were looking at her differently. Initially, she had put this down to the fact that they'd heard about her court appearance. But then she'd realised that her carefully selected residents, all Little Englanders of the first water, rarely concerned themselves with the world outside of the village. Most didn't even know what was happening in neighbouring towns unless it warranted an appearance in the *Shapcott Basset Mercury* on a Wednesday. It was highly unlikely that any of them knew what had happened to her. No, it was her change of appearance that they were noting, and maybe her new persona too. There was no doubting the fact that Marcheline's demeanour seemed more relaxed. To Stan Twimbley's surprise she didn't even mention the fact that his shop door was sticking, even though she'd repeatedly asked him to get it mended and he'd repeatedly not got around to doing so. She walked at an average relaxed pace, rather than her usual brisk march. She smiled more. She looked happy.

Her next stop was the village hall for 10.30am, where she'd asked the members of the Village Council, with the notable exception of Berkeley – whose apologies she tendered on account of his recent illness – to assemble for a short informal meeting.

Her new-found self-awareness was a double-edged sword. On the one hand, having seen the world from the perspective of the underdog, she'd become more sympathetic to other people's feelings and viewpoints. But, on the other, it had made her realise just how bullish she'd been in forcing the residents of her village to adhere to her rules and idiosyncrasies. Her treatment of Benjamin, her arrest and court appearance and the knowledge that she had possibly been a factor in driving her brother to take such cruel and drastic action had not only tumbled her from her high horse, it had also slaughtered and knackered the metaphorical animal and rendered it down into glue. Who was she to dictate how people should live their lives? It was time for the Village Council to take control of its own destiny. And so, when they had all arrived, she explained that, due to unforeseen circumstances, she was no longer able to justify a position on said council and promptly resigned her seat. After the initial surprise over her change of appearance, this came as a complete shock.

'Are you sure, your Ladyship?' said the Reverend Freacke, who had noted her absence at Sunday service. 'If you're having some kind of crisis, perhaps there is something we could help you with?'

'Hear, hear,' said Major Crantlemain who was quietly worrying whether Marcheline's resignation would result in him having to do some work. She had always been the powerhouse behind most of the council's projects.

'Really, there is nothing at all that any of you can help with,' said Marcheline. 'Kind though the offer is. It's a personal matter and, as such, mine to deal with. I will also be resigning as Chair of the Residents' Committee as well.'

'You're doing what?' said publican David Tubby, fiddling with his hearing aid.

'Resigning as Chair of the Residents' Committee,' said Marcheline, loudly.

'Oh! Surely not?' said Tubby.

'I'm afraid so,' said Marcheline. 'And as this group comprises around ninety per cent of the Residents' Committee, I wonder if you'd be so kind as to pass on the news to absent members? Barring my brother of course. I'd be much obliged.'

'Well, I have to say that this has knocked me for six,' said the Reverend Freacke. 'Are you sure we can't persuade you to stay?'

'I am,' said Marcheline. 'You'll all understand why in due course. For the moment, all I ask is that you respect my wishes. You'll do a wonderful job without me, I have no doubts about that.'

'In that case,' said the Reverend, 'I suppose that it only remains for us to thank you for all of your sterling work over the years and to say that your seat will always be available if you ever choose to come back.'

'Hear, hear,' said Crantlemain.

'Eh?' said Tubby, straining to follow the conversation.

'Three cheers for Lady Cockering,' said the Reverend. 'Hip hip!'

When the cheers had died down, and following a resounding chorus of 'For she's a jolly good fellow', Marcheline shook each of the council members warmly by the hand and left.

'Well, what do you make of that?' said Tubby.

'Extraordinary,' said the Reverend.

'Young people today. No staying power,' said 'Toosey' Cornock.

'I must say that I like her new look,' said Tubby. 'She was always a handsome woman, but now...'

'Perhaps Berkeley is more poorly than we thought?' suggested Bertie Barsted.

'I'm sure I'd have heard if he was,' said Dr Pallister, who worked at the cottage hospital. 'Besides, she offered his apologies for not being here today. She didn't say that he was resigning the Chair, which suggests that he's well enough to continue in post.'

'That's true,' said Barsted.

'Oh dear, I do hope it's nothing serious,' said the Reverend. 'But, whatever the reasons are for her leaving, it means, I'm afraid, that we'd better look at how to apportion her workload among us. She did do an awful lot.'

Major Crantlemain harrumphed.

Marcheline's next rendezvous was with Benjamin, whom she collected from Brill Farm. As the Rover lurched away and headed towards Shapcott Bassett, an unmarked police car pulled out from a nearby lay-by and followed at a discreet distance.

'You do know that the car has two other forward gears don't you?' said Ben as they drove slowly and noisily along the Morbridge Road.

'I could never get the things to work without the most fearful grinding noise,' said Marcheline.

'That's because you need to double clutch on these older cars,' said Ben. 'Our truck is the same. It's a bit tricky to begin with but you soon get the hang of it. Dip the clutch and put the car into neutral. Then, give the accelerator a little touch. Then dip the clutch again and move up into third.'

'Oh dear, that sounds complicated,' said Marcheline.

'It really isn't,' said Ben. 'Try it with me. Dip the clutch and move the gearstick into neutral…'

Fifteen minutes later, the Rover's six-cylinder 2.1 litre engine was purring in top gear and, for the first time in her life, Marcheline was driving at very near the speed limit of fifty. It was exhilarating. They arrived in Shapcott Bassett in record time and Ben jumped out.

'Thank you,' she said. 'I can't tell you what a difference this is going to make.'

'I'm sure anyone would have shown you if you'd asked,' said Ben.

'I'm sure they would,' said Marcheline. 'But the old me would never have asked anyone. God, I was such a pompous old sow. Now, do you understand what you have to say to Berkeley? It's important that the story sounds convincing.'

'Yes,' said Ben. 'I have it all memorised.'

'Good. Here's the first cryptic clue. I'm rather proud of it.' She handed over a slip of paper and Ben read it.

'Well, that's completely opaque,' he said. 'I have no idea what it means.'

'Good. If you don't know the answer it gives us plausible deniability. Your confusion will make you sound more genuine and get his devious little mind going. Here take this too.' She handed Ben a small gold bar.

'Is that real?' exclaimed Ben.

'I bought it at a jeweller's this morning,' said Marcheline. 'It's only a ten-gram bar, but it will be sufficient bait for someone as greedy as my brother. Give it to Berkeley and tell him that I gave it to you as a present and as proof that I really do have a hidden hoard. While you're doing that I'll pop home and plant the next clue.'

'You are a bad girl.'

'I am. Which is why I also have the painful duty of visiting the Clerk of the Court this morning to explain my resignation as Chief Magistrate.'

Ben leaned in through the car window and kissed her on the cheek. 'Be strong,' he said.

Marcheline nodded bravely, started the car and drove out of the village towards Cockering Manor. Ben phoned for a taxi to take him to Pardley.

Berkeley was waiting in the saloon bar of the Green Man nursing a gin and tonic and a regal headache. He was exhausted and hungover. Sunday had been his first full day on his feet since his heart attack and he'd spent most of it drinking. He'd got home from the hospital at 6pm and found the house empty. Mrs Shandcreek apparently had the day off and, realising that he'd have to cook his own evening meal, he'd decided to reach for the Scotch instead. He'd made a pile of cheese sandwiches and then ignored them while he filled the void in his stomach with a good single malt. He'd eventually fallen asleep in his chair, only to be woken by the sound of Marcheline's car coming up the drive at 10pm. Too drunk to care, he'd drifted off once again; his dreams filled, as they often were, with crimson visions of his sister being mangled in a variety of interestingly gory ways. After several uncomfortable hours asleep in his chair, he'd been woken again at 5.15am by the sound of a car crunching on the gravel drive outside. For the briefest of moments he wondered where on Earth Marcheline could be going at such an ungodly hour, but then tiredness once again overwhelmed him. He'd woken with just enough time to manage a shower and a change of clothes before heading off to meet Ben.

'*Grab old format LPs to be broken by a monkey on the bottom of the sea?* What the hell does that mean?' he said as he read the slip of paper that Ben had given him. The production of the gold bar had convinced Berkeley that at least Ben believed her story. 'We couldn't be further from the bloody sea.'

'Well, that's what she gave me,' said Ben. 'It's a cryptic clue, obviously, and presumably one that she is sure that I don't have a hope in Hell of cracking. She wouldn't have given it to me if she did.'

'Marsh is very good at cryptic clues,' said Berkeley. 'We've both done the *Times* crossword every day since we were teenagers. Tell me again what she said, and in what context.'

'We were having a picnic by the folly,' said Ben. 'And I said to her that it reminded me, a little bit, of Rosslyn Chapel. Then I said, "This would be a great location for one of those stories; you know, where the hero and heroine have to solve a series of cryptic clues to find a buried treasure or a secret Nazi base or something." And she said, "I love codes and ciphers and, actually, I do have a hidden treasure. Gold bars, as it happens." I said that I didn't believe her, and she said that it's true and that she'd invested the family surplus in gold when there was all that panic with banks collapsing a few years ago. So I asked her what she meant by "hidden treasure" and she said that only she knows where the gold is stashed. "I've left details of where the gold is hidden with my solicitors, in case I go before Berkeley," she said. "But he's not getting it easily! I've left him a set of cryptic clues to follow to make him work for his money for a change."'

Berkeley harrumphed.

'Anyway, I said that I still didn't believe her and that was that. But then, the next day when I saw her, she gave me that clue and this little gold bar, and said that I could keep it if I solved the clue.'

'Why on Earth would she do that?' said Berkeley. 'She hardly knows you.'

'She knows me pretty well, trust me,' said Ben, winking. 'That's what you want isn't it? For her to get close to me?'

'Of course. Just don't get too close to her,' said Berkeley. He looked again at the slip of paper containing Marcheline's clue.

'She said that it was a good way of testing how good her

cryptic clues are,' said Ben. 'So I said that I'd have a go but, frankly, she's wasting her time. I haven't got a clue. I did wonder whether it had something to do with the folly, it being all covered in sea shells. After all, they were once on the bottom of the sea. And we had been sitting right beside it the day before.'

'Too obvious,' said Berkeley. 'And it's on a public right of way.'

'Unless it's a double bluff?' said Ben. 'Maybe the gold is hidden in plain view.'

'Not very likely. There are always ramblers and metal detectorists around the folly,' said Berkeley. 'That field was the site of some inconsequential skirmish during the English Civil War, and the occasional shoe buckle or lead shot turns up now and again. No, she'd never be so literal, my sister. It'll be something to do with... Ah! Brill Farm!'

'Where the circus is?'

'Brill live on the bottom of the sea.'

'What's a brill?' said Ben.

'It's a flat fish, like a turbot. Delicious in a butter and saffron sauce.'

'I'd never have got that in a million years,' said Ben. 'Look, I've got to go. I'm supposed to be having afternoon tea with her.'

'You make sure to let me know if she says anything else,' said Berkeley. 'Keep her occupied while I get searching. You won't find me ungrateful.'

Ben left the pub and called for a cab. But as he waited, he spotted a nondescript black Vauxhall parked on the far side of the village square. The averagely priced saloon car was jarringly out of place, as Pardley was even more salubrious than Shapcott Bassett. Ironically, the make and model had been chosen by the South Herewardshire Constabulary for its ubiquity and anonymity. But here, in affluent Pardley, parked among the Jaguars and Mercedes, it could only have been more conspicuous if it had sported a flashing blue light. Ben recognised the car immediately. Just a few nights ago, he'd stood naked in front of it while attempting to extricate himself from the clutches of the demonic penis pump. His heart sank. Of course. Blount was following him. He'd made the DS look foolish in front of his colleagues and his superiors. The man was unlikely to rest until he had something to pin on him.

To take his mind off the detective, he considered Marcheline's riddle. What did *Grab old format LPs to be broken by a monkey on the bottom of the sea* mean? 'Broken' was usually a hint that there was a concealed anagram or anagrams. After a minute or two of doodling, he'd turned 'format LPs' into 'platforms' and 'grab old' into 'gold bar'. But 'gold bar platforms' didn't make much sense and, as he couldn't make head nor tail of the rest of the clue, he gave up and allowed himself a satisfied smile. Berkeley was going to find this whole treasure hunt hugely frustrating. Served the bugger right for trying to blackmail him.

Berkeley was frustrated. Just like Ben, he'd figured out the anagram part of the clue and was now trying to figure out the rest. Among the 'bottom of the sea' ideas currently vying for pole position in his brain were Brill Farm, a delicatessen in Chepping Frogmoor called The Continental Shelf, and Floor C of the multi-storey car park in Morbridge because 'Floor C' was a reversal of 'sea floor'.

He took a taxi back to Cockering Hall and went into his study to consider the problem over a brandy or two.

Marcheline arrived at Mrs Dillby's tea shop to find Ben already waiting for her. She apologised for her lateness.

'So how did it go?' asked Ben.

'Better than expected,' said Marcheline. 'They seemed genuinely sad to see me go. But there was no getting away from the fact that my position on the bench is no longer tenable. And, do you know what? I thought I would be upset, but I'm not. These last couple of days I feel as if the weight of the world has been lifted off my shoulders.'

'That's great news,' said Ben, smiling.

'And I've planted the second clue to Berkeley's treasure hunt.'

'Already?'

'No point in hanging about,' said Marcheline, 'He might figure out the first clue quickly, in which case I had to have the second one in place. How did your meeting go?'

'I told him the story, passed on the clue and he put on a bit of a front and tried to make me think he's already got a fair idea of where to look, but I don't think he has. Unless it's at Brill Farm.'

'Brill Farm? Ha! Not even warm,' said Marcheline. 'But we must not underestimate him. My brother may be many things but he isn't stupid. Devious minds can solve devious puzzles.'

'I'm obviously not devious enough then,' said Ben.

'You still haven't figured it out?' teased Marcheline.

'A bit of it. Maybe,' said Ben. 'I think the first bit is an anagram of gold bars and platform. Or platforms and gold bar. I can't make any sense of the bottom of the sea part.'

'Well, you're right so far,' said Marcheline. 'So, what's another name for the bottom of the sea?'

'The ocean floor? The sea bed?'

'What do sailors call it?'

'Erm… the deep? Twenty thousand leagues?'

'Twenty thousand leagues isn't a measurement of depth. It's distance. It's how far Captain Nemo travelled in the Nautilus.'

'Ah. I learn something new every day.'

'What do pirates call the sea floor?'

'Oh, ah…'

'The clue was in monkey. Spelled with a double E?'

'Monkee? Oh! Davy Jones! Davy Jones' Locker!' said Ben, triumphantly. 'Gold bars platform in Davy Jones' locker?'

'You're nearly there,' said Marcheline. 'Add the 'to be' back into the middle.'

'Okay. Gold bars. Platform. 2B. Davy Jones' locker… a locker in the name of Davy Jones on Platform 2B?'

'Well done,' said Marcheline. 'At Uttercombe train station.'

'Incredible,' said Ben. 'What on Earth made you think of that?'

'I heard *Daydream Believer* on the wireless in the car. It all sort of flowed from there,' said Marcheline, with a suddenly wicked grin. 'Now, I thought we'd head to a little travel tavern that I know just outside Hoddenford. They do a lovely afternoon tea. And they rent out day rooms.'

Ben smiled, and decided not to mention the fact that he seemed to be being followed by the police. There was no sense in worrying Marcheline for the moment.

Chapter 31

When Berkeley woke on Tuesday morning he found that Marcheline hadn't been home, presumably because she was shacked up in some love nest with Ellis. He ate a light breakfast of cereal and toast and endured a perfunctory conversation with Mrs Shandcreek before turning his attentions once again to his sister's abstruse puzzle.

Like Ben, he'd figured out the anagram part fairly quickly, but had only worked out the 'monkey at the bottom of the sea' reference very late the night before. He imagined that the 'Platform 2B' referred to in the clue was probably at Uttercombe railway station; it was notable for the bank of old 1930s wooden lockers in the waiting rooms. Not many stations had them these days but, back in those days, businessmen had used them to store things like umbrellas, raincoats and hats for use in inclement weather. Hardly anyone used them these days for fear of theft, which, ironically, made them a great place to hide valuables as no self-respecting thief ever bothered to check them out when there were richer pickings elsewhere. Besides which, there was CCTV now and you needed a valid ticket to even get on to the platform. These were the same barriers that Berkeley was now considering how to circumvent. He could hardly crowbar the locker open. Therefore, he used Marcheline's absence as an opportunity to visit her office and, in her desk drawer, he found a locker key with a tag saying 'Property of Midwestern Railways'.

'Bingo,' he said to himself. Pocketing the key, he took a taxi to Uttercombe Station, bought a return ticket to Hoddenford and quickly located the lockers on Platform 2B. None had names on them and Berkeley was pretty sure that none of the station staff would break any confidences by revealing which one might have been rented by a 'Mr Davy Jones'. On a hunch, he tried the key in the second locker on the second row – a repeat of the 2B clue – but that didn't work. Then he wondered if 'Davy Jones' was like a crossword clue answer: Davy Jones (4, 5) – four across and five down maybe? To his delight, the locker door opened and he stifled a cheer of self-congratulation. There were very few people about but, even so, the sight of a grown man whooping with delight because he'd managed to open a locker might attract unwanted attention. Inside he found what looked like a shoebox. He lifted it out, its surprising heaviness raising his spirits still further. He returned to his taxi, which was waiting outside.

The journey home felt interminably long. He was desperate to open the box to see what was inside, but he didn't want to pique the driver's interest. In the meantime, it had suddenly occurred to him that Marcheline might have come home while he was out. What if she'd discovered the missing key? He'd have to cross that bridge when and if he came to it.

After what seemed like an age, the taxi pulled up on the gravel drive outside Cockering Hall. To Berkeley's relief, Marcheline's old Rover was nowhere in sight. He went inside, popped the key back in Marcheline's desk drawer and took the shoebox to his room, as excited as a child on Christmas morning.

Bert was feeling similarly excited. While foraging for some mushrooms and wild herbs for his breakfast, he'd come upon a treasure-trove of useful materials. On the edge of an informal car park – an area of scrubby grass where bird watchers often left their vehicles while visiting the woodlands that partially clothed the Big Knapper – he found an unsightly pile of fly-tipped rubbish. But to him it was anything but ugly; to him it was the promise of a comfortable future. True, the old mattress and sofa were damp and musty, but they didn't look as if they'd been there long and they could be cleaned – to the old clown's standards of cleanliness anyway – and dried out easily enough. There was an old wooden cable drum and a stack of broken pallets too. He knew that if he could pull the nails it would be simplicity itself to turn the wood into a working door for his cowshed, and maybe even a bed frame. The cable drum would make an excellent table. The problem was how to get the materials back to his new home. He wondered whether he'd be able to borrow one of the circus vehicles, maybe during the Wednesday performance when no one would miss it? And in considering this, he came back to the vexing issue of the fire and the fact that the evidence pointed to Ben as the culprit. Why had the circus owner burned down his own caravan and, allegedly, attempted to burn his too? Bert wasn't a great one for forming emotional attachments; his Red Army bosses had had him examined by a psychologist who'd described him as 'somewhere low to medium on the scale of psychopathy,' which was great news for his career as a professional killer but not so good for the likelihood of him forming deep and lasting relationships. However, despite this, he regarded Ben Ellis as a friend and assumed that the circus owner felt the same. However, he was not so attached that it didn't cross his mind that there was possibly a deep vein of guilt that he might be able to mine in order to persuade Ellis to let him borrow a truck.

Special Constable Arthur Pews was cycling from Snipeton to Shapcott Bassett after one of his regular overnight 'enquiries' with Mrs Tiggs when he spotted Marcheline's Rover coming down the Hoddenford Road at a trajectory that would see them meet at an approaching T-junction. Pews was somewhat surprised to note that the car was moving quite extraordinarily fast; within the speed limit admittedly, but still much faster than he'd ever suspected the car could go. For one horrible moment he wondered whether the Rover had been stolen. But soon he was close enough to see that it was indeed Lady Cockering at the wheel. He was so shocked by the change in her appearance that when she waved at him and shouted a cheery good morning, all he could do was open and close his mouth like a goldfish. Her appearance once again lit the fires of lust within him. Perhaps he ought to pay her a visit at the hall? He could always use the pretext of offering crime prevention advice or something like that.

It was another ten minutes before he arrived in the village and opened up the tiny police station for business. His first customer was Dr Pallister, who was checking to see if anyone had handed in a pair of spectacles that he'd lost.

'We did have a pair handed in,' said Pews, rummaging in a cardboard box of odds and ends that completely broke police regulations regarding the safeguarding of lost and found property. 'Here we are. These yours?'

He produced the pair of glasses that Bertie Barsted had found. 'Yes! Those are mine. Excellent,' said the doctor. 'So, how are things with you Arthur? That's a cracking black eye you have there. The villains keeping you busy are they?'

'It's been a troubling week on many counts, Doctor,' said Pews. 'Any news on Lord Cockering? How is he?'

'Discharged from the hospital. It was a mild heart attack, but enough to give anyone a scare. Or so you'd think. I've told him that it was a warning. but I doubt that he'll take any heed. I can see him back in hospital within six months if he doesn't lose some weight and cut down on the booze, cigars and rich foods. He needs to think very hard about how he lives his life if he wants it to extend beyond the next few years. You could stand to shed a few pounds yourself, if you don't mind me saying so, Arthur.'

'Yes, I know,' said Arthur, keen to change the subject. 'I saw Lady Marcheline on my way into work. She looked well, anyway.'

'Did you hear that she resigned from the village council and the residents' association?'

'She did?'

'It's all very odd,' said the doctor. 'What with that and her physical transformation, I shouldn't wonder if she's having some kind of a midlife crisis. Maybe Berkeley's heart attack made her more aware of her own mortality? A shock like that can make you reassess your life. I'd like to think that it would do the same for her brother. Anyway, must dash. Thanks for the specs.'

Dr Pallister left and Pews made himself a cup of tea and settled down in front of the police computer to catch up on the overnight alerts from Divisional HQ. Not much had happened over the weekend: a handful of burglaries, a few shoplifting cases, a drunk and disorderly or two, and all of them had occurred in or around Morbridge. Nothing had been reported in his small sub-division since the fire at the circus, which was just how he liked things. Idly he turned to the court reports for the county, hoping for some juicy scandal, and nearly spat his tea.

'What the...? Lady Marcheline Leticia Cockering and Mr Benjamin Anthony Joshua Ellis...' he read aloud, skimming through the report. 'Breach of the peace and lewd behaviour at the Hogman's Arms Travel Tavern... fined £250 each and bound over to keep the peace for twelve months. Costs awarded...'

Pews sat back and considered this new information. Marcheline and that circus owner. Lewd behaviour. Dr Pallister was obviously on the money; Marcheline was clearly having some sort of midlife crisis. And with the circus owner of all people! He suddenly realised that he was feeling decidedly envious, but with that realisation came the thought that if the skinny circus owner stood a chance with Lady Cockering then so might he. A fling with Marcheline was no longer an unattainable fantasy – and maybe more than just a fling. Arthur Pews quite fancied the idea of living in comfort and splendour as the master of Cockering Hall.

At the Hall, the current master had opened the shoebox and been rewarded with a second gold bar and another cryptic clue.

'Not so clever after all, are you old girl?' he said, secretly hoping that this wasn't the template for the rest of his treasure hunt. One bar at a time was a very slow and tiresome way to amass a fortune and the longer he took to find them all, the greater the chance of Marcheline discovering his involvement. He decided that he would put the gold bar back in the station locker, so as not to tip her off that he was on the trail. But first, he'd have a crack at this next puzzle.

Written on a piece of paper was a curious message which read:

DS OV NP YE BL MI NX VH MU XK

The groups of two letters were a dead giveaway. Berkeley immediately recognised the Playfair cipher, a mid-nineteenth-century encryption system that was still occasionally used in some puzzles and crosswords. This was good news because, once you had guessed the coder's keyword, Playfair was a cinch to decode. He grabbed a piece of paper and a pen and drew a five-by-five grid. Guessing that the keyword might be GOLDBARS, he filled in the first eight boxes and then completed the grid using the remaining letters of the alphabet in order. Then he began trying to decrypt the message in blocks of two letters. The first two letters of Marcheline's clue – DS – translated into the letters L and C. As no word started like that, the keyword was wrong. He drew a new grid and tried the codeword TREASURE. On this occasion, DS translated as IT. This was more promising so he moved to the next two letters. But OV decoded to LZ so that was wrong too.

'Confounded woman,' he growled.

Marcheline watched as Stan Twimbley endeavoured to cut, jam and dollop some cream on his scone single-handedly. She desperately wanted to help him, just by holding the scone steady on the plate at least, but she knew from long experience than Stan was fiercely independent and would not welcome the offer of assistance. He was determined to show the world that one industrial injury in his twenties did not define his life nor make him any less able than someone with two arms. However, he was making such a frightful mess of things that Marcheline felt the need to distract him for a short while.

'I'm pleased to hear that the rebuilding is going well,' she said.

'As well as can be expected,' said Stan. 'Thankfully, the structure of the shop hasn't been affected, so the work won't be too complicated.'

'And how is young Eric?'

'If I'm being honest, Lady Marcheline, his welfare has not been uppermost in my thoughts,' said Stan. 'I'm finding it very hard to forget the sight of those beastly magazines and films he had. In my flat.'

'Technically, my flat,' said Marcheline.

'But those handcuffs and hoods and those… those rubber… those… things…'

'… were things he only used on himself,' said Marcheline. 'We shouldn't be too harsh on the boy. His humiliation has been punishment enough I suspect and, really, he was doing no harm.'

'I must say that I'm quite surprised to hear you say that,' said Stan. 'I had no idea you were so liberal.'

'To be honest, nor did I,' said Marcheline. 'But each to his own, Stanley, each to his own.'

'Yes well, Agatha and I, we're simple folk and we don't hold with such goings-on,' said Stan. 'Therefore, if you have no objections, we would really prefer not to take him back as a lodger.'

'I understand. Although I very much doubt that he'd want to, given that he put on such a public show,' said Marcheline, finishing her tea. 'Right, I must cut along. I may have stepped down from the village council but I want people to know that I am still your landlady and that I do not take the responsibility lightly. I am, I hope, a fair and approachable one who cares about the welfare of her tenants.'

'We've never had any complaints,' said Stan Twimbley,

biting his tongue. Marcheline's obsession with everything being just right in the village had made him curse her name more than a few times over the years, but he couldn't say that she was a bad landlady. A bit overbearing to be sure, but always with the welfare of the village at heart.

'Good. I'm glad we've had this little chat, Stanley. Now, you won't forget to do me that little favour with your camera will you?'

'I won't. I do wonder why, though.'

'All will be made clear in due course,' said Marcheline. 'Give my regards to Agatha.'

Having completed all that she had to do in the village, Marcheline's thoughts turned immediately to Benjamin and remembrance of the passions of the past twenty-four hours. Her normally stoic heart was singing – she had never felt quite so alive and so happy before. And yet, at the back of her mind, there still remained a tiny nagging doubt; a feeling that this was all too good to be true and that maybe her brother's machinations were still in play. She immediately suppressed the idea. There was no possible way, unless he was the very finest actor, or a sociopath of some description, that Ben could have faked his emotions and reactions so consistently for four days. Was it really only four days, she thought? It seemed so much longer. The fact that she'd only been home once in all that time and hadn't bumped into Berkeley since his discharge from hospital made it seem even longer. Unfortunately, she was going to have to face him today, as she needed a change of clothes and to arrange for a company to come and empty the septic tanks. It occurred to her that, of the two tasks, talking to Berkeley was the more onerous.

It was with a resigned sigh that she left the tea rooms and

walked to where she'd parked her car in the small huddle of spaces under the shadow of Big Bessie. She was rather surprised to find Special Constable Pews standing nearby, in an attitude that almost suggested that he was waiting for her.

'Good morning, Arthur,' she said, fumbling in her bag for her car keys.

'Looking good,' said Arthur in a style that he hoped made him sound sophisticated and cosmopolitan. In truth it made him sound like a bad actor doing an accent that was somewhere between the Bronx and deepest Somerset. He followed the statement with a curious finger gesture that almost looked like he'd shot her with a fake gun.

'Thank you,' said Marcheline. 'You're looking very well yourself.'

'Just so you know... you can always call on me if you need help with anything,' said Pews. 'Anything at all.' He winked salaciously.

'Thank you Arthur, that's... very comforting,' said Marcheline.

'I must pay you a visit sometime,' said Pews. 'To check out access to your entrances and exits. For security reasons, obviously.' He winked again.

'That's a very kind offer,' said Marcheline. She quickly slid inside the car and started the Rover's engine. As she pulled away, she saw Pews mouth the words, 'See you soon... I hope.'

'How extraordinary,' said Marcheline, with a knowing smile. Her new look really did seem to be having an effect on the boys.

Chapter 32

Ben was keen to see how preparations were going for the circus's final performance and so Marcheline had dropped him off at Brill Farm while she'd gone into Morbridge on business. On the whole, things were going very well indeed. Almost everyone was fit enough to perform, barring one of the Flying Mannings, who had slipped a disc, and both of Colonel Sanders' tigers, who had picked up infections from tick bites and were therefore listless, lethargic and hard to control. Sanders didn't mind too much. His cats were getting too old for it all and, anyway, he was going to have his hands full directing Della the elephant to perform some new tricks with the Daughters of Epona.

The sight of his old friends so happy and enthused had put a big smile on Ben's face. The only dark cloud hanging over his morning was the knowledge that he was being watched; spotting the nondescript black car parked in the lay-by nearest the farm entrance had confirmed his suspicions that Blount was definitely tailing him. He wondered why the man seemed to be so obsessed with him and the circus. Surely there were other, more important crimes that required his attention? All Ben could think of was that it had become a matter of professional pride. Circumstances had made Blount look foolish in front of his colleagues and his best chance of recovering his credibility was obviously to prove that he'd been right all along. All of which meant that he was unlikely to give up the chase anytime soon. Ben considered whether he should make a complaint of harassment. After all, in the eyes of the law at least, he'd done nothing wrong. But that seemed unnecessarily spiteful. And, besides, it might make the detective even more dogged in his desire to pin something on him. Who knew to what depths he'd plumb if he felt desperate enough? No, it was safer just to keep his nose clean and to not do anything that would give Blount an inch.

'Psssst!'

Ben started, and looked around to locate the source of the noise.

'Pssssst! Boss!'

An old man, possibly a tramp, was beckoning to him from behind a caravan. It took Ben several seconds to recognise who it was.

'Glupi?'

'Shhhh! Come here.'

Ben scurried over and hoped that Blount wasn't watching through binoculars. The police very much wanted to have a word with Glupi about his illegal still and, by associating with the man and not reporting the fact, he could be seen as withholding evidence. Blount would love that.

'Is that you, Glupi?'

'I's callin' myself Bert now.'

'I've been worried about you,' said Ben. 'Where have you been for the last week?'

'I's been around an' about. I hear the circus is retirin' so I's been making plans and findin' a house, seein' as mine is out of bounds.' He pointed to his caravan, which was still surrounded by police tape. 'I hears someone tried to burn it.'

Ben's heart skipped a beat.

'You did?'

'Yeah. I also hears nasty stories sayin' you was doin' the burning but I cannot believe this. I say that you are my best friend. You are best friend, yes?'

'Yes,' said Ben. 'Best friend.'

'Yeah, so I says to them you wouldn't do that to your best friend. I says it ain't true but they is not convinced.'

'People? What people?' said Ben, desperately hoping that some of the clown's week long disappearance hadn't been spent in police interview rooms.

'Jus' circus people. Some of thems think you done it,' said Bert. 'But I says, "He burn his own van. Why he burn his own van?" I tells them that no way would my best friend want to burn his own van. And then I says no way my best friend burn my home an' all my stuff either. Right, Boss?'

'Right.' Ben looked at the clown's sad and bloodshot eyes and felt waves of guilt wash over him.

'So I was wonderin' if I can borrow truck.'

'A truck? What for?'

'I has got some gear I need to move to my new gaff,' said Bert. 'I only needs it for an hour an' then I won't be botherin' you no more.'

'Well, I don't know…'

'I could do it when the show is on tomorrow night an' no one will knows.'

'Yes, but it's not up to me, is it? I don't own a truck. You'd have to ask one of the others.'

Bert played his 'sympathy eyes' card once again and wondered whether to use the term 'best friend' a few more times.

'But I guess you could use the Colonel's truck,' said Ben, resignedly. 'It's the only vehicle I have a spare set of keys for.'

'Tha's great.'

'So where are you living?' said Ben.

'I has a little place not far. Is free. I's very comfy. When show is all over an' circus folk is all gone you come visit. I have it all nice by then.'

'I'm envious,' said Ben. 'I have no idea where I'll go or what I'll do after tomorrow. You will come to the wrap party though? We're having a few beers after the show to say goodbye.'

'I use truck, then I return it an' come to party,' said Bert.

'It wouldn't be the same without Glupi the clown,' said Ben.

'I not Glupi no more. Glupi, he is dead,' said Glupi.

'End of an era, eh?' said Ben.

'I is happy enough,' said Bert. 'I always happy if people leaves me alone.'

'That reminds me,' said Ben. 'Just outside the main gate there's a black Vauxhall parked up. It's a police car and there's a detective inside it who's keeping an eye on us.'

'I seen him.'

'Good. Because you probably don't want to get yourself spotted. Not that they'd recognise you. I hardly recognised you myself.'

A week of being off the booze and a prolific growth of white stubble had transformed the former clown's tanned and deeply-lined face. All remnants of the greasepaint that he had worn for decades were gone and he looked just like any other old lush that you'd find sitting on a park bench in any town in the UK. Glupi really was no more.

'I get past police easy and they not see me,' said Bert. 'Now, can I have keys to truck, best friend?'

Marcheline parked her Rover on the drive and took a deep breath to prepare herself for her first meeting with Berkeley since she'd visited him in the hospital. So much had happened since then and she had so much to be angry about, but she could not let him know that she had uncovered his plot. She had the perfect opportunity to teach her brother a lesson. It would mean no more moans about family money, no more attempts to irritate and annoy her, no more bullying about selling off the village. But everything depended upon him not knowing what she knew. Not yet, anyway. She composed herself and walked into the Hall.

She found Berkeley on the grand staircase, peering closely at the lowest part of the frame containing the portrait of fiery Elizabeth Cockering. He was concentrating so hard that he didn't hear her arrival at first. The sight of him probing and prying gave Marcheline a boost in confidence. Obviously, he'd figured out the cipher. There was no other reason for him to be examining the painting.

'What on Earth are you doing?' she snapped in her customary voice.

Berkeley had indeed cracked the code in her second clue. By figuring out that the keyword was MARCHELINE, the cipher had revealed the message 'Gold is under Elizabeth' and, as the only Elizabeths that came readily to mind were the Queen, Elizabeth 'Big Bessie' Cockering, and the marble cow unofficially named after her, he figured that the portrait was probably his first port of call. He'd barely started to poke around when Marcheline had unexpectedly returned home. Having no good or logical reason for doing what he was doing, he immediately went on the offensive.

'Good grief woman, don't make me jump like that! I have just had a heart attack you know.'

'What on Earth are you doing up there?'

'I was… trying to remember the name of the artist who painted the portrait of Big Bessie,' he said, walking down the stairs. 'There was a painting on some antiques show on TV that looked to be in the same style. It sold for a pretty penny too, I thought that if this was the same artist, it might affect the insurance valuation.'

Marcheline smiled inwardly at her brother's inventiveness. The man had guile in spades. She wondered how far she could test his nerve before the cracks in his lies began to show.

'Everything is about money with you isn't it?' she said. 'So who was the artist they mentioned on the TV show?'

'I can't remember,' said Berkeley.

'So what use would it be to you to find a name on the painting?' asked Marcheline, frowning.

'I'm sure I'd remember it if I saw it,' said Berkeley, sweating slightly. 'It's on the tip of my tongue. If I can find a signature I'll know if it's the same name even though I can't remember what the artist's name was right now.'

'I'll put you out of your misery,' she said. 'It was painted in 1909 by Thadeus Bultitude, a Royal Academician. Is that the name on the tip of your tongue?'

'I'm afraid not,' said Berkeley.

'Oh dear,' said Marcheline. 'What a disappointment for you.'

'It was just a thought,' said Berkeley. 'You look nice, by the way. Done something with your hair?'

'I fancied a change,' said Marcheline.

'Any particular reason?' asked Berkeley.

Marcheline was suddenly aware that, with just two questions, Berkeley had somehow regained the upper hand. She was now being forced to account for herself. While every fibre of her being yearned to slap his face and vent her spleen at his appalling behaviour towards her, she swallowed her anger and decided to let him believe that he'd won this clash of wits. Pretending to lose one small battle would not lose her the war.

'No, no reason,' she said and scurried into the kitchen.

Berkeley smiled triumphantly. However, the fact that she was at home meant no more treasure-hunting for the time being. It also meant that it would be difficult to smuggle the shoebox out of the Hall and replace it in the locker at Uttercombe Station. He would have to wait until she left the house again, which, he was sure, she would do as soon as she could. If half of what Ellis had claimed was true, she was now completely besotted with him. Her change in appearance was a clear indication that the circus owner was not exaggerating. Berkeley now knew that he could utterly destroy his sister's life and break her heart with one phone call if he chose to do so. But, even better than that, if he could get her married and then divorced, he'd be quids in for the rest of his life. The sudden rush of power made him feel ten feet tall.

As the sun began to set on the circus's penultimate day in business, Ben watched the final run-through of all of the acts and felt, if not entirely contented, certainly the happiest he'd been for many years. The millstone that was the welfare of his friends was to be lifted from around his neck. He'd met a wonderful woman and was soon to spend another night with her in a delightful little guest house beside the lakes at Doughton Regis. For the first time in his life he was in love. Despite the very short time that they'd known each other he knew that she was the woman with whom he wanted to spend the remainder of his life. He wondered if she felt the same. Neither of them had yet dared to say 'I love you'. Were her feelings as deep and profound as his own? At times, it seemed that she checked herself and pulled back on the reins of her emotions. He suddenly remembered a snatch of a W B Yeats poem:

'O never give the heart outright,
For they, for all smooth lips can say,
Have given their hearts up to the play.
And who could play it well enough
If deaf and dumb and blind with love?
He that made this knows all the cost,
For he gave all his heart and lost.'

Knowing that Marcheline's weasel of a brother had engineered the scenario that had brought them together surely didn't help; he could barely imagine the tangled mess of feelings that Marcheline was having to cope with. Surely, at the back of her mind, there must lurk the awful suspicion that he was still doing Berkeley's dirty work? Ben hoped she didn't believe that. He really had given her his heart, and desperately hoped that he didn't lose her as Yeats had lost his lover. His introspection was rudely curtailed by a loud *thud* as a knife embedded itself in the caravan he was walking past.

'Sorry!' shouted Genaro Coltello. 'The knife ricocheted off Sybella's thigh.'

Once Marcheline had left the Hall, Berkeley got busy. Firstly, he returned the shoebox to the locker at Uttercombe Station. Then he returned to Cockering Hall to resume his search for the gold 'under Elizabeth'.

He quickly discovered what he was looking for on the picture frame directly underneath Elizabeth's painted feet. The frame was made of old dark wood decorated with ornate plaster mouldings, all covered in gold leaf. In the century since it had been painted, various Cockerings and their children and staff had, here and there, knocked off a few of the high points, clumsily disguising the damage with a lick of gold paint. In some places, entire chunks of moulding had needed to be reattached. And it was one particularly large section, identifiable by deep cracks, that Berkeley had found. The cracks tapered inwards from bottom to top of the moulding, meaning that the replaced section was held in place without the need for screws or glue. It also meant that it could be prised off the frame with ease. Berkeley carefully levered the plaster away with a butter knife and gently lifted the piece free. In the space left behind was a folded piece of paper. But, to Berkeley's dismay, there was a complete absence of gold bars. However, the paper revealed yet another cryptic clue and hinted strongly that this was the final test of his intelligence. If he cracked this, it would lead him to the hoard. The note contained a quote and a poem:

'The longest journey starts with a single step, but also ends with one. Every goal could be just a single step away.'
– G R R Hendrie

'Gone from its stronghold
Is the glorious Sun
Denuding the sky's heart
Held down to Earth and chained fast
Only for the eyes of rich men to see
Like a blinding bonanza;
Beatified wealth.'

'Oh for Heaven's sake,' snapped Berkeley. He studied the note again. The allusions to wealth, to the rich, and to the Sun being brought down to Earth were obvious references to gold. But the fact that this final clue took the form of a poem meant that, presumably, there was a cipher hidden somewhere within it.

His first thought was that it might be an acrostic so he checked the first letter of each line but GIDHOLB meant nothing. Even after using those letters as an anagram, all he could find was 'GOLD HIB' and 'HID BLOG,' which might have sounded feasible if Marcheline knew anything about the internet. He then tried the last letter of each line and got DNTTEAH, which proved to be even less amenable to rearrangement. THAT DEN? TNT HEAD?

'You are not going to beat me,' he growled, pointing an angry finger at the portrait of Elizabeth Cockering. It seemed to him that, more than ever before, she bore a striking resemblance to his sister.

In Market Square, Marcheline planted her final clue, and then drove off out of Shapcott Bassett with a smile on her face. Berkeley was about to learn a very painful lesson.

Chapter 33

Wednesday morning felt a little like the first day of autumn. After the unseasonably warm first half of September, a northerly chill was in the air; not enough to have people reaching for their thermostats, but certainly enough to make them take a jacket if they went outside, just in case. It was a grey and downbeat start to what the circus folk hoped would be a joyous occasion.

The news that Benelli's Circus was to perform its swansong had proven to be an excellent crowd puller. The incident of the fire had helped too, as had the business with the elephant and the revelations of Eric Clacketer's secret life. In a sedate and law-abiding area like Morbridge, anything more exciting than a controversial decision at the annual vegetable show was of huge interest. The box office – manned by Astrid the hormonal un-bearded lady – had done a roaring trade as people who wouldn't normally have considered going to the circus had turned out in droves. Almost the entire populations of Doughton Magna and Chepping Frogmoor were in attendance, along with people from Snipeton and Morbridge, all drawn in by morbid curiosity. There were even reporters from the local BBC radio station on site and a photographer from the *South Herewardshire Mercury*.

By 8pm, the Big Top was nearing full capacity, a fact that brought on another panic attack for Tonto the Human Telephone Directory, who locked himself in his caravan and refused to come out. For the other performers, however, it was a dream come true. Their excitement was palpable.

In Snipeton, Arthur Pews adjusted his uniform tie in the mirror and tried to avoid the reflection of Beryl Tiggs' Rubenesque body on the bed behind him. His mind was a seething cauldron of mixed emotions and beastly passions. His newfound amorous feelings for Lady Marcheline and an early evening romp with Beryl had combined to leave him confused and frustrated.

'But why? Why do you have to go to work now?' she asked.

'I have to be there,' said Arthur. 'I represent law and order in this part of the county. I have to show my face.'

'But it's all bruised still. Can't you take the evening off?'

'I'm afraid not, Beryl. Duty calls.'

'But I get so lonely at night,' said Beryl. She opened the front of her Winceyette nightie. 'Come back to bed. You were magnificent tonight. A stallion.'

'I can't.'

'Oh, Arthur… don't you think it's about time we dropped this charade? You've been regularly staying the night here for nearly a year. I'm sure the neighbours know the truth. Why can't we be open about our relationship? You keep saying that we'll get engaged but when, Arthur, when?'

'We'll discuss it later,' said Pews, 'I have to go now. Bye.'

He rushed out of the house and tried to remember what his last excuse for not getting engaged had been. Not a very convincing one, he suspected. Ten months of constant bullshit meant that his excuses were wearing very thin, but he could hardly tell Beryl the truth. She was the closest thing to a wife that he'd ever had, not that his frequent visits to her bed had ever stopped his sleeping with, or peeping at, every indiscreet wife or non-discerning widow in the borough. Besides which, he had new feelings to consider. Lady Marcheline filled his thoughts, and his seedy fantasies had brought a new ardour to his lovemaking.

At Cockering Hall, Berkeley had spent the morning puzzling over the poem. His efforts had been rewarded just after lunch by discovering that if you took the first two and last two letters from each line and put them all together they made the sentence 'Gold is under the stone Elizabeth'. This time, there could be no doubting that the Elizabeth mentioned was the marble statue of Big Bessie. And Marcheline had overseen the planting of new flower beds around the statue just over a year ago. It was obvious that something lay buried somewhere under those beds; maybe even the full hoard of gold. And what a clever place to hide it, he thought. It was always in sight and so anyone attempting to dig it up was sure to be spotted. Therefore, it would have to be done at night and very quietly, of course, which meant digging by hand. Berkeley abhorred manual labour, but while it was tempting to get someone in to do the digging – Ellis perhaps – his greed overcame any qualms he had about blisters or dirt. He wasn't going to share this with anyone. Thoughts of Ben reminded him that he'd promised to go and watch the circus's final show. And why not? He couldn't attack the flower beds with a shovel until the wee hours anyway.

*

Blount had also decided to attend the performance, partly because it was the only way that he could keep his eye on Ellis, but also because, having spent nearly a week observing the campsite, he had developed a grudging admiration for the elderly performers. Even if their boss was a crook, they deserved a good send-off. Or, actually, even if their boss wasn't a crook, for that matter. The thought had crossed Blount's mind many times, during the six uncomfortable, sleepless nights he'd spent in his car, that maybe Ellis wasn't the bad guy he thought he was. Maybe he'd set out to be a bad guy but, despite forming the intent, hadn't been able to go through with it. Everyone, at some time in their lives, fantasised about doing bad things. but you couldn't be locked up for that. But then he'd remember Ellis's curious involvement with the Viscount Morbridge and his sister and, all of a sudden, his coppers' hunch would start throbbing again. It was his relationship with Lady Cockering that was the most puzzling. On the one hand, they seemed to be a couple; they had spent yet another night together at a hotel before she had dropped him back at the circus this morning. But, on the other, he'd seen the terror on the man's face outside the Hogman's Arms travel tavern. And how any of this related to Berkeley Cockering was anyone's guess.

Blount had finally resigned himself to the fact that he might not get an arrest at the end of his enquiries, but he had resolved to stay the course – if only to satisfy his own curiosity.

Backstage, Benjamin Ellis carefully lowered his battered top hat onto his still sore head wounds. The past few days had been full of extraordinary events. But now it was time to forget all of that, to focus on the task in hand, and to do his level best to make Benelli's Circus shine one last time. The lights dimmed and a drumroll sounded. He stood up straight and took a deep lungful of air. He strode into the centre of the ring and bowed low before the expectant crowd.

'Ladies and gentlemen, boys and girls! Welcome!' he shouted, 'Welcome to Benelli's Circus... the greatest show on Earth!'

Accompanying a clumsily played rendition of Sousa's *Liberty Bell* by Summersmith Mudd on his mighty organ, the performers limped, hobbled and shuffled into the ring to perform the opening parade one last time. Or they would have done if Della the elephant's sedatives had worn off. As she reached the centre of the ring, she suddenly sat down heavily. This was bad news for the Daughters of Epona, who'd replaced their absent horses with the elephant, and who were balancing in various poses on the animal's back. Joan Angel, in the middle of her *pièce de résistance* – a single-handed handstand – landed with a painful thud on the sawdust floor of the ring. A moment later, Hilda was the next to fall, quickly followed by Maureen, who landed clumsily on her feet. As she clutched at her painful and possibly broken ankle and wailed for assistance, clowns Grimpen and Cronk came running on to stretcher her out of the ring, At this point, Della flopped down asleep and her incontinence struck once again. The horsewomen found themselves sitting in a rapidly growing puddle of warm elephant urine. Colonel Sanders was soon similarly soaked to the skin and slipped over twice while attempting to wake his snoring elephant by prodding her with his *thotti*. But it was Flamo and Dirk who suffered the worst indignities, as they took centre-stage to keep the audience amused and distracted with their fire-eating act. Having positioned themselves a little too closely to the dozing elephant's rear end, they suddenly found themselves in direct line of fire as she broke wind with an intensity and power that belied her gentle personality. As the powerful gust hit their burning torches, they were both momentarily engulfed in a bloom of spectral green flame. It was an exotic prelude to the larger and altogether more violent sheet of orange flame that followed as Dirk's bucket of petrol ignited. Della was immediately awakened, and thundered from the ring, accidentally colliding with the raised platform upon which Summersmith Mudd was playing his Wurlitzer. With a deafening crash and a last wheezing minor chord, the platform and organ fell to the ground and broke into a thousand fragments. Mudd himself clung to a remaining upright and feebly screamed for a ladder before his frail osteoarthritic grip gave way. Flamo and Dirk, for their part, emerged partially naked and wholly blackened from the fireball, with only the slightest indication that they'd ever once possessed any hair on their bodies. To the appreciative applause and cheers of the crowd, the fire-eaters were doused with water and Summersmith Mudd was rescued by a human pyramid formed by the acrobatic Bonzini Brothers. However, the dodgy hamstring of Barry Bonzini chose this moment to twang, and brought the entire structure down in a curiously accurate human re-enactment of the organ platform collapse. Among the tangle of bruised and battered acrobats, Summersmith Mudd struggled for breath and lapsed into unconsciousness. Professional to the end, the heap of injured performers waved to the audience and smiled through their pain. However, the uproariously drunk Grimpen and Cronk, in deciding to join in the waving, unfortunately chose to wave with the same hand at the same time, thereby dropping one side of their stretcher. As Maureen Angel fell to the ground with a loud and appreciable 'Oof', the crowd cheered and roared their appreciation. Believing that everything they were seeing was scripted, it looked by all accounts to be an amazing show ahead, and the price that they'd paid for their tickets appeared to be money well spent.

Sat amongst a gang of popcorn-throwing and cola-splashing Boy Scouts from the First Morbridge troop, who seemed to be going out of their way to be ear-shatteringly loud, Blount found himself experiencing a modicum of sympathy for Benjamin Ellis. If this was the sort of thing he had to cope with on a daily basis then it was amazing that all he'd tried to burn down was Glupi's caravan. Or maybe that had simply been a test run for burning down the whole circus? Ellis's story about the insurance policy had sounded genuine enough but maybe money wasn't the motive. Maybe Benjamin Ellis was simply just sick and fed up with the whole business.

Blount looked around at the crowd and noted their laughter. *Schadenfreude*, that's what the Germans called it, he thought. Taking pleasure in other's misfortunes. Although, saying that, they hadn't had the advantage of watching several days of rehearsals like he had so it was more than likely that the majority would be assuming that the parade of continuous disasters was 'all part of the act'. It was all too insane to be unplanned.

Across the ring he spotted a large red-faced man who was swigging from a silver hipflask between bouts of gusty laughter. It was Berkeley, the Viscount Morbridge, and the third partner in whatever shifty business his sister and Ben Ellis were engaged in. Next to him and laughing just as hard was the local uniformed officer, Pews, and a portly dishevelled man who looked a bit like Sid James but with a large and bulbous drinker's nose.

*

For his part, Bert was thoroughly enjoying the show from a rare audience perspective. Finding himself sitting beside the police constable had made him nervous at first, but he'd soon realised that the man only had eyes for the circus and, in particular for the large urine-soaked ladies in tutus who were currently exiting the ring. Besides which, he'd only met Pews once before and doubted the officer would recognise him. His attentions had therefore turned towards the fat man sat on the other side of Pews, whose loud and braying laugh was only half as annoying as the fact that he was drinking what smelled to be a very palatable single malt and wasn't passing the hip flask around. Bert hadn't tasted booze in days. To take his mind off the cravings, he slipped out of the back of the tent to where the circus vehicles were parked. It was time to collect his new furnishings.

Berkeley hadn't laughed so heartily in years. He'd seen Ellis's fiasco of a circus perform once before at the Royal Middenshire Show and had been so impressed by their hilarious ineptitude that he'd persuaded them to come and perform at Brill Farm. Marcheline was such a frightful snob that she'd be up in arms at having 'circus types' on her land. But, even better than that, if half the stories he'd heard were true, Benelli's Circus brought chaos, litter, damage to property, lawsuits and unpaid bills everywhere they went – just the kinds of things that would make Marcheline incandescent with rage – and they hadn't disappointed so far. But this final show, where they were trying so hard to achieve new levels of performance and technical skill, was priceless. Almost everything had gone wrong so far and Berkeley's stomach and ribs ached.

In the lull between acts, he looked around the Big Top and couldn't help noticing that almost everyone he knew from the village was in attendance, including the Reverend Freacke, Fred and Bunty Clacketer, Bertie and Janet Barsted, and Stan and Agatha Twimbley. Dr Pallister was there too, as were Major Crantlemain, Gerald Ostridge and Dr Sleight and his wife, Kay. It suddenly occurred to him that Shapcott Bassett was probably empty. The sight of publican David Tubby and his staff also meant that the King's Head was shut for the evening. And Arthur Pews was here too. The only other people who lived around the Market Square area were Miss Dillby and old Mr Cornock, but they would probably both be in bed by 9pm. No, the village would be all but deserted, which meant that, if he could slide away mid-show, it would be the perfect opportunity to dig up the flower beds. Perhaps he might even make it back in time for the finale. That would provide him with, if not a perfect alibi, a damned good one.

To this end, he made an effort to catch the eye of anyone he knew and to wave to them. If asked at a later date, they would swear on oath that they had seen him there during the show. He waited until the next act came out – a strange little man dressed as a penguin – and then slipped out of his seat and out through the exit.

Having decided on this new course of action, his only problem now was how to get back to Shapcott Bassett. Booking a taxi was problematic. If he was implicated in any sort of crime at a later date, the cab company had records and all of their drivers knew him. On the other hand, it was too far for him to walk. Idly, he wondered if anyone hitch-hiked any more. It was then that he noticed that, above the sound of the Big Top's generator, there was a lorry engine running. He sought out the sound of the noise and found an elderly gentleman climbing into the cab.

'Excuse me, I don't suppose you're going anywhere near Shapcott Bassett, are you?' said Berkeley.

Bert stood up. 'Maybe,' he said cautiously.

'If you are, could I perhaps sponge a lift?' asked Berkeley. 'I'm happy to pay you the same as I'd pay a taxi. Ten pounds?'

'Hops in,' said Bert, smiling at the ten-pound note and having no clue whatsoever who the man was. He looked sort of familiar, but the old clown had met a great many fat, posh men in his lifetime and his memory, seasoned by decades of bad alcohol, wasn't what it was. 'I's going that way an' I can drops you there,' he said, taking the bank note.

In the circus ring, things were improving a little. In a desperate attempt to look professional and to divert people's attention away from the cleaning-up, the Flying Mannings had taken to the air. They were putting on a stunning show. On the ground, Penguin Boy was as amusing as ever with his 'flipper feats' and the audience was delighted.

In the wings, Grimpen the clown prepared for his surprise finale. Having been drinking for most of the day and having downed half a bottle of Glupi's Highland Fling before the show, he had become fixated upon the idea of performing one last time as the Great Bazoom. After all, he'd never get another chance and he had a rare full house. So, while the other performers were engaged in clearing up the circus ring, he busied himself pulling the dust covers off the cannon.

'You are nuts,' said Cronk. 'You're not seriously thinking of going through with this are you?'

'Just once,' said Grimpen. 'For old times' sake.' He squinted as he tried to read the instructions on a container of black powder. 'I wish I'd brought my glasses. How much gunpowder do we use?'

'How would I know?' said Cronk.

'Someone else used to do this for me,' said Grimpen. 'Some

exotic dancer we picked up in Frothington. Candy I think her name was. Went off with some RAF bloke. I have no idea how she set this thing up. I just climbed inside and *Bang!* I was flying.'

'No use asking me,' said Cronk. 'I thought it was all done with springs or compressed air or something.'

'She definitely used gunpowder,' said Grimpen. 'I just don't know how much. There was a three in it I think. Does three ounces sound right? It can't be. A mouse weighs more than that. Three pounds maybe?'

'That's still only half a baby,' said Cronk. 'You'd need a ton of TNT to lift your lardy arse into the air. Just forget the whole idea and stick to the clown act. Let's do the fire brigade sketch. Audiences love getting soaked.'

'The problem with you is you have no sense of adventure,' said Grimpen, hefting a bag of black powder to gauge the weight. 'I reckon there's about five pounds in each bag. Four bags maybe?'

Cronk shrugged.

Having decided that his highly scientific method of measurement was close enough, Grimpen proceeded to pour it down the cannon's open barrel.

'You're fucking mad,' said Cronk.

At Cockering Hall, Marcheline drew herself a deep, hot bath and lit some scented candles. She'd decided not to show her face at the circus tonight for several reasons. Uppermost was the fact that Berkeley would be there, and she had no desire to sit with him while he guffawed at the show. Secondly, she simply didn't find circuses remotely entertaining. Clowns and captive animals were not her idea of fun and, even with Ben's reassurances, she still didn't want to see tigers and elephants performing tricks. And then there was Ben himself. The Ben Ellis she knew was a kind, witty, sensitive and caring man; an artist with a great novel pent up inside him waiting to burst forth. She liked that Ben. If she dared admit it, she might even love that Ben. She had never seen him in his role as circus master and worried that if she did see him in that guise it would taint her view. Therefore, secure in the knowledge that it was his final show and that Ringmaster Ben was no more from this day forward, she had excused herself and bid him good luck. In fact she'd said, 'Break a leg!' and had then wondered whether it was an appropriate thing to say for a circus performance. 'Inevitable given the age and brittle bones of some of my performers,' had been Ben's reply. And so, having decided upon an indulgent pampering evening instead, Marcheline slid down among the perfumed bubbles – another little luxury she'd learned to appreciate in recent days – and dreamed of her future happiness.

Back inside the Big Top, Ben watched his performers with mixed emotions. On the one hand, the constant struggle was over. But, on the other, these people had shared their lives with him and had become his friends. It was like saying goodbye to a family; a dysfunctional, argumentative and occasionally bothersome family to be sure, but a family all the same. All that was now left of the circus his father had loved and bequeathed to him was a handful of aged performers and a shabby tent that smelled of elephant urine and singed dwarf. It was a sad legacy. But at least, he thought, they'd go out with a bang.

With a perfectly executed triple somersault, Geraint Manning plunged into the safety net and the crowd clapped long and loud. The Flying Mannings' performance had been exemplary, maybe one of the best of their careers, and Ben applauded as loudly as anyone else. The Mannings took their bows, but the audience's attention was already diverted by the sight of a long barrel sliding between the rear flies of the circus tent. In the open mouth of the cannon was Grimpen the clown, wearing a yellow crash helmet that sported a single red lightning flash. He waved happily. The crowd cheered and waved back, as the rejuvenated and horribly drunk Great Bazoom and his mighty cannon were clumsily manoeuvred into position by Cronk, using the beaten-up old VW Beetle to push the carriage along.

Ben Ellis realised that he was standing with his mouth wide open. No one had told him about this and he was very much concerned that two drunk clowns were probably the worst people in the world to be operating such a very dangerous piece of equipment. He skipped briskly across the circus ring.

'What are you two idiots doing?' he hissed through a fake smile to the crowd.

'He wants to do his cannonball act one last time,' said Cronk, climbing out of the car.

High above, in the end of the barrel, Grimpen burped noisily.

'Are you insane?' growled Ben. 'He hasn't done it for years. And he's clearly pissed!'

'He figured if he didn't do it tonight he'd never get another chance,' explained Cronk. 'I did try to tell him. I said, "Grimpen, you're fucking mad and…"'

'Get this thing out of here and sober him up!' snapped Ben. 'I'll tell the crowd that it's malfunctioned or something. Go. Go!'

As Ben walked away to face the crowd, Cronk looked up at his colleague and shrugged.

'The boss says no,' he said.

'Fuck the boss!' said Grimpen. 'It's my act and I want to do it one last time.'

'Yeah, but…'

'But nothing. Look, there's a safety net and a big crowd. What can go wrong? And what's he going to do if we disobey him… fire us?' said Grimpen. 'Heh… fire me! Go on… fire me!'

And with that, he pulled his WWII fighter pilot goggles down over his eyes, adjusted his crash helmet and wriggled down inside the ever-so-tight barrel. Cronk suffered one last, small dose of second thoughts and then shrugged and pulled a box of matches from his pocket. 'I guess he knows what he's doing,' he said.

'Sadly, the price we pay for bringing you the greatest show on Earth is that occasionally, just occasionally, things do go wrong,' explained Ben, working the crowd. 'Our stunts are so daring, so death-defying, that even the slightest error could cost someone their life. And so, it is with great regret that I have to announce that tonight's human cannonball act will not be going ahead as pla–'

Anything else he had to say was lost in the explosion.

In her bath some three miles away, Marcheline heard a distant boom and wondered what on Earth it was. Thunder perhaps? But it was a minor distraction, soon forgotten as she returned to her bubbles and candles.

Chapter 34

Bert was driving along the dirt track towards the fly-tipping area when he heard a loud explosion in the distance. He slowed to a stop and listened, but the only sounds now were from the babbling River Gew and a few randy owls in the nearby woods. There was another noise too, very faint, almost like people screaming. Mating foxes, no doubt, he thought to himself. The noise they made was horrendous. Mind you, it was a bit early; they usually did all that stuff during the winter months and it was only September.

He drove on to the car park, the big cats' cage trailer rattling noisily behind the truck as it passed over the bumpy unmade road surface. It had annoyed him at first that he hadn't been able to unhitch the trailer from the truck; the lever that locked the coupling to the tow bar had been far too stiff and rusty for his old hands to operate. The trailer made it a lot harder to manoeuvre in the small car park but its size did have one advantage; it meant that he could take all the items that he wanted in just one trip. And, as he wanted to have the truck back before the end of the show, knowing that he only had to make one trip speeded things up considerably.

He parked as close as he could to the rubbish pile, slipped the bolts at the rear of the cage and lowered the tailgate ramp. The first item to go on the trailer was the cable drum. Despite its size and weight, it could be rolled quite easily. This also meant that it was likely to move around on the trailer, so he decided to put it on first and then wedge it in place with the sofa. With some effort, he rolled the large bobbin up the ramp and gave it a solid push to send it down to the dark far end. What he didn't expect at this moment was a sudden roar of surprise and for three frightened tigers to suddenly rush at him.

As the startled animals ran off into the night, Bert got up from the ground, towards which he'd instinctively thrown himself, and dusted his clothes off. He'd been so sure that the big cats would form part of the show's finale that he hadn't even considered checking whether the trailer was empty.

'I is so in the shits now,' he said.

In an eerily quiet Shapcott Bassett, Berkeley was looking around for something to dig with. The village was never noisy like a town was but there were usually a few people about at this time of an evening, walking dogs or sauntering to and from the King's Head. But the pub was shut and every sound he made seemed to be magnified by the eerie silence. Having been fairly out of touch with events for a few days, Berkeley hadn't seen the extent of the damage inflicted upon the rear of Twimbley's, but the scaffolding meant that builders were at work, and where there were builders there were probably tools. He walked down the alleyway between the grocery store and Barsted's Bakery and very quickly found what he was looking for propped up against a cement mixer. Returning to the flowerbeds with the shovel, he began to dig.

A sudden distant boom, like a giant firework going off, made him look towards the Morbridge Road.

'Hell, I hope that's not the finale already,' he cursed.
He began to dig faster.

The gout of flame from the exploding cannon had punched
a very large hole in the Big Top, and the old, dry fabric
had quickly caught fire. The flames quickly spread across the
entire roof of the tent, engulfing all in their way. As guy
ropes and wooden support poles burned through, parts of the
Big Top began to fold in on themselves, setting even more
areas of canvas ablaze. Burning fragments fell from the canopy
like rain and, in their panic, audience members and circus
folk alike stampeded towards the exits, trampling over anyone
that had been unfortunate enough to either fall over or be
blown off their feet by the explosion. One such was Special
Constable Arthur Pews, who tried to get up but was then
rendered unconscious by a burly man's walking boot
connecting with his temple. The smoking remains of the
cannon, and of Grimpen and Cronk, sat at the bottom of a
shallow crater and the front stalls nearest to it were littered
with the dead and dying. An occasional groan or the sounds of
sobbing were barely audible over the roar of the flames above.
Two or three brave souls, including Ben Ellis himself, had run
back into the tent, with coats over their heads to protect them
from the burning smuts, and had rescued as many people as
they could, but it had now become simply too dangerous for
amateurs.

Outside the tent, the crowd watched in horrid fascination as,
with a loud crack, the tallest point of the Big Top collapsed
inwards and fell. In the distance sirens could be heard as the
emergency services raced to attend. The first fire engine was
nearly on scene but, as it sped along the Morbridge Road,
the driver became aware of something large and grey hurtling

towards his engine in the opposite direction. Della the elephant was blindly running for her life and nothing was going to get in her way, not even an equally large red thing with flashing blue lights. She lowered her head and charged. Suddenly finding himself playing chicken with three tons of terrified elephant, the driver stamped on the brake pedal and swerved off the road in a screech of tyres. With a loud crash, the fire engine toppled and rolled into the very same ditch that Glupi had slept in just a few nights earlier. A second engine appeared shortly afterwards. It stopped to ensure that all of the firefighters were unharmed, if dazed and bearing a few minor injuries, before continuing, double-crewed, to the circus.

The Big Top was still ablaze and half-destroyed when the fire engine arrived. Some of the crew quickly ran inside to rescue any last survivors and to pull out as many victims as possible before the tent collapsed completely. Meanwhile, the remaining crew trained the hose on the fire itself. Another engine from Uttercombe arrived and soon the blaze was starting to abate.

Ben watched as the orange flames licked against the sky and wondered what he had done to deserve this. All he had ever tried to do was look after his staff and to keep the circus afloat. It was enough to make a man cry. And he did. As fat tears welled up and rolled down his red cheeks, he felt a hand on his shoulder.

'I guess you know what I'm going to say next,' said a bloodied but unbowed DS Blount.

Bert had decided that, with discretion being the better part of valour, he would leave the truck and trailer where they were so that, when they were found, it would be assumed to be a simple case of joyriding. He considered wiping down the truck but, as he'd quite often driven the vehicle – he was considerably better at manoeuvring it into parking spaces than was Colonel Sanders – it was hard to know where to wipe, as his fingerprints were legitimately all over it. Having decided that it wasn't worth the bother, he grabbed up anything from the rubbish pile that was portable enough to carry and set off for his cow shed, all the while looking out nervously for yellow cat-like eyes in the darkness.

He needn't have worried. Colonel Sanders' tigers were more terrified than terrifying and, finding themselves abandoned in unfamiliar territory, had started to make their way towards distant lights in the hope that it was the circus. Even if they encountered anyone en route, it was highly unlikely that they'd hurt them. The tigers were very tame, having been raised among people. One of them, the oldest, had barely any teeth left in her head. All they wanted was somewhere warm, comfortable and safe in which to curl up, fall asleep and forget the upsetting events of the evening. To that end they nervously stalked their way through the grass towards the lights of Cockering Hall.

Berkeley was getting more and more frustrated. He had now dug up three of the four flowerbeds and had discovered nothing of any interest. There had been one small moment of excitement when his spade had struck something solid in flower bed number two, but a furious five minutes of excavation had revealed only a time capsule, planted by the villagers in 1977 for the Queen's Silver Jubilee. There was no gold in there, only a copy of the *Radio Times*, a commemorative mug, several newspapers, and lots of individually hand-written letters and family photos. There was treasure of a kind in the form of valuable collectibles like the very first issue of *2000AD* comic and a pristine cinema poster for *Star Wars*. Best of all was a rare A&M label copy of the Sex Pistols' single *God Save the Queen*. These had been known to fetch up to £10,000 at auction. But Berkeley wasn't in the know and, blinded by the promise of an imagined hoard of gold, he continued to dig. Once or twice he stopped at the sounds of sirens – police or otherwise, he didn't know, but the last thing he wanted to have to do was explain himself to anyone. Thankfully they seemed to be some distance away.

He finished turfing up the final flowerbed and sat down, exhausted. He took a long hard drink from his hipflask. The flowerbeds were ruined and soil was thrown all over the road but, despite a good forty minutes of digging, it had all been for nothing. There was no buried treasure. All of a sudden, the thought struck him that maybe he hadn't interpreted Marcheline's clue correctly. What if 'Gold is under the stone Elizabeth' didn't mean the flower beds? What if she'd meant something else? The only other things that could be said to be 'under' the statue were the plinth upon which it stood, the flower beds, a handful of parking spaces and the ornamental horse trough. Berkeley examined the plinth first, in particular the bronze plaque that explained that the statue was a gift to Lord Marlbury Cockering from the British Dairy Industry 'on behalf of the grateful children of Herewardshire'. He felt all around the letters and edges of the plaque in the vain hope that it might be removable and have a secret recess behind it, but the plaque gave no clues and seemed to be very firmly attached to the stone. Even trying to prise it off with the shovel didn't budge it an inch; all it resulted in was a bent shovel blade and some deep scratches in the bronze. Berkeley therefore turned his attentions to the granite horse trough. The thing was far too heavy to move, so he knelt down and felt all around underneath it. His hand knocked against what felt to be a box of some kind. Using the spade handle to push it out from under the trough, he discovered a small, plain metal tin sealed inside a zip-lock waterproof bag. He removed the tin and opened it. Inside was a letter that said simply:

Dear Berkeley,

Congratulations. If you are reading this, then you have successfully solved all of the clues and have proven yourself to be clever and resourceful. You have also proven that you are a thief, a coward and someone with whom I am thoroughly ashamed to share a surname and a bloodline.

I have tried very hard not to believe some of the things I've heard said about you over the years but I can deny the truth no longer. You are a greedy, manipulative and beastly little man and you deserve to be punished. And thanks to G R R Hendrie (did you spot that fishy anagram?) you now will be.

The only reason you are able to read this note is that you followed a trail of clues that I wrote, and the only possible reason for you to have done so was because you intended to steal from me. And now I have physical proof of your guilt.

If you look across to the front of Twimbley's, you'll see that the security camera has been repositioned to record everything that happens in Market Square. This includes a video recording of everything that you have just done prior to finding and reading this letter. I could hand the footage over to the police if I considered it in the public interest. And, short of breaking into Twimbley's to steal the video, an act which surely will mark you as even more guilty and which, circumstantially, could only point to you as the culprit, there really isn't anything you can do about it.

There is no gold and there never was. You have been 'done

up like a kipper,' as they say in the criminal underworld that you delight in skirting around but would never be man enough to be part of.

I look forward to discussing the terms of your surrender.

Your 'loving' sister Marcheline.

Berkeley sat for a long time, his mouth hanging open in shock and the note still clutched tightly in his quivering hand. She was right. By focusing exclusively on decoding the poem, he had completely missed the fact that the author of the accompanying quote – G R R Hendrie – was an anagram of 'red herring'. Marcheline had completely wrongfooted him. She had sent him on a wild goose chase specifically designed to lead him here, to the marble cow that many people associated with Elizabeth Cockering and the rise of women's liberation. Here, underneath this symbol of female empowerment, he'd been made to look a fool and had completely incriminated himself by his actions.

Berkeley put his head in his muddy hands and swore. She had beaten him, and no mistake. The only possible interpretation of events that any right-minded person would accept was that he had set out with the express intention of stealing his sister's gold. Whether the gold actually existed or not was immaterial. His intentions were clear and, in the eyes of the law at least, he had attempted to commit theft. The very best case scenario he could envisage was that, even if the theft charge didn't hold, he'd still be prosecuted for the criminal damage to the flower beds and the bronze plaque. The evidence was there for all to see and it had all been captured on camera.

He drained his hipflask, picked up the shovel, hefted its

weight in his hand and stalked off murderously towards the
lane that led to Cockering Hall.

Chapter 35

The fire was finally out. Approximately two thirds of the physical structure of the Big Top had been burned to ash and, with no wind to move it, a great dark cloud of smoke hung over the campsite.

An Army bomb disposal team had been called to ensure that there was no more explosive material in the crater and, once they had declared it safe, police forensic officers had moved in. They'd erected a kind of pop-up tent in the pit and were currently filling plastic bags with as many pieces of clown as they could find. Another tent had been set up in which to store the bodies of the unfortunate victims. There were nine in all and they included two abattoir workers from Doughton Magna, a brewery man from Morbridge, a heavily tattooed animal rights protestor called 'Revvin' Kevin' whose dedication to the cause had wavered somewhat and who had snuck in to watch the show, and a retired school teacher from Chepping Frogmoor. Summersmith Mudd, whose old heart had finally given up the ghost and who, sadly, would now never retire to the seaside, was the sixth victim, and young Eric Clacketer had become the seventh when his skin-tight and constricting rubber underwear had prevented him from running fast enough to avoid the largest piece of cannon as it fell out of the sky.

Grimpen and Cronk completed the tally, although there was little evidence of their demise as they had been distributed across a wide area. Some of them had ended up covering the ample frame of Arthur Pews, whose unconscious and bloodied body had initially been misidentified as one of the dead and placed in the makeshift mortuary. Upon waking and discovering a decapitated slaughterman's head resting against his shoulder and apparently winking at him, he'd screamed for a full minute before being sedated by a paramedic.

Berkeley arrived at the front door of Cockering Hall and fumbled for his keys. Throwing the door wide open, he staggered exhaustedly into the grand entrance hall.

'Marcheline!'

In her bedroom, Marcheline heard her brother's shout and took a deep breath. She'd been preparing for this confrontation and was ready for it. She'd spent the last half an hour staring at herself in a mirror and wondering what it was that made some people good and others evil. What were the influences that turned this child into a saint and that child into a serial killer? And on the sliding scale of morality where did Berkeley lie? And where, for that matter, did she?

She considered her life to date and made a quick mental list of all the sins she had undoubtedly committed. Pride and anger topped the charts; the pride she'd had in her village had made her run roughshod over anyone else's opinions and ideas. And anger at her situation had driven her to physically abuse Ben and now to turn on her own brother. Not that he didn't deserve it. Look at what the sins of greed and envy had driven him to do. She concluded that no one was good and no one was bad. The human condition was to find your way through a shadowy grey world where uncertainty was king and where circumstance, not biology, dictated whether you were saint or sinner.

'Marcheline!'

It was time. Marcheline threw on a dressing gown and glanced at herself in the mirror once more. The person who looked back was not a defenceless young girl. Nor was it the pompous, arrogant shrew she'd once been. It was a powerful, middle-aged woman who looked back at her, a caring, strong woman with the tenacity and courage to do what had to be done to protect herself, her family and her heritage. She couldn't imagine for a minute that Berkeley might physically assault her. She couldn't even imagine him attempting to seriously threaten or intimidate her. But he was angry and he was manipulative and she would need all of her wits about her. She walked out of her bedroom and along to the balcony overlooking the entrance hall.

Berkeley, red-faced and wild-eyed, was pacing up and down, brandishing a shovel like a two-handed broadsword. He looked dishevelled and filthy, and a trail of dirt and muddy scuff marks on the marble showed where he'd been stomping around. For one moment, Marcheline wondered whether he'd been in some kind of terrible accident.

'Berkeley? What have I told you about carrying mud into the house?' she barked. 'You should use the boot room to…'

'Shut up!' he shouted.

This was unexpected. Marcheline stopped in her tracks, shocked by the uncharacteristic violence of his response.

'I beg your pardon?'

'Don't you dare talk to me in that holier-than-thou voice!' shouted Berkeley. 'Not after what you've just put me through, you mad cow!'

'What are you talking about?' said Marcheline, affecting total dismay.

'Don't you dare! Don't you dare play the dumb blonde with me! You know only too damned well what I'm talking about! At least have the backbone to admit it.'

'Have you been drinking?'

'Don't change the subject!'

'I assume that you mean my treasure trail? I take it that you've completed your nasty little attempt to steal from me?'

Berkeley glowered at her. 'You've been playing me!' he shouted.

'Yes. And can you blame me?' said Marcheline walking slowly down the grand staircase. 'I've watched you turn from a good man into a spiteful and nasty little stoat, Berkeley. And all because of money.'

'Yes, my money!' said Berkeley. 'The money you've kept from me! The money you have all tied up in your fucking oh-so-perfect village!'

'No, the money that I was entrusted with,' said Marcheline. 'It isn't your money and it isn't my money. It's the family's money. The money that I've prevented you from spending on drink, gambling and loose women.'

'Oh you're so fucking perfect aren't you?'

'No, I am not. But I'll admit to a sense of duty,' said Marcheline. 'All these years it's been me looking after our properties, me running the businesses, me protecting our investments. It's been me who's had to sit through interminable business meetings and complaints from tenants. It's me who's had to keep the books straight and work with the accountants. And all because I want the Cockering name to still stand for something in this shallow, modern world where mediocrity is celebrated, and where morality and privacy are seen as anachronisms. That's what I've been doing, Berkeley.'

With each sentence, she moved closer and closer to her

brother who backed slowly away, holding the shovel in front of his body as a shield.

'If you'd got off your lazy backside and worked with me, you might have earned yourself some money on top of your more than generous allowance,' she continued. 'But no, you didn't. You left all the work to me. And what have you been doing instead, eh? Casinos and gentlemen's clubs, golfing holidays and cocktail parties. You haven't even tried to find a suitable partner. That's all you had to do, Berkeley, get married and produce the heir to the family name. It's your one function as Viscount Morbridge and you haven't even bothered to do that. Why is that, Berkeley, eh? Is it because you can't bear the idea of being tied down by the responsibilities incumbent upon a husband? It's all I can do to get you to come to council meetings, so God only knows how you'd handle fatherhood. Or is it something else I wonder? Impotence perhaps?'

'No it damned well is not!' snapped Berkeley. 'There's nothing wrong with my virility! I could father a child if I wanted to! But I don't. That's right, I don't want to.'

'You have a duty to the family.'

'What family? There's only you and me. And I'll be damned if I'm going to pollute the world with any more Marcheline Cockerings and their old-fashioned fucking moralistic dogma.'

'You forget that I could have a child,' said Marcheline. 'And they could inherit the title when you die – which judging by the throbbing blood vessels in your head and neck, won't be far away.'

'You? You have a kid? Don't make me fucking laugh.'

Marcheline sneered and took another step forward. Berkeley raised the shovel and levelled it at her.

'Don't you come near me, you old sow!'

'As if you'd ever have the guts to hit me with that thing,' said Marcheline. 'You are pathetic.'

'I'm pathetic? I'm pathetic?' ranted Berkeley. 'So who do you think is going to be brave enough put a bun in your oven, eh? What kind of desperate maniac would get you up the duff? I had to bribe some pikey from a fucking circus to get you into bed, you're such a two-bagger.'

'I am finding it increasingly difficult to keep up with your obscure colloquialisms,' said Marcheline, dangerously.

'A one-bagger is a woman so foul that you have to put a bag over her head before you can shag her,' said Berkeley. He smiled maliciously. 'A two-bagger is when you wear one too… just in case hers falls off.'

He waited for the inevitable explosion of anger and hatred but Marcheline was not going to give him the satisfaction.

'There are nobler creatures than you living in a tramp's beard, Berkeley Cockering. There are wittier creatures than you eating their own faeces in the zoo.'

'Now you just hol–'

'You are a parasitic worm living in the backside of humanity and I wash my hands of you. And if your morals are as flaccid and pathetic as I suspect your penis is, then perhaps you are right. The family name deserves to die.' And, with that, Marcheline turned her back on him and, in a perfect display of *savoir–faire*, walked back upstairs.

'Don't you fucking walk away from me!' yelled Berkeley. 'I haven't finished with you yet.'

'But I have finished with you,' said Marcheline. 'Forever. And tomorrow, we'll see what the police have to say about a certain video. Sleep well.'

At the sound of her bedroom door being firmly locked, Berkeley roared with anger and attacked the marble bust of Buxton the Blackshirt, knocking it from its plinth and beating the cold stone pointlessly with the shovel until the wooden shaft broke in two. Red faced and panting hard, his heart pounding in his chest and his arms buzzing from the repeated shock of metal hitting marble, he staggered up the stairs to his own room and reached for the decanter of Scotch on his bedside table. Eschewing the formalities of a glass, he began to drink.

'So, what have we got, Brian?' asked the Custody Officer at Morbridge Police Station. Blount smiled triumphantly.

'This man is responsible for the deaths of at least five people, maybe more. Two for certain,' he said.

'Okay,' said the Custody Officer. 'Let's get him booked in then.' He opened a blank charge record on his computer screen. 'Name?'

Ben sighed. 'Benjamin Anthony Joshua Ellis. Born February 18th 1971, London. No fixed abode. Male. White British. Six foot tall…'

'Whoa, whoa! Slow down,' said the Custody Officer. 'I'm only a two-finger typist here. I guess you've done this before, eh? Have a history of crime do you?'

'No. But I have a history of being arrested by him for things I haven't done,' said Ben, nodding accusingly at Blount.

'Not this time,' said Blount. 'I have you bang to rights.'

DI Nicola Banton appeared in the custody suite.

'I understand we have a suspect in for homicide? Ah, hello Brian.'

'Ban… Ma'am.'

'So, what's the story?' asked Banton.

Blount explained in great detail the circumstances of the explosion and subsequent fire. The Custody Officer listened intently, scribbling occasional notes on a pad as he did so. When Blount had finished, the Custody Officer sat back in his chair and put his hands behind his head.

'That's a hell of a story,' he said.

'It is,' agreed Banton. 'However, I'm struggling to find any connection between this man and the deaths you've described.'

'He's in charge of the circus,' said Blount. 'He owns the cannon.'

'No, that belongs... belonged to Grimpen the clown,' said Ben. 'He used to be the Great Bazoom. Human cannonball.'

'So did you fire the cannon?' asked Banton.

'That was another clown. One of the other victims.'

'But you authorised the use of the cannon?'

'I did not,' said Ben. 'If I'd had any idea they were going to use it I'd have been horrified.'

'Didn't you try to stop them?' said Banton.

'I most certainly did,' said Ellis. 'Ask anyone who was there. I specifically ordered Grimpen not to go ahead with the act. I even told the crowd that the human cannonball act wouldn't be going ahead. You must have heard me say that? You were in the audience.'

Blount was forced to concede that he had.

'Can I have a word with you, Brian?' said Banton. 'In private?'

Berkeley woke up with a thumping headache and pins and needles in his left arm. He felt as if someone had pushed him through a combine harvester. More worryingly, he couldn't move his left arm. Panic gripped him. Was this the prelude to another heart attack? He rolled over onto his side and was surprised to find that someone was in his bed and lying on his arm. That was why he had pins and needles. But who could it be? And how had they got into his bed? As far as he was aware only he and Marcheline had been in the house and it was hardly likely to be his sister. The only other person who had keys was Mrs Shandcreek and for one awful moment he imagined her naked under the bed clothes. Had Meg taken advantage of his inebriation to seduce him? He didn't feel like he'd been seduced. To start with he was still fully clothed and nothing seemed to be unzipped or unbuttoned. And besides, Meg rarely came to the house after 7pm as she 'knew her place' and respected their privacy. No, she'd be tucked up in bed in her home in one of the estate's twin gatehouses.

So, who was in his bed? Surely not someone from the village? The choice of possible bedfellows in Shapcott Bassett was somewhat limited and largely superannuated and he hoped to God he wasn't being stalked by some predatory old woman. Cougars, they called themselves. Tentatively, he reached over and pulled the sheet back from the head of his unexpected guest and found himself face to face not with a cougar, but a tiger. A sleeping and gently snoring Bengal tiger.

His first reaction was to scream, but he bit his lower lip hard and squeakily broke wind instead. Screaming might upset the big cat. And what a big cat it was lying there on its side, the skin around its mouth pulled back into a grimace revealing yellowed three-inch long dagger-like teeth. The tiger twitched and snarled in its sleep, presumably dreaming primeval dreams of hunting down some soft, fleshy prey to despatch with those terrible jaws.

Very, very gently, Berkeley pulled his arm out from under the tiger and stepped carefully and quietly out of bed. It took a second for him to gain his balance – he really had drunk an enormous quantity of liquor – but then his foot brushed against something warm and furry. Knowing that he didn't own a pair of furry slippers, he looked down and bit his lower lip again. A second tiger was sound asleep on his bedroom floor and, if it was possible, this beast was even bigger than the one in his bed. He tiptoed past the sleeping cat and tried desperately to form any kind of coherent explanation for why there should be two tigers in his bedroom. It had to be Marcheline's doing. Yes, she'd got her boyfriend to release the tigers into Cockering Hall in the hope that they would eat her troublesome brother. It was the only explanation, surely. His insistent bladder was telling him that it needed emptying and, if he was honest, his bowels weren't feeling too settled either. There was no way that he was going to risk using his en suite, so the Hall's main bathroom would have to do. He made a quick inspection of the hallway and, finding it clear of large predatory mammals, began creeping silently along it. Or as silently as he could manage. Despite the instantly sobering effect of finding tigers in his bedroom, he was still very drunk and uncoordinated. Gingerly, he pushed open the bathroom door and found his sister glaring at him from the bathtub.

'Berkeley! What in God's name have you done!' she hissed, covering herself strategically with a pair of flannels.

'What have I done!' said Berkeley, swaying gently.

'Shhhh!' said Marcheline, pointing to the tiled floor where yet another tiger lay asleep.

'Fuck!' said Berkeley.

'Keep your voice down!' whispered Marcheline as loudly as she dared. The tiger made a low rumbling growl. 'You've gone too far this time, Berkeley.'

'What do you mean I've gone too far?' hissed Berkeley. 'You let the bloody things in here to kill me.'

'What? I did no such thing,' whispered Marcheline. 'You let them in to kill me.'

'I did not.'

'Then who did?'

'I don't know. Ask your bloody boyfriend. It certainly wasn't me.'

'Pass me a towel and help me out of this bath. I've been in here for over an hour and the water has gone stone cold.'

Berkeley passed her a towel and she stood slowly up. Every splash of water, every squeak of flesh against porcelain made the tiger twitch in its sleep. Taking her brother's hand, Marcheline stepped from the bath tub and quietly followed him out onto the landing. Together they tiptoed down the stairs and into the drawing room.

'I woke early and fancied a bath and I must have dozed off,' she explained. 'When I woke that tiger was sleeping on the floor. I didn't dare move.'

'I expect it was the under-floor heating that attracted it,' said Berkeley, reaching for a decanter of sherry.

'Is that wise?' said Marcheline. 'You already look to be as soused as a herring.'

'Perhaps a red herring like Mr G R R fucking Hendrie, eh?' said Berkeley, pouring himself a large glass of Palo Cortado. 'That was a good one that was. I missed that bugger didn't I?'

'Can we just put aside our differences for the moment and focus on the problem in hand?' said Marcheline. 'There are three tigers in our house. I think we should call the police.'

'Call the police? Oh yes, that's a good idea,' said Berkeley sarcastically, throwing back a large mouthful. 'Aherm. "Excuse me officer, but I have three tigers in my house. Could you possibly come around and get rid of them for me?" Oh yes, that's the sort of call they get every day, I expect. They're bound to believe that kind of story.'

'With you sounding as drunk as a skunk I very much doubt it,' said Marcheline. 'But we must do something.' While her brother had been talking, she'd used her mobile to phone Ben, but he wasn't answering his phone.

'Phoning the boyfriend are you?' asked Berkeley. 'He's

probably fast asleep in bed. Probably worn out after all the exercise he's been having recently, eh? Eh?'

'Oh do shut up,' said Marcheline, dialling again. 'And stop drinking! That isn't going to help.'

'It's helping me.'

'He's still not picking up,' said Marcheline. 'I still don't understand how those tigers got into the house. You did shut the front door last night, didn't you?'

'Oops,' said Berkeley sarcastically.

'Typical. Though Lord knows why there should be tigers roaming the grounds in the first place. Right, let's get organised.'

'That's right. Let's get to bossing people about.'

'Oh do grow up,' said Marcheline. 'I suggest that we lock ourselves in the kitchen, where we have food and access to the toilet in the utility rooms. We can hole up there until help arrives.'

'What help?' said Berkeley.

'Despite your ridiculous assertions, I am going to call the police and they will come,' said Marcheline. 'I am a... well, I was a magistrate after all.'

'Good luck with that,' said Berkeley, refilling his glass. 'I'm going to stay right here. Oh, and while you're in the kitchen, check how much milk we have in the fridge.'

'Milk? What for?'

'Because,' said Berkeley. 'When those beauties wake up, if we haven't woken them up already, I expect they'll be hungry and it might be a good idea to provide them with something to eat and drink. After all, my dear, we are made of meat.'

'But there must be something you can charge him with,' said Blount. 'Anything!'

'Like what?' said Custody. 'You heard DI Banton. She's been through all of the evidence and witness statements we've had in so far. None of it implicates this Ellis chap in any wrongdoing. In fact, he's come across as a bit of a hero in some accounts. Apparently, he ran back into the burning tent and hauled some old duffer to safety.'

'But people are dead!' said Blount. 'He has to be held accountable for that surely?'

'There may be a breach of health and safety regulations, I suppose.'

'You're damned right there was a breach of health and safety regulations,' said Blount.

'But that's a civil matter,' said Custody. 'And even if he is successfully prosecuted in due course, it is still not a criminal matter. We don't have the powers to deal with health and safety breaches. I can't hold him.'

'So you're just going to let him walk out of here, scot-free?'

'Best I can do is bail him pending further investigation,' said Custody. 'Unless you find something that shows wilful negligence or malice aforethought, I can't do a thing more. I'm sorry, but the law is the law.'

'And we all know the law is an arse,' said Blount, rubbing his forehead.

'You look tired,' said the Custody Officer. 'Perhaps you need a holiday. I heard about that nasty business with the murder investigation in Nasely a few years back and…'

'I don't need a fucking holiday! I need that bastard locked up!'

'Then get me something I can –'

'Hey Sarge! Sarge! Come and listen to this!'

A young male officer had barged into the custody suite and was beckoning towards the station's control room.

'What is it?' asked Custody.

'You won't believe this – there's some mad woman on the phone who claims her house has been invaded by tigers!'

'Tigers?' said Blount. 'Let me hear that.' He and the Custody Officer walked through to the control room and indicated for the communications officer to put the call on the speaker.

'... Yes, tigers!' said a female voice. 'You do know what tigers are don't you?'

'Tigers! Fucking great big stripy cats with teeth like traffic cones and claws you could rip open a can of beans with! Tigers!' shouted a male voice.

'I do know what tigers are, sir,' said the comms officer. 'There's really no need to swear.'

'You wouldn't say that if you had three of the fucking brutes loose in your house!' said the male voice.

'Shut up Berkeley, you're not helping,' snapped the female voice.

'Hilarious eh?' said the young officer, laughing.

'Is it?' said Blount. 'If I'm not mistaken that is the voice of Lady Marcheline Cockering and the other voice belongs to her brother Lord Berkeley Cockering, the Viscount Morbridge and a personal chum of the Chief Constable. Neither of them, as far as I know, are pranksters. So If I were you I'd wipe that stupid grin off your face and get someone around to Cockering Hall pronto, before you find yourself in a world of pain.'

The colour drained from the young officer's face.

'Yes, ma'am, we understand. Units are on way,' said the comms officer into the phone, as his colleague directed every available free unit to descend on Cockering Hall.

'And about time too,' said Marcheline's voice over the speaker. She hung up.

'Tigers. Training school didn't tell us anything about how to deal with tigers,' said the young officer. 'I wouldn't know where to start.'

'Luckily I know someone who knows exactly how to manage tigers,' said Blount to the Custody Officer. 'Release Ellis into my custody. I'm going to give the bugger one last bit of rope with which to hang himself.'

Chapter 36

Back at the Hall, Berkeley had decided on a new and rather more drastic form of action.

'If the buggers come near me, I'll let them have both barrels,' he mumbled as he attempted to load his shotgun with cartridges. Three times he fumbled it and dropped the ammunition before he managed to get two into the breach.

'Put that thing down before you kill one of us,' snapped Marcheline. 'You're a rotten shot when you're sober.'

'Ah, but a tiger is considerably bigger than a woodcock or a snipe,' said Berkeley. 'Did you know that's how snipers got their name? If you can take one of those tiny bastards out of the air, you're some kind of a shot, you are. Mystic powers, I reckon. The bird flies like it's drunk. Now, tigers on the other hand...'

'... are a mite more dangerous than snipe,' said Marcheline. 'But not nearly as dangerous as you are right now. Put the thing down.'

'Not a chance.'

'Then that's it. I'm not staying around you for a minute longer,' said Marcheline. 'I'll be in the kitchen if you need me.'

'Need you for what?' said Berkeley and he sat down heavily

in his chair, the broken shotgun across his knees. 'Bloody coward,' he snarled.

In the kitchen, Marcheline tried Ben's mobile once more and this time was rewarded with a reply.

'Oh thank God!' she said. 'I've been trying to get hold of you for hours.'

'Long story,' said Ben. 'I guess you haven't heard what happened at the circus tonight.'

'Tell me later. I don't have time right now,' said Marcheline. 'There are three tigers in the Hall and –'

'Yes, yes I know. I'm on my way there with the police,' said Ben. 'Listen Marsh, the tigers… they're pretty tame. They're like big pussy cats really. Just don't startle them, that's all. Like any startled animal, they revert to instinct. Just sit tight, don't upset the cats and we'll be there in ten minutes.'

There was a sudden loud report.

'What the hell was that?' said Ben.

'Oh dear God. I think Berkeley might have bagged one of them,' said Marcheline.

'What?'

There was another loud bang.

'Marcheline?'

Berkeley hadn't bagged anything. One of the tigers had been awoken by the sound of people talking downstairs. Slinking on to the landing and down the stairs, it had been startled to see someone that it didn't recognise. The big cat decided to therefore creep back upstairs, but not before emitting a low growl that caught the ear of Berkeley Cockering. Upon seeing the animal – or animals, thanks to him having polished off the crusted port – he stood up unsteadily, pointed the gun at a

257

spot directly between the two tigers and pulled the trigger. As the hopelessly misdirected volley of buckshot tore into Thadeus Bultitude's painting of Elizabeth Cockering, Berkeley was knocked backwards off his feet and the tiger raced up the stairs. The other two tigers, equally terrified of the loud gunshot, were instantly awake and left Berkeley's bedroom nervously, meeting their fellow on the landing. One of them was brave enough to look around for an exit and, finding none, moved towards the staircase.

Berkeley had just got to his feet when he saw a tiger once again at the top of the stairs. He raised the gun, and this time it was Judge Parsden whose portrait was shredded.

'Berkeley! What have you done?' said Marcheline, emerging at a run from the kitchen.

'I've saved our bloody skins, that's what I've done,' he said, getting once more to his feet and breaking the gun ready for another attempt at loading.

'You've done more than enough damage,' said Marcheline, dashing forward and attempting to wrestle the gun from his hands. Her momentum knocked the already wobbly-legged Berkeley over onto his back and the two of them rolled on the hard marble floor as she attempted to gain control of the weapon. In a sudden act of desperation, Berkeley swung a fist at his sister's face, which glanced off her cheek, causing her to release him. He scrambled to his feet, but not quickly enough. Even before he had regained his balance, Marcheline landed a solid haymaker on his jaw and he was once again thrown to the floor. She picked up the gun and removed the barrel from the stock, throwing each half to opposite ends of the entrance hall.

'That's it! That is fucking it! I quit!' shouted Berkeley, standing up and wiping the fresh blood from the corner of his mouth. 'I've had enough. I quit as Lord Cockering. I quit as your fucking brother. I'll take you to fucking court to get my half of the estate!' He staggered towards the front door.

'Where do you think you're going?' said Marcheline.

'Anywhere that doesn't have you in it,' snapped Berkeley as he left.

In the garage, Berkeley searched for the keys to his Jaguar. He knew that Marcheline kept all the car keys hanging on a peg somewhere, but it was dark and he had somehow managed to bypass the light switch.

Blount's nondescript Vauxhall pulled up on the gravel outside the hall just as the three tigers appeared in the doorway, their lithe and dangerous figures silhouetted against the light. They had crept down the stairs and past Marcheline, who had ignored them as she'd been advised to do. Now they were looking for a way to escape. Cautiously they emerged onto the driveway sniffing the air.

'Shit!' said Blount.

Marcheline appeared at the doorway, still clad in just a towel.

'Shoo! Shoo!' she shouted.

As one, the terrified tigers loped off into the darkness.

Berkeley's hand suddenly alighted on the car keys and he pressed the button to open the car doors. The interior lights of the Jag illuminated the garage. He found the switch that opened the garage's electric doors and climbed into the driver's seat of the Jaguar. He turned on the ignition and the car's powerful engine roared into life.

*

Marcheline heard the car start and ran towards the garage, but she was too late. With a squealing wheel spin, Berkeley shot out of the not quite fully open door, putting a large dent in the car's roof, and raced off down Cockering Lane towards the village.

As the Jaguar tore between the two gatehouses that marked the boundary of the estate, Berkeley's mind was once more filled with thoughts of freedom. He remembered that just before his heart attack he'd been fantasising about life on a yacht in the Caribbean, thousands of miles away from Marcheline and damp, dull South Herewardshire. Well, he would have his freedom, no matter what the cost. He would drive to London, employ the very best barristers that money could buy and he would get legal access to his half of his inheritance. Fuck Marcheline and her stupid village.

He drunkenly threw the car into the sharp corner by the grocery store where Cockering Lane joined Market Square when, all of a sudden, six glowing eyes shone out at him from the darkness.

'Fuck!' shouted Berkeley as he swerved to avoid the tigers. The car's rear end spun out and made contact with the outside wall of Twimbley's. As Berkeley wrestled to bring the car back under his control, the Jaguar skidded on the mud that he'd thrown on to the road earlier, careened through the destroyed flowerbeds and smashed into the plinth that supported the marble statue of Big Bessie.

Bloodied and broken, his face ashen and pushed up against an inflated air bag, Berkeley knew that he'd been terribly injured, possibly even fatally. The Jaguar was equipped with excellent safety features but the human body was not designed to withstand a 40mph collision with several tons of solid Portland Stone and white marble. That said, he noted with some satisfaction that the plinth had been cracked by the impact and that a good third of it had fallen away, leaving the cow balancing precariously on three legs.

'Well... built... car,' he groaned.

Another crack appeared, and then another. They crept towards each other like twin rivers cutting through loose soil. With a loud crack, the plinth split from one end to another and Bessie the cow began to topple over.

'*Ut sementem feceris, ita metes*,' said Berkeley as the marble statue crashed heavily onto the roof of the Jaguar, breaking into several pieces and ending the life of the Viscount Morbridge.

A police car, responding to the call at Cockering Manor, screeched to a halt. The driver jumped out of his vehicle and was running towards the Jaguar just as the cow fell. The officer grimaced at the sight of the victim within and radioed for an ambulance, even though he knew it was too late.

Back at the hall, it fell to Brian Blount to break the news of Berkeley's demise to his sister. He found her sitting on a stone bench by the front door, holding hands with Ben Ellis.

'I'm sorry, Miss Cockering, but I have some bad news regarding your brother.'

'I know about the crash. I heard the radio,' said Marcheline. 'He's dead, isn't he?'

'I'm afraid so. I'm very sorry.'

'He was such an awful man at times, and we didn't get on at all these last few years,' said Marcheline, trying to hold back her tears. 'His last words to me were that he wanted to be anywhere that didn't have me in it.'

'Well, he kind of is now,' said Blount.

Marcheline buried her head in Ben's shoulder and started to sob.

Blount sighed resignedly. 'Good luck, son,' he said and walked back to his car.

Chapter 37

It had been nine months since the tragedy at Benelli's Circus.

The inquest into the deaths of Vincent Balding and Christos Ionnacuo (aka Grimpen and Cronk) and the seven other victims had run for three of those months, with much evidence-gathering and interviewing as the coroner and the police had attempted to establish whether the tragedy was the fault of anyone or anything other than the clowns and their own drunken stupidity. The court had heard evidence from witnesses and from the nephew of the cannon's original manufacturer – a company long since gone out of business – who had revealed that the machine was designed to launch its user by way of a sprung platform. A small pinch of black powder was used only to create a small bang and a puff of smoke for dramatic effect. The barrel had not been designed to handle the pressures involved in setting off a large amount of explosives inside it, which was why it had split open like a peeled banana, decapitating a member of the audience, incinerating Cronk, and turning 'The Great Bazoom' into something resembling raw liver. In the end, the verdict had been given of death by misadventure and Ben had been cleared of all responsibility.

In the meantime, Ben had begun the unenviable task of sifting through what was left of the circus and selling it all to raise money for his performers to retire. The fire had destroyed not only the Big Top but also a number of the performers' caravans, along with a lifetime of memories and all of their worldly possessions. Most of them were, understandably, still in shock. The Salvation Army had come to the rescue with temporary accommodation, food and camp beds at the Shapcott Bassett Village Hall, but it wasn't ideal and social services had been called in with a view to rehousing the elderly performers. Ben had spent a great deal of his time visiting his colleagues to make sure that they were as comfortable as possible in their digs. Surprisingly, a lot of the circus's remaining props and equipment had made good money at auction, having attracted antique collectors from all over the globe, and Ben's insurance policy had paid off too. On top of that, the story of the geriatric circus performers had caught the public's imagination. Someone had started a charity webpage and the donations had been rolling in. Each of the performers had come out of the ordeal with a modest nest-egg. And as the Coltellos, the final act to leave Benelli's Circus, set off to begin a new life in sheltered accommodation near the coast in South Wales, Ben finally allowed himself to relax.

Berkeley's funeral had been an affair of mixed emotions. Attended by many of his hedonistic, party-loving friends that Marcheline didn't know and didn't want to know, it had taken place at St Lydwina's on a cold, grey afternoon, and was administered by the Reverend Grimson Freacke. In his eulogy he spoke warmly of Berkeley's fondness for the village and its inhabitants, and of his pride in the local dairy industry.

In her pew, Marcheline grieved for the loss of a brother she had once loved while simultaneously suppressing the urge to correct the vicar on pretty much all counts. The interment had been followed by an impromptu wake at the King's Head that Marcheline was happy not to attend.

Arthur Pews still hadn't fully recovered from his experiences. Suffering from a form of post-traumatic stress disorder and temporary deafness, he'd spent all of his first week in hospital hearing nothing but a loud and continuous ringing tone, which had made communication with the overworked staff at the cottage hospital difficult. His ability to attach names to faces had also been affected, which had resulted in him proposing to Beryl Tiggs in the mistaken belief that she was Lady Cockering, a mistake he found himself unable to rectify after Beryl had introduced her two enormous and dangerous-looking sons to their new daddy.

Like Ben, Bert had also been exonerated of all charges. Returning to the fly-tipping dump to gather his supplies, he'd been surprised and delighted to find that the tigers had found their way back to their trailer, miserable and shaking and desperate to be somewhere safe. He had therefore triumphantly returned the truck to Colonel Sanders with the lie that he'd driven it away from the fire to save the animals. He had been rewarded with gratitude and a humanitarian award from the RSPCA. Once his heroic deeds had been plastered all over the front page of the *South Herewardshire Mercury*, the police had dropped all charges deciding that, on balance, prosecuting hero pensioners for daring to make a bit of whisky on the side was not in the public interest. To his extreme annoyance, Blount was given the task of presenting Mr Adalbert Szewczyk with the award at a small press conference. He chose the platform to also announce his retirement from the force. Enough was enough.

And so, normality returned to the little village of Shapcott Bassett, with its WI bake sales, pottery classes and flower shows where Bert's green fingers often resulted in him winning a rosette or two. Ben and Marcheline had taken him on as groundsman for the estate and he had made it bloom. He'd also converted an old potting shed into a new distillery, but kept that particular innovation to himself.

At Marcheline's insistence, he'd moved out of his draughty cowshed and into the vacant gate house opposite Mrs Shandcreek's. The two of them had struck up a lively friendship, and maybe a little more.

And there had been some changes in the village too. Big Bessie had been repaired and remounted and now bore a second bronze plaque. It was dedicated to Berkeley Cockering and Marcheline had insisted on writing the curious inscription, of which she was rather proud. It read:

'Keen sword did not slay this man
Nor bullet, spear or murd'rous hand,
Or problems cardiovascular
But three tigers and a Jaguar.'

Marcheline had also decided to dissolve the residents' committee and to put the late Jack Clancaster's cottage onto the open market. It had attracted a slew of potential buyers, all keen to move into such an idyllic environment, and was eventually sold to a charming young couple, whose twin three-year-olds had injected some life back into the village. The death of old Mrs Rabberley, creating another 'Local woman dies of natural causes' headline for the local paper, saw another young family move in just two months later. Marcheline's perfect village was being brought back to life. And, besides, it was only right that her child, the future Viscount Morbridge, should have other children to play with.

At the hall, Marcheline shared a philosophical brew with Mrs Shandcreek.

'Meg. Do you remember, nearly a year ago now, we sat here just like this and you read my leaves?'

'I dunno. Memory ain't what it was, my dear.'

'Well, I remember it very clearly. You said that things lost would be found and that something dark would be brought to light. You predicted change. And death.'

'The leaves don't often lie,' said Mrs Shandcreek. 'All depends how you look at what they say. Don't take it all so literal. Look at yourself. You've changed. And you found something you thought you'd lost. And I said there would be babies.'

'Yes. You did didn't you?' said Marcheline. She rubbed her hands over her round tummy and smiled. 'Meg! It just kicked!'

'Gonna be just like his father,' said Mrs Shandcreek. 'He's been kicking himself for not having done what he loves doing afore now.'

'It's never too late to pursue the things you want from life,' said Marcheline as the baby kicked again.

In his study, two floors above them, Benjamin Ellis sat back in his chair and read over what he'd typed. His new book, entitled *Inhuman Laughter*, told the story of an ageing clown whose only desire was to drink away the memories of his time as a Nazi guard in the death camp at Treblinka. Ellis wiped a tear from the corner of his eye and looked out of the window to where Bert was taking a break from forking horse manure onto a rose bed. The old clown had never looked so fit and happy. Ben read through what he'd written again and smiled. It was his best work yet. His first book, *Ghosts of Tigers*, had recently made the longlist for the Man Booker Prize. Who knew what this new book might achieve?

He saved the novel to his hard drive, switched his computer off and went downstairs to join his fiancée for supper.

The Playfair Cipher

The Playfair cipher was created in 1854 by Charles Wheatstone (1802-1875) and named after his good friend Lord Lyon Playfair (1819-1898), who heavily promoted its use. There is a splendid story that when Wheatstone offered it to the Foreign Office they rejected it because it was too complex. Wheatstone stated that he could teach a schoolboy to use it in just 15 minutes, to which the Under Secretary of the Foreign Office allegedly replied, 'That is very possible, but you could never teach it to attachés.' Despite this inauspicious start, and mostly thanks to Lord Playfair's involvement, the cipher did go on to be used by the British during the second Boer War and by the Allied forces in both World Wars. One huge advantage of Playfair is that it requires no special equipment – just a pencil and paper.

Playfair works by substituting pairs of letters, or *digraphs*, instead of single letters. There are a number of variant versions, but here's a description of the one that I've used for this book.

First you draw a five-by-five grid. Then, starting in the first box, you write your *key word*. Repeated letters are left out or, if there's just one duplicate, it can be replaced with an X for an extra layer of encryption. You then fill the remaining boxes with the other letters of the alphabet in order. The Q isn't used and I and J are interchangeable and share the same square. So, a grid using the keyword of PLAYFAIR would look like this (Note that the X replaces the repeated A):

P	L	A	Y	F
X	I/J	R	B	C
D	E	G	H	K
M	N	O	S	T
U	V	W	Y	Z

To encode a message – for example MARCHELINE – you break the message into pairs of letters e.g. MA RC HE LI NE. If there's an odd number of letters, add a Q somewhere e.g. the codeword TELEPATHY could be written as TE LE QP AT HY or TE LE PA TH YQ.

Then look at the grid and find the first two letters; in this case the M and A of MARCHELINE.

P	L	A	Y	F
X	I/J	R	B	C
D	E	G	H	K
M	N	O	S	T
U	V	W	Y	Z

Note that they make a box that has P and O at the other corners. These are your substituted letters. M is on the same line as O and A is on the same line as P, so MA becomes coded as OP. Any two letters that form a box will use the letters at the other two corners as substitutes.

Now find R and C. These don't form a box as they are on the same line. So what we do is substitute the letters immediately after R and after C, so they become B and X (because C is at the end of the line, the next letter (X) is found by wrapping around to the start of the same line). So MA RC is now OP BX.

P	L	A	Y	F
X	I	R	B	C
D	E	G	H	K
M	N	O	S	T
U	V	W	Y	Z

The next two letters are H and E. Because they are also on the same line, the same rule applies. So H becomes K and E becomes G. So our code now reads OP BX KG.

P	L	A	Y	F
X	I	R	B	C
D	E	G	H	K
M	N	O	S	T
U	V	W	Y	Z

Next come L and I. These occupy a vertical line. Just like the horizontal lines, you take the letter immediately after (below) the L, which is I, and after the I, which is E. Our cipher has now rendered MA RC HE LI into OP BX KG IE.

P	L	A	Y	F
X	I	R	B	C
D	E	G	H	K
M	N	O	S	T
U	V	W	Y	Z

Finally, we have N and E which, like the previous two letters are on the same vertical line. So we take the next letters after the N (V) and, because the next letter after the E is N, we use that.

P	L	A	Y	F
X	I	R	B	C
D	E	G	H	K
M	N	O	S	T
U	V	W	Y	Z

So, the fully coded MA RC HE LI NE becomes OP BX KG IE VN. You can further encode the message by breaking it into blocks of four using Qs as fillers e.g. OPBX QKGI EQVN (The decoder would know to discount the Qs).

To decode a message, you simply reverse the process: OP on the grid makes a box where the other two corners are MA etc. And, for two letters on the same line, horizontally or vertically, you read the two letters before.

The message that Berkeley had to decode had the key word of MARCHELINE so the grid looked like this:

M	A	R	C	H
E	L	IJ	N	X
B	D	F	G	K
M	O	P	S	T
U	V	W	Y	Z

Which translates like this:

D S D O N P Y E B L M I J N V H M B Z X

G O L D I S U N D E R E L I Z A B E T H

'G O L D I S U N D E R E L I Z A B E T H'.

*

We hope you enjoyed your visit to South Herewardshire.

Here are two bonus short stories featuring characters from *Cockerings* that first appeared in the anthology *The Nearly Invisible Man (and Other Stories)*.

Potato Salad Days

(THIS TAKES PLACE BEFORE THE EVENTS IN *COCKERINGS*)

'I'm really not sure that we should have left the organising of the food to Stella,' said Lady Marcheline. 'She is getting on and she can be… well, a bit forgetful at times.'

'I reckon she's earned the right to have the occasional lapse,' said Bunty Clacketer.

'It wasn't a criticism,' said Marcheline. 'More of an observation. Anyway, I'm surprised she wanted that kind of responsibility at her age.'

'She volunteered. She's too frail to get involved in any physical way but she wanted to help. All she had to do is work out a menu and then ask people to prepare a particular item. What could go wrong?'

'Well, everything is in order out here. Let's go and see how preparations are going up at the Hall.'

'It's going to be a lovely day,' said Bunty.

It was midsummer in the village of Shapcott Bassett and preparations were well in hand for the annual charity music concert held, as always, at the foot of the low chalk hills known as the Big and Little Knapper. The Knappers stood within the grounds of Cockering Hall, a grand eighteenth-century manor house set in forty-five acres of landscaped park, and took their name from the many shaped and worked flints found there, from Stone Age hand axes to strikers for use in flintlock pistols. The Big Knapper wasn't that big and the Little Knapper was little more than a crescent-shaped bump; but they were considered high ground when compared to most of the county, which was almost uniformly flat. Within the curve of the Little Knapper there had once been a hamlet of flint knappers' cottages, now long gone. All that stood there now was Cublington's Folly, a scaled-down replica of the Basilica di Santa Maria del Fiore in Florence, and covered from base to tip in bleached white seashells. It was here, in this natural amphitheatre, that the stage had been erected so that music lovers had a great view from the slopes of the bigger hill. Highlights for this year's concert included the world famous Factum Quartet and a rare appearance by the reclusive Cornish tenor, Trevellyan Lillicrap.

Overseeing the organisation of the event was Lady Marcheline Cockering, older sister of Lord Berkeley Cockering, the Viscount Morbridge, and joint owner of the Cockering Estate. Berkeley had sloped off for a week's golfing holiday in Vilamoura, as he always did at this time of year, to ensure that he couldn't be roped into doing any work. But Marcheline didn't mind; the Viscount was effortlessly and predictably unreliable and, to her mind, more hindrance than help. She was quite capable of doing it all by herself and, indeed, the majority of the work was done. The stage was erected and the lights and PA were installed, a small village of stalls and food wagons had parked around the Folly and were setting out their wares, and the first concert goers had arrived to camp overnight and to stake the best plots on the Big Knapper. Having walked around the site with her deputy, redoubtable butcher Bunty Clacketer, Marcheline headed back to her family home. The celebrities, all of whom were being put up at the Hall, were due to start arriving at six and she wanted to be sure that their needs were going to be adequately catered for. To this end, she had decided to lay on a banquet.

However, it soon became clear that all was not as she might have liked it to be. One quick glance at the dining room table revealed that, unless the guests' needs were very particular indeed, her lack of faith in old Mrs Rabberley's organisational skills had been justified after all.

'She asked me to make potato salad,' said Agatha Twimbley.

'She asked me to make potato salad, too,' said Demelza Ostridge.

'And me,' said Doris Spatting.

'I have potato salad too,' said Beryl Tiggs.

'Has anyone brought anything other than potato salad?' asked Marcheline, a nervous quaver causing her voice to rise ever so slightly in pitch.

No hands were raised.Marcheline looked again at the table, covered from end to end with clingfilm-sealed bowls of potato salad and nothing more. Mrs Rabberley's memory had become much worse of late and words like 'dementia' were starting to be used. Today had clearly been one of her bad days.

'Oh dear,' said Bunty Clacketer. 'I'm sorry Marcheline, it looks as if you were right.'

'I remarked to Stan that we'd sold a lot of potatoes this week,' said Agatha Twimbley. 'Normally we sell about twenty bags. This week we sold over sixty. I doubt there's a potato left in the village.'

'Yes, well, there's no use crying over spilled milk,' said Marcheline. 'Our guests are due here in two hours and unless we expect them to sit down to a cold meal completely composed of carbohydrates, we need to get weaving.'

'I could roast some chickens,' said Bunty. 'And there are plenty of roasting joints in the shop.'

'And there's plenty of other veg at our shop,' said Agatha Twimbley.

'That's good,' said Marcheline. 'Who else has time to cook? We have two hours.'

Hands were raised.

'Excellent,' said Marcheline. 'Those of you who are cooking, head over to Clacketer's and see what's there. Bunty, Agatha, I'll see that you are both suitably reimbursed. The rest of you, see what else you can pull together while the meats are cooking. I will organise the vegetables here and will happily accept some help. Everyone back here at 6pm.'

The next two hours were a flurry of activity as Clacketer's was raided and half-emptied and the good womenfolk of Shapcott Bassett searched every corner of every kitchen cabinet, pantry, larder and fridge to find things to cook. Joints were roasted and sausages fried. Kidneys were devilled, salmon kettled and prawns potted. Marcheline organised the distribution of free potato salad to the food vans to provide an extra garnish for their burgers, hot dogs and pies before she and her cook, Mrs Shandcreek, tackled the mountain of vegetables purloined from Twimbley's grocery. By the time the ladies returned to Cockering Hall, the dining table had been transformed into something that even the most hedonistic of Tudor monarchs would have recognised as a damnably fine feast.

'It's perfect,' said Marcheline. 'Just perfect. I've always said that there is no problem so large that it cannot be defeated by the good women of South Herewardshire. Give yourselves a huge round of applause.'

'It looks lovely, just as I imagined,' said old Mrs Rabberley, who'd come along to see if she was needed. She clapped as loudly as everyone else.

'Yes, you did a grand job,' said Marcheline, kindly. She looked over the table groaning under the weight of warm meats, piles of cabbage, broccoli, and cauliflower, dishes of sweet carrots and peas, mashed swedes and Yorkshire puddings and felt very proud of what had been achieved.

'Oh, but did no one do any potatoes?' said Mrs Rabberley. 'You can't have a roast without potatoes. I'm sure I must have mentioned potatoes to somebody.'

Five go to the Captain's cottage

(THIS TAKES PLACE DURING THE EVENTS IN
COCKERINGS)

Captain Jack Clancaster (Merchant Navy ret.), known as
'Saucy Jack' by those ladies who had vainly attempted to best
him on the bowling green, was dead. Quite when he'd died
wasn't known, but he was a popular man in Shapcott Bassett
and his absence from village life had been noticed very quickly.
Mrs Spatting, the neighbour who had gone to check on him,
reported that she'd found him slumped in his favourite
armchair as if asleep. He appeared to have died painlessly and
contently alone in his little cottage in Creamery Walk.

And no one could argue that he hadn't had a good innings;
born in 1925, he'd spent most of his life at sea but, on his
occasional sojourns to dry land, he had managed to get married
and divorced three times and to sire five children, all of whom
paid regular visits to the village to see their father. He'd even
somehow managed to maintain good relations with his ex-
wives and those in the know claimed that they were not averse
to staying overnight at his cottage. Saucy Jack was saucy to the
end and many would miss the cheeky twinkle in his eye, even

if they didn't miss his practical jokes and occasional suggestive comments.

Following a well-attended funeral at St Lydwina's, a small group of his closest friends gathered at the King's Head to splice the mainbrace in his memory.

'Oh dear,' said the Reverend Freacke, 'It's barely past one.'

'You can't send an old sailor off on his final voyage without a toast,' said Major Crantlemain. 'Tradition is tradition and, as an ex-military man myself, it's important to honour his service.'

'Perhaps a small sherry, then,' said the Reverend.

'Can't splice the mainbrace with sherry,' said Crantlemain. 'Got to be rum. A tot of grog to see the old sea dog off.'

'Oh very well,' said Reverend Freacke. 'But a small one.'

'The Navy has a different toast for every day of the week you know,' said Professor Ostridge. 'As today is a Saturday it should be "To our families". It used to be "To our wives and girlfriends" and the reply to the toast was "May they never meet"!'

'Very appropriate,' said Bertie Barsted. 'Jack was something of a lad in his day. Ha! Jack the Lad!'

'I don't think I could, in all conscience, drink a toast to adultery,' said the Reverend, 'But a toast to families is very agreeable.'

'Very well then,' said Crantlemain. 'To Captain Jack and to families.'

The five men clinked their glasses together and downed their tot of rum in one. All except the Reverend Freacke who sipped at his like a bird at a pond.

'I'm intrigued by this reading of the will business,' said Stan Twimbley. 'Surely he can't have left us any money? He had five boys and three ex-wives and I don't imagine he was a rich man.'

'He was certainly never first to the bar,' said the Major.

'Tight as a ferret's chuff,' he added, earning a wagged finger of admonishment from the Reverend.

'Perhaps he amassed a secret fortune?' suggested the Professor. 'You do hear stories. There was that chap in America a few years ago, lived modestly but left over seven million dollars in gold to his cousin, a teacher who'd never met him. In fact, as I recall, she didn't even know he existed.'

'Seven million eh? That would be damned useful,' said the Major.

'Between five of us,' said Stan Twimbley.

'Still a decent wad,' said the Major.

'This is all rather mercenary isn't it?' said the Reverend. 'I'm rather hoping he bequeathed something for the church roof.'

'Some tiles?' said Barsted, laughing.

'I've never been to a reading of a will before,' said Professor Ostridge. 'It's something I've only ever seen in films.'

'You mean like in one of those daft movies where you can only inherit if you spend the night in a haunted house?' said Bertie Barsted. 'As if things like that ever happen.'

'The terms and conditions of the late Captain Clancaster's last will and testament are quite clear and unambiguous,' said Mr Mallord, senior partner at the firm of Tremens, Mallord, Hacker and Budge, Solicitors, Commissioners for Oaths and Notary Public.

'We have to spend the night in his cottage?' said Bertie Barsted.

'From sunset to sunrise on the first Saturday following Captain Clancaster's death, which would be tonight,' said Mr Mallord. 'On completion of this task, Captain Clancaster asked that you each be given one thousand pounds.'

'What a strange thing to ask of us,' said the Reverend.

'Extraordinary,' said Professor Ostridge.

'Is the cottage supposed to be haunted or something?' asked Stan Twimbley.

'Do you believe in ghosts?' asked the solicitor.

'Not at all,' said Stan.

'Then it's not haunted is it?' said Mr Mallord with a wry smile.

Saucy Jack's tiny cottage stood sandwiched between the equally tiny police station and Mrs Spatting's converted dairy house on the corner of Creamery Walk and The Pastures. The cottage garden was one of the smallest in the village but could certainly boast the highest concentration of plants per square foot. The Captain had never been much for gardening, and the place had returned to Nature sometime in the early 1990s. The jungle of tall grasses, brambles, nettles and cow parsley had also claimed his garden furniture, pulling the rotten timbers apart and providing pulp for the wasps and damp, musty homes for woodlice and earwigs. Things were barely any less crowded inside the one-bedroom cottage. The downstairs consisted of a sitting room and a small kitchen and every single surface was covered in mementoes from his many years spent at sea. On the mantelpiece over the fire stood a tacky plastic hula girl from Hawaii, a ship in a bottle, a snow globe of the Statue of Liberty, a scrimshaw-decorated sperm whale tooth and a fat wooden smiling Buddha. Elsewhere there hung countless hats, tribal masks and dangerous-looking spears, shelves were piled high with postcards and books, and drawers were filled with sea shells, foreign coins, bottles of strangely coloured liquors, badges, broken watches and other trinkets and gewgaws. Among the more macabre items on display were a kangaroo-scrotum purse, a stuffed mongoose facing up against a cobra, and a 'Jenny Haniver' – a dried skate carved to look like some kind of mermaid figure. Upstairs, the story was no better.

There was only a bedroom and a bathroom but these too were filled floor to ceiling with the clutter of Captain Clancaster's long and peripatetic life.

'It's not so much a question of trying to sleep in this place as figuring out where,' said Bertie Barsted. 'There isn't a bit of space to lie down.'

'There's a double bed upstairs,' said the Reverend Freacke. 'Two of us could share?'

'I'll be damned if I'll lie in a dead man's bed,' said Major Crantlemain.

'He didn't die in bed. He died in his armchair,' said the Reverend.

'Damned if I'll sleep in that either,' said the Major. 'I've brought my own sleeping bag.'

'I brought some sheets and a duvet,' said Bertie Barsted. 'I don't mind sleeping on the bed as long as I'm not in direct contact with the old boy's mattress.'

'I don't mind either,' said Stan Twimbley. 'I have a sleeping bag. That will be fine on the bed.'

'Well, that's two of us accommodated,' said the Reverend.

'I'm not tall. I'll happily take the bath,' said the Professor.

'Which just leaves you and me,' said the Reverend. 'And if you don't want the armchair, Major...'

The Major harrumphed. 'Nothing wrong with the floor,' he said, at once regretting it when he saw the state of the carpet.

As the sun dipped below the horizon, the five friends sat around the Captain's dining table and were thankful that he hadn't died in the depths of winter, when sunset to sunrise would have been almost twice as long. Even so, it was early September and sunrise was a good ten hours away. There wasn't even an opportunity to cheat; Special Constable Arthur Pews, who lived above the police station next door, had volunteered to monitor the house to ensure that no-one left until after 6.30am.

'The thing to do is get some sleep and get the damned business over with,' said the Major. 'It'll be dawn in a trice and we'll all be a thousand pounds richer.'

'We shouldn't just be thinking about the money,' said the Reverend. 'In a way, we're spending our last night with him. We should treasure this time.'

'Did anybody bring any cards?' asked Bertie Barsted. 'A few rounds of whist would help pass the time.'

No one had and a quick rummage through Clancaster's possessions failed to find any.

'I found this though,' said Professor Ostridge, laying a box on the table.

'*Cluedo*? I haven't played that in years,' said Stan Twimbley.

'What fun!' said the Reverend.

'It's perfect,' said Bertie Barsted. 'And look, we have a real-life Reverend Green, a Professor Plum and a Colonel Mustard right here around this table!'

'Good show,' said Crantlemain, relishing his promotion.

'So who am I?' said Stan Twimbley.

'I guess we'll have to be the ladies,' said Barsted.

Having agreed that Bertie Barsted would be Mrs White and Stan Twimbley would be Mrs Peacock, the five friends set out the board, placed the murder weapons randomly around the various rooms and selected the three cards for the envelope at the centre. The game then progressed at its usual pace with each of the players taking turns to ask to see other people's cards and slowly but surely reducing the number of suspects, murder weapons and crime scenes to the point where a reasoned guess could be made. It was the Reverend Freacke who arrived there first.

'I accuse Mrs Peacock of committing the crime in the

Dining Room with the Candlestick,' he said triumphantly, reaching for the small black envelope. At that moment, the cottage was plunged into darkness.

'Power cut,' said the Professor.

'I don't think so. The lights are on everywhere else,' said Bertie Barsted peering out of a window.

The Major struck a match and walked into the kitchen to look for the fuse box but had no luck. He did, however, find several candles which he lit and glued to some saucers with wax.

'Curious that it's just this house,' said the Professor. 'Perhaps he was on a meter?'

'And it's just run out?' said Barsted. 'That would be an odd coincidence.'

'Spooky,' said Twimbley.

'A power cut isn't spooky,' said the Professor.

'You don't suppose this is planned do you?' said Barsted. 'Like some kind of a test?'

'Test? What sort of test?' asked the Major.

'Like a test of nerve. To make us leave the house early and lose the money,' said Barsted. 'Maybe Jack paid someone to knock the power off?'

'Why would he do that?' asked Professor Ostridge.

'One of his practical jokes?'

'That would make sense if we were in a supposedly haunted castle,' said the Professor. 'But we're not. We're in a rather shabby cottage that has no reputation for anything supernatural.'

'And anyway, what would be the point of a practical joke?' said the Major. 'He's dead and can't enjoy our discomfort.'

'Okay, how about his sons?' asked Barsted. 'If we were to fail to stay here overnight, they'd stand to inherit five thousand pounds more than they currently do. Five boys, five grand.'

'That's true,' said the Major.

'Surely not?' said the Reverend. 'I've met the Clancaster boys and they are all nice young men. One is a doctor.'

'Greed can make even the most honourable man into a thief,' said Barsted.

'I still don't believe it,' said the Reverend.

'All I believe is that the sooner it's sunrise the better,' grumbled the Major. 'I'm going to get my head down. Bagsy first for the bathroom.'

By Midnight, all five men were tucked up in their makeshift beds for the night and the candles had been snuffed. The waxy smoke mingled with the cottage's musty staleness and smells of leather and old wood, and an ever-so-slight hint of the seaside given off by the many stuffed and desiccated specimens on display, which included a mummified pufferfish and the wall-mounted snout of a sawfish. Major Crantlemain was the first to drop off and his rasping snore reverberated around the cottage. It was soon joined by the Reverend's gentle purr and Bertie Barsted's asthmatic wheezing. The Professor was also sound asleep in his bath tub but was mercifully silent as the tiled walls would have amplified any sound he made. Only Stan Twimbley remained awake, awkwardly trying to avoid body contact with Bertie Barsted on the bed and listening nervously to scratching noises coming from the attic. Even though he knew that it was probably just mice scurrying around, his imagination constructed terrifying images of nameless skeletal things clawing at the wooden floorboards with bony talons. But he eventually dropped off at 2am and the night passed by.

Professor Ostridge was the first to wake and look at his watch. It was 7.25am and well past the official sunrise time of 6.30am.

He stepped out of the bath tub and stretched his aching back. It hadn't been the most comfortable night but it was a small price to pay for a decent reward. He used the toilet and sound of the flush woke Bertie Barsted who then had to pay a visit himself. By 8.15am, everyone was awake except Major Crantlemain and congratulations were in the air.

'Easiest money I ever made,' said Bertie Barsted.

'You speak for yourself. My back is going to be playing me up for a week,' said Professor Ostridge. 'Best we wake the Major up, I suppose. The solicitor said that he'd be here at half-nine. Still no electricity I suppose?'

Barsted checked the light switch.

'Shame,' said the Professor. 'I could murder a cuppa.'

Mr Mallord arrived at the cottage at exactly half past nine carrying a large brown envelope. The electricity still wasn't on but Professor Ostridge had identified the cause – a mouse that had fatally electrocuted itself while chewing through a power cable. With some excitement the five prospective recipients gathered around the dining table and waited to hear the good news.

'Most wills are very straightforward,' said Mr Mallord. 'So this has been a welcome change from routine. It's been rather fun hasn't it?'

'I'll let you know when I can stand up straight,' said the Professor.

'Right, to business,' said the solicitor, pushing aside the Cluedo board and laying the brown envelope on the table. 'As you've all done as Captain Clancaster requested – and I have verified that fact with the police constable – I can now open this envelope. I have no idea what is inside. I feel almost as excited as I'm sure you do.'

With a flourish, he tore open the envelope and reached inside, producing five smaller envelopes addressed to the Reverend Grimson Freacke, Major Menzies Crantlemain, Bertie Barsted, Professor Gerald Ostridge and Stan Twimbley. The solicitor distributed them to the five friends who excitedly tore them open. Inside, rather than the cheques they'd been hoping for, there was a letter which read:

Dear friend,

Are you familiar with that old expression, 'To know me, walk a mile in my shoes?' That's what you have just done.

When I was alive, I was always too embarrassed to invite you back to my home for a drink or even a meal. I've been to all of your houses, of course. I've eaten Agatha's delicious fish pie on Stan's veranda, drunk pink gins at the Major's, shared a sherry or two at the Vicarage, sampled Bertie and Janet's wonderful sourdough fresh from the bakery oven, and marvelled at the Professor's skill with a smoker. But never once could I play 'mine host' because, truth be known, I was ashamed. I am a hoarder. I'm told it's a psychological affliction. All I do know for sure is that I could not bear to part with any of my treasures. My boys and my wives tried to help me get better but they couldn't. My obsession cost me three marriages and took over my life. Then it became my life.

But now I am dead and I am no longer in any kind of a position to oppose a damned good clear out. I therefore, somewhat cheekily, am leaving it to you – my best friends – to dispose of the detritus of my life. I finally got to invite you to my home and you can now see the enormity of the problem I lived with every day. I have instructed my solicitor to tell you that each of you is entitled to a thousand pounds – that's a half of one short ton – of my possessions to be sold, dumped or otherwise disposed of.

Oh… did you think I meant a thousand pounds in cash? I'm afraid not! One last prank from Saucy Jack, eh? However, many of my knick-knacks are worth quite a lot of money, I imagine, and I'm confident that each of you will earn a great deal more than a thousand pounds from your thousand pounds.

Thank you for the years of friendship and laughter.

Jack.

'That poor man,' said the Reverend. 'I had no idea.'

'A practical joker to the last,' said Bertie Barsted. 'I can see a lot of car boot sales in our futures.'

'Not necessarily,' said Professor Ostridge, picking up the scrimshaw whale tooth. 'This alone is going to be worth around a thousand pounds and it weighs just ounces. We are potentially all going to do very well out of this.'

'The crafty old sod,' said the Major, with a smile. 'Getting us to clear his house as part of his will. You have to admire his cheek.'

'You seem pensive, Reverend,' said Stan Twimbley.

'What? Oh sorry,' said the Reverend Freacke, idly fingering the edge of the Cluedo board. 'I was just wondering… was it Mrs Peacock in the Dining Room with the Candlestick after all?'

Afterword

One of the most enjoyable activities for any writer is world building. J R R Tolkien loved doing it. So did Terry Pratchett, Edgar Rice Burroughs and Frank Herbert. I imagine that Iain M Banks and Douglas Adams did too, and they built entire galaxies. And George R R Martin is still at it, creating continents and countries, and a cast of characters – human or otherwise – that live, die and get gratuitously naked in them. Even TV shows like *The Simpsons* exist inside their own worlds, each with its own internal logic and rules.

But even if your books are set in the real world, it's still possible to indulge yourself with a modest amount of deity-like behaviour.

Me? I created an English county.

South Herewardshire is located somewhere in the west of England; it's not Wiltshire or Somerset or Gloucestershire, but it's somewhere over there and down a bit. It's a tiny anonymous piece of rural old England, peppered with pretty market towns, crumbly villages and flat green fields full of plump livestock. Most Britons would find it hard to point to on a map. Like Bedfordshire.

It's far enough away from the metro-bubble of London to be

unconcerned with politics and other complex modern issues. It's a place where people know their neighbours, where gossip travels faster than light and where mobile phone reception is patchy. And it's populated with salt-of-the-earth farmers, avuncular pub landlords, snooty lords and ladies, beefy butchers, bombastic schoolmistresses and eccentric vicars – people who, in my head, are played by the likes of Terry-Thomas, Joyce Grenfell, Alastair Sim, Sid James, Hattie Jacques, Margaret Rutherford and Kenneth Williams. South Herewardshire is old-fashioned, quintessentially British, and very content to be so.

My inspiration comes from classic British comedy films like *The Naked Truth*, *Too Many Crooks* and *School for Scoundrels,* and from novels like *Porterhouse Blue, Cold Comfort Farm* and *Three Men in a Boat*. With South Herewardshire I wanted to create a place where you wouldn't be surprised to find Tony Hancock bemoaning the missing last page of *Lady Don't Fall Backwards*, or Henry Wilt pretending to murder his wife using a sex doll as a substitute, or Judith Starkadder casting a baleful eye over the flowering of the sukebind.

My stories are set in a nicer, fairer, happier and undivided Britain; a Britain where people still believe in 'playing the game'. Most British comedy is underpinned by a strong moral code, which is why Peter Sellers and his gang lose the proceeds of their heist in *Two Way Stretch*, why Basil Fawlty's attempts to out-snob everyone always result in him falling on his arse, and why there's that delicious twist in the final minute of *Kind Hearts and Coronets*. Justice is always served: the pompous get pricked, the wicked get punished, the unlikely love story is consummated and, of course, the underdog always comes out on top. You can root for the bad guys if you want to but, no matter how loveable they are, they will never quite get away with it. *The Italian Job* is the perfect example of this.

I guess that what I'm endeavouring to write is Ealing comedies for the twenty-first century. I grew up with those films – and others from that era made by British Lion, Bryanston, London Films, Eros, Anglo Amalgamated, Mario Zampi etc. – and they were funny, charming and beautifully written. Did you know that T E B 'Tibby' Clarke won the 1952 Academy Award for best screenplay for *The Lavender Hill Mob?* That's something very few British writers – let alone comedy writers – have ever achieved (*and* he was previously nominated in 1949 for *Passport to Pimlico*). Then, in 1956, William Rose was nominated for *The Ladykillers*. They may have been comedy films but they were Oscar-worthy British comedy films and they didn't have to be edgy, or bloodthirsty, or stuffed full of digital effects or fart gags to please an audience. They just had to be good stories, made well and acted brilliantly.

Now, I would never be so bold as to compare my writing to Clarke's or Rose's or to the works of any other British comedy writer – but they are the guiding stars by which I steer my modest course. And if, along the way, I can visit the silliness of P G Wodehouse, the farce of Michael Frayn, the eccentricity of Stella Gibbons, the wit of Alan Coren, the gentle satire of David Nobbs, the savagery of Tom Sharpe, and the warmth and charm of Sue Townsend, I'll be a very happy man.

As Sharpe once said, 'I don't claim to be a serious writer. I just want to make myself laugh.'

I feel exactly the same.

Hopefully I've made some of you laugh too.

Stevyn Colgan

Gerry's Club, Soho, January 2020

P.S. If you've read my previous novels, you'll know that I like to pepper them with 'Easter eggs' – things to find among the text. As a tribute to the Golden Age of British comedy, I've taken the names of over a dozen fictional railway stations that have appeared in comedy films, sitcoms, books and radio shows and sprinkled them throughout *Cockerings*. I wonder how many you can spot?

Find the answers at http://amurdertodiefor.blogspot.com/2016/05/putting-you-out-of-your-misery-part-3.html

Acknowledgements

My heartfelt thanks, as always, to Dawn for putting up with the long hours I spend locked away in my study, and to my sounding boards and beta readers Terry Bergin, Jo Haseltine, Andrew Hodge, Steve Hills, Sarah Marr, Erica McAlister, Linda Nagle, Phil Speechley, Janice Staines, Mark Vent, Paul Waters and Huw Williams. And, as always, a massive thank you is due to Michael Dillon at Gerry's Club, Soho, for the many happy evenings of gin-steeped 'inspiration'. He has all the best stories.

Special thanks go to Chris Hale, to whom this book is dedicated. Back in the late 1980s Chris and I shared an office at Hendon Police College. We were members of the Met Police's training and curriculum design team and part of our workload consisted of writing scenarios for mock police promotion exams so that prospective candidates could have a practice before they faced the real thing. These took the form of 'Knowledge and Reasoning' tests in which a policing situation was described in detail. The candidates would then have to prove their mettle by identifying which, if any, offences were being committed and by describing what course(s) of action they would take. We wrote a new K&R test, once a month, for several years and it was enjoyable work because it involved a creativity and freedom that was absent in much of our daily workload. But then, responsibility for writing them was taken over by the Home Office and we were told that we could write just one more. So Chris and I decided that we'd go out with a bang. For our final K&R, we set out to create the maddest, most ridiculous (though not completely impossible) scenario ever. It involved a geriatric circus, a catastrophic fire, drunk clowns, a troupe of aged trapeze artists, escaped tigers, an incontinent elephant and so much more. The promotion candidates loved it. And, afterwards, I realised that the idea of a geriatric circus was just too good to throw away. So, with Chris's blessing, I wrote a short comic story about the circus which, over the course of the next couple of decades, expanded and grew into a novel.

And then, while playing round with ideas for naming the circus, I discovered the marionettes of the late, great British puppet maker Stan Parker (1926-2004). The characters who performed in his *Stanelli's Super Circus* were wonderfully eccentric and many looked quite old. They quickly became a source of inspiration for me and I'm delighted that, upon Stan's death, a grant from the National Lottery allowed them to be saved for the nation. They now reside at the Up Front Gallery Puppet Theatre in Cumbria (www.up-front.com).

All of which brings us to now.

It's been nearly 30 years since Glupi, the Flying Mannings, Penguin Boy, Le Tosseur and all the other aged entertainers from Benelli's Circus first came creaking and grumbling into my life and they feel like old and much-loved friends. I'm glad that I now finally have the chance to share them with you.

Thanks also go to my agent, Piers Blofeld, who believed in this book from the start, to Bruce Hood, my speaking agent. Also to Xander Cansell, Mat Clayton, Catherine Emery, Anna

Simpson and Andrew Chapman at Unbound who helped to make the book into the beautiful item you're now reading. The cover art is by Mark Ecob. My excellent editors were Russel McLean and Philip Purser-Hallard who did an epic job.

But, most of all, thank you to my Unbound subscribers who, once again, made this book a reality through their generosity and belief in me. There's a list of them on the following pages. If I could arrange a fanfare for every name that appears, I would.

Let the parade of patrons begin!

(Hours and ticketprice is make know at circuscash.)

Unbound is the world's first crowdfunding publisher, established in 2011.

We believe that wonderful things can happen when you clear a path for people who share a passion. That's why we've built a platform that brings together readers and authors to crowdfund books they believe in – and give fresh ideas that don't fit the traditional mould the chance they deserve.

This book is in your hands because readers made it possible. Everyone who pledged their support is listed at the front of the book and below. Join them by visiting unbound.com and supporting a book today.

Nev Kramt
Mit Lahiri
Amy Lord
Mathew Lyons
Alistair Mackie
Pamela McCarthy
Alice McVeigh
Alice Meadows
Joel Meadows
Jesper Meisner
Andrew Merritt
Margo Milne
Carlo Navato
David Perez
Jennifer Pierce
Justin Pollard
Trevor Prinn

Becca Read
Colette Reap
Val Reid
Danny Scheerlinck
Sue Sharpe
Louise Shearsby
Ed Silvester
Graham Stanley
Andrew Tees
Mike Scott Thomson
Cara Usher
Mr Ken Vat
Barry and Maxe Wake
Derek Wilson
Wendalynn Wordsmith
Nicole Wright
Rachel Wright